I0762065

HENRY

By

PAUL EBERZ

Cover Design — Asya Blue Design
Line Editor — Carrie Murgittroyd

Printed in the United States of America
First Edition 2021
Copyright 2022 TXu 2 306-515. HENRY — Paul Eberz
A Just Sugar Production

Paperback ISBN 978-1-7352566-6-5
Hardcover ISBN 978-1-7352566-9-6

DEDICATION

Florence Simon Eberz
My mother, my hero

HENRY

PAUL EBERZ

1

MARCH 2, 2002
PHILADELPHIA, PENNSYLVANIA

Spring had no chance of showing up because winter continued to batter Northeast Philadelphia. A snowfall might have made the cold more tolerable, but the white stuff was in short supply. There was no white Christmas and only dustings through February. The kids didn't get a snow day from school or get to slide down a hill in Pennypack Park. They just waited for the school bus every day in the cold. Adults braved the harsh weather with about as much enthusiasm as the kids, hustling everyday against a wind that always seemed to be blowing just above a turned collar and slightly below the brim of a hat.

It was morning. The sun was up and a Philadelphia unmarked police car returning to the precinct provided heat to Detective Robert Aimer and his partner, Sergeant Michael McFee. They had been on an all-night stakeout of the apartment of the girlfriend of a suspect in an ongoing homicide. The vigil had been fruitless.

Aimer had one hand on the wheel and one covering a yawn.

"Yeah, me too." McFee cracked the side window of the passenger side of the soon to be removed from service 1995 Ford Crown Vic.

The cold air instantly widened their eyes, driving off the fatigue of a ten-hour shift.

Seven years ago, the vehicle had a new car smell. Now, however, it smelled like old spilt coffee, sweat, and the fabric from grandma's old chair. Adding to the bouquet was the back seat where passengers in handcuffs had contributed the odor of urine and vomit.

Aimer shot a look at his watch. "Ya wanna grab some breakfast before we report in?"

McFee appeared to ponder his decision as he stared out the window and rubbed his rounded, non-departmental-sized, belly.

Michael McFee had been promoted on the same day that his much thinner and much younger partner made detective. McFee passed the sergeant's exam on his fifth try while Aimer aced his test on his first effort. They had been partners since Aimer was assigned to the 15th Division, but that was soon to end.

McFee's promotion meant a desk was waiting, which both men recognized was the right outcome. Michael was a cop's cop. He was loyal, righteous, and always had his partner's back, but his age and weight made him a couple of steps slower.

Aimer looked over at the distracted sergeant and smacked his arm. "Do you want to eat or what?"

McFee snapped at his partner. "How dare you strike a superior officer?"

Aimer laughed. "Tell me, did those new sergeant stripes on your sleeve come in extra-large?"

"Fuck you. And... yes, I want breakfast."

"That was a huge decision. I can understand why you were hesitating."

"Again... fuck you. And... I was considering the home fries at Melrose Diner."

"It's a good thing nobody else heard you say that. We are cops from northeast Philly and cops go to Jack's Diner or Tony's on Levick."

"Fuc—" McFee's third fuck you of the morning was cut short by the crackle of the police radio.

"Car 318—respond to a 10-35 at 4245 Chandler Street, Rawnhurst. Meet the inspector, 10-18."

McFee keyed the mic. "Car 318 responding to 4245 Chandler Street, 10-18."

Aimer's face tightened and he gripped the wheel so hard his knuckles turned white.

McFee hit the lights and siren. "A 10-35 major crime and an inspector on the scene already? Must be big." He looked over at Aimer who was still staring straight ahead. "Wait... that address isn't in our district. Why would they want two cops from the 7th there, 10-18-urgent?"

Aimer spoke through a clenched jaw. "They don't want us... they want me."

Four squad cars with flashing lights blocked the intersections of each end of the 4300 block of Chandler Street. Two vans, one from KYW TV and the other from Action News had taken positions and discharged their correspondents who were hoping to get sound bites for the nightly news broadcasts.

Aimer slowed and a uniform approached as he lowered his window. "We've been summoned."

The officer nodded, then jumped into one of the blue and whites, and backed it up, letting car 318 through the blockade. The beat-up, unmarked 1995 Crown Vic drove down the street to where four sleek and shiny unmarked 2002 Vics were parked irregularly in front of a row house.

Aimer jammed the gearshift into park, leaving the door open behind him when he jumped out. He passed six uniforms, all with drawn, serious faces, pointlessly guarding the sidewalk as he hustled up the cracked concrete pathway toward the steps leading to, what he instinctually knew, was very, very bad news.

McFee was several paces behind, moving quickly, but already red-faced from the effort.

A uniform posted at the door pushed it open and stood sideways, letting the detective pass.

The red brick rowhouse was narrow and three rooms long with stairs to the second floor. A living room opened to a dining room and a doorway led to the kitchen. It was brightly painted, neat and once had smelled of flowers and scented candles. Now it was jammed with men and smelled of Old Spice and stale tobacco.

The Inspector, tall, distinguished and dressed in a perfectly creased suit, stood in the middle of the living room. One of the two smaller, similarly dressed but less notable men, flanking the man in command, touched the Inspector's arm and whispered while pointing.

The Inspector nodded then took on an in-charge voice. "Detective Aimer."

"Sir." Aimer came to attention.

"I've been told you know who lives here?"

"Yes, sir. This is the residence of Henry Smokehouse, his wife Helen, and their son, Henry."

No one spoke.

"Hrummp." The Inspector made a noise instead of speaking.

The suit on the right spoke next. "Detective, I'm Captain Conners of the 15th. We've called you here from the 7th to help us with our investigation. Your Captain has been made aware of the situation."

Again, no one else spoke.

"How about making me aware." Aimer bristled, but remained at attention.

The Inspector frowned and the suit on the left took over. "I'm Lieutenant Panacci of the 15th. I'm heading the investigation."

McFee had just caught up and stood next to his partner. "What's up, Bobby?"

Continuing to stare straight at the superior officer, Aimer responded to his partner's question. "I have no fucking idea."

Lieutenant Panacci glanced at the Inspector but then addressed the insubordinate Aimer. "Detective, do you know the whereabouts of one Henry Smokehouse?"

The official suspect question hit Aimer like a punch in the face.

"Staff Sergeant Henry 'Smoke' Smokehouse, U.S. Army, is at this moment, and has been for the past nine months, in Afghanistan looking for Osama Bin Laden. Sir."

Panacci made a face, appearing to weigh the answer for loopholes. After the moment of contemplation, he looked at the Captain, then to the Inspector, both of whom gave a go-ahead nod.

Panacci turned back to Aimer. "This morning the next-door neighbors noticed the front door of this house was standing open. Both the husband and wife came to investigate. They looked downstairs, then the husband went upstairs and found her body and called 911."

Aimer emitted a breath that carried his worst fear. "Body?"

The lieutenant pulled out a small notebook and began reading. "When the EMTs arrived, she was unresponsive but had a weak pulse. She was rushed to Nazareth Hospital but died in the ambulance. Time of death was 7:35 this morning. The ER physician at the hospital said her wounds indicated she was beaten and sexually assaulted over several hours before she was stabbed to death. The working theory is a break-in occurred the night before, probably in the early evening. It's too soon to establish if there was more than one perpetrator but it's clear they stabbed her after the assaults." The lieutenant looked up from his pad. "He also said she must have tried to fight back, because there was evidence of defensive wounds on her arms and hands."

Everyone in the room was now not only silent, but motionless.

"Body?" Aimer's voice was stronger.

The lieutenant flipped his notebook closed. “Detective?”

“You said body, not bodies. Where’s Henry?”

“Ah…um, we believe the baby was kidnapped.”

Aimer turned on his heels and walked toward the stairs.

“Detective,” the lieutenant’s voice became commanding, “this is an active crime scene.”

Aimer gripped the handrail as he ascended. “And I’m an active detective.”

McFee looked at the three suits and shrugged.

A uniform, diligently guarding the top of the stairs from an unseen threat, nodded toward the direction of the crime.

Aimer stopped cold when he saw the bed. Helen’s blood had painted her outline on a white sheet then disappeared into the mattress leaving behind a horrible, black, crusted-over silhouette of one of the finest people he had ever known.

He closed his eyes and shook his head, fighting off the emotions, suppressing the rage. The horror he saw would never leave his mind’s eye, but now he had to be a cop, a detective. He needed to find answers. Retribution would come later. He walked the room slowly, step by step, scanning every inch of every surface. Beside the bed, a chair was broken and lay on its side, the mirror on the dresser was smashed, and a sheet had been ripped and used as restraints. There was blood spatter on the walls and floor.

He circled the room then walked out and down the hall to the nursery. The blue painted room, unlike the bedroom, seemed undisturbed, nothing out of place. He opened the closet door and every drawer of the dresser.

He came out of the nursery and stood in the hall, head down, hands at his side. He was silent and still. Eventually, he took a breath and looked up. The stair-guard cop, who looked like a rookie, his face reflecting perhaps his first murder, nodded. There were no words, nothing to say. Aimer passed him by and went down the stairs.

Aimer walked towards the three suits and they stopped talking.

Lieutenant Panacci spoke in a command voice. "Detective, I have been told you knew the victim, but let me be very clear. This is a 15th district case and I'm in charge of the murder investigation of Helen Smokehouse and the kidnapping of the baby. Is that clear, detective?"

"Taken." Aimer contradicted his superior.

"Excuse me?"

"They took his clothes... diapers, bottles, everything. There won't be a ransom demand. He wasn't kidnapped, Lieutenant... he was taken."

McFee stepped up and stood beside his partner.

Aimer looked at the higher-ranked suits. "For the record, I am their friend, a very good friend. And also, for the record, my name is Robert and the baby's name is Henry... Robert... Smokehouse."

Detective Aimer turned back to face the Lieutenant-in-charge Panacci. "And... I'll investigate anything I fuckin' want to."

2

6,804 MILES AWAY, THE SAME DAY
MARCH 2, 2002
SHAHI-KOT VALLEY, AFGHANISTAN
OPERATION ANACONDA

Staff Sergeant Henry Smokehouse, Sergeant Felix Upton Grant, and the rest of the 87th Infantry Regiment were ready for battle. A light snow was falling when they jumped out the backs of the transports and now their platoon, along with twenty-five Afghan troops, sat nervously waiting to begin an attack. Some were checking their weapons, a few were smoking, and some sat with eyes closed, chins lifted and silently praying.

High-ranking Coalition leadership, based on the best intelligence available, had determined Al-Qaeda and Taliban forces were in control of the entire Shahi-Kot valley. The enemy had taken up positions in caves and on top of ridges along the five-mile-long basin in the mountains bordering Pakistan.

The operational plan was scheduled to begin with a predawn aerial bombardment, followed by three platoons of U.S. and Afghan regulars attacking the enemy mountain positions from the south, east, and west. The platoon attacking from the south included two fifteen-man squads commanded by Staff Sergeant Henry Smokehouse. Following a barrage from B-1B bombers, his squads were to attack the enemy positions and drive them north where three additional platoons of Coalition forces would be waiting to cut them off before they could escape into Pakistan.

Like every battle plan in the history of warfare, it did not unfold as designed.

The first flaw was that the intelligence reports dramatically underestimated the opposing force. What was expected to be from 100 to 150 troops, in fact, was more like 1,000.

The second flaw was a typical snafu— situation normal, all fucked up. Before dawn and before the ground assault began, a fifty-five-minute Air Force bombardment nicknamed 'hammer and anvil' was to rain fire and destruction across the valley. However, the strafing fell well short of that goal. The number of bombs actually dropped was six.

The seventh of the five hundred bombs that were to fall from the sky got stuck in a bomb bay of a B1-B. Procedure called for the bomber with the constipation problem to call for and receive permission to manually jettison the bomb, then go around and begin again. However, in that process the bombers and their fighter escorts, F-15E Strike Eagles, received a misinterpreted "knock off" call directing them to cease the bombardment.

The bombers indicated an attack was coming and Smoke's squads of Coalition troops were visible on the road below.

The rising sun gave the enemy clear targets and they opened fire.

Immediately, the need for air support was radioed in, but Apache helicopters attempting to suppress enemy mortar teams were met with stinger missiles, rocket propelled grenades, and a wall of 12.7 antiaircraft groundfire.

Smoke's squads were pinned down. The trucks that got them there became the cover that was keeping them alive. As the mortars and rifle fire zoned in on the road and the troop transports, the soldiers scrambled to find cover behind rocks and boulders on the snow-covered ground.

Smoke slid down next to Felix who was lying behind a rock just off the road. "How many got hit?"

"Six maybe seven. Hoskins and Butler took a mortar—they're angels. I saw McDonnel get it in the leg. Ronner and Gorman, and a couple more, not sure who."

Three mortars exploded near them. They buried their heads further into the mud as rocks rained down and a cloud of dirt covered their camos.

Smoke's ears were ringing. "We're taking fire from every direction and so are the choppers—they can't get in."

The rifle fire intensified and somebody behind them screamed. "I'm hit."

"Fuck." Smoke looked around and saw an M-ATV communications vehicle still intact. The communications officer stood near the open door screaming into a mic. The truck blew up just as the officer said, "Now... right fucking now."

The din of the explosion masked the sound of Felix getting hit. His body rose and fell with the impact, and he went face down into the mud.

Smoke flipped Felix over, saw that he had taken a round in the side, and put pressure on the wound. He pulled out a pressure bandage, covered the bleeding hole, and pressed down hard, then yelled, "Medic."

"Christ that hurts." Felix moaned.

Smoke stayed hunched over his friend a minute, formulating the next move. He saw that most of the enemy fire power concentrated on the trucks and troops behind him. Although the platoon was pinned down, they were returning fire which meant they were also drawing fire and attention— away from him.

Smoke saw a medic maneuvering towards them. He grabbed Felix's paw and put it on top of the wound. "Keep pressure on that."

He looked again and saw the medic was close. He looked at his friend. "I'll be back."

"That would be funnier if you did it with a Schwarzenegger accent."

"Gutshot and still making jokes."

"Always," Felix grimaced then gripped Smoke's hand as another wave of pain hit.

Smoke dropped to the ground and crawled to the lead truck in the caravan. Crouching low, he sprinted across the road, diving into a rocky creek bed on the other side. He didn't draw any fire. The enemy must be concentrating on the platoon instead of him.

He caught his breath then turned his M4 carbine around with the butt near his face so no debris or mud could get into the barrel and started crawling up the incline. He was hidden in the creek, which was muddy and smelled like rotting vegetation. Ragged brush that looked like desert tumbleweed provided additional cover. He headed toward the gunfire above. It was cold. A mixture of mud and snow had penetrated his clothes and worked its way down into his boots. The sound of the enemy gunfire was getting louder.

He poked his head up and looked around. He saw movement and muzzle flashes. A woosh from a mortar preceded an explosion down the valley slope. It sounded like the round hit a truck.

I need to get above and behind them.

He crawled another fifty feet, then fifty more. He crept as flat as possible until the sound of the fire was behind him, then he got up into a crouch, and quickly moved out of the creek, across the slope, stopping in the middle of the moving bodies below.

He hid behind a boulder, checking his weapon. The stock was full of mud but the barrel was clean. He took a breath, checked the magazine slide, then the six ammo clips on his belt.

He allowed his mind to drift to Helen and Henry, but only long enough to say goodbye. Another woosh from a mortar brought him back to reality. He brought the M4 to his chest then came out from behind the boulder.

It had been twenty minutes since the first mortar hit the convoy. The battle, in what was to be later called the 'Valley of Death,' would be over in ten more.

There was a 120-page report on form OMB No. 0704 filed by the Chief of Staff on Operation Anaconda which took place from 2 March 2002 through 16 March 2002. It was written in the same military/political fashion as the reports on Enduring Freedom, Noble Eagle, and Iraqi Freedom. It was mostly accurate, in as much as any battle report written by the victor could be. The report included chapters named; *Planning for Operation in the Khowst-Gardez Region*, *Persistent Close Air Support*, and *Renewing the Attack*. Within a chapter named *The First 72 Hours* was a subheading titled *Taking of the Shai-Kot Valley*.

About halfway through that chapter the narrative described how a platoon of Coalition troops, pinned down under heavy fire, began taking casualties from Al-Qaeda and Taliban forces who had superior numbers and held the high ground position. It stated that air support had been ineffective and the situation became dire. However, one individual turned the tide.

Staff Sergeant Henry Smokehouse crawled up the mountainside, got above the Al-Qaeda and Taliban forces, then attacked. He flanked the enemy position, and overcame their stronghold. The team surveying the battle aftermath determined he faced two squads of approximately twenty-five soldiers each stationed in two separate bunkers. Using the element of surprise, he took out eight enemy who were using rifle and machine guns on the platoon below then disabled the mortar fire with hand grenades. He took the second bunker using a Russian 7.62 x 54R machine gun he took from the first bunker.

When the gunfire that had held them in check ended, the Coalition troops immediately began up the mountain. As they approached, they encountered and engaged a group of twenty enemy in full retreat from their bunkers. When the platoon arrived at the enemy stronghold, they found Staff Sergeant Smokehouse badly wounded and unconscious. The last of his injuries were suffered in hand-to-hand combat. The enemy sustained twelve killed and fifteen wounded from the estimated fifty enemy soldiers manning the positions.

Coalition casualties numbered twelve wounded and five killed in action.

The last chapter in the report titled *Final Assault* summarized the efforts of the Coalition Forces that took the valley but were unable to prevent most of the enemy from escaping into Pakistan.

"You were hit pretty bad, Sergeant."

"Doc, I feel okay, but I can't feel my toes." Smoke sort of recognized his own voice. The words were slurred and came out much slower than he was thinking them. Smoke knew the Doctor was talking to him but he felt like he was talking about someone else.

"Yeah, that would be the drugs. They'll be wearing off soon and you won't be so fine in another hour or so."

Smoke looked around the room.

The doctor saw the puzzled look on his face. "You're in Kabul, Daound Khan Military Hospital. Long way from the mountain, huh?"

Smoke nodded then looked to his left. A body with a huge head covered with close cropped white hair was laying on its side in the bed next to his.

"Hi ya, bunky." Felix smiled.

The sound of footsteps approaching caused the Doctor to turn and snap to attention.

"Uh oh, here come the brass." Felix winced, grabbed his side, and pointed at the incoming bevy of officers.

"This is him, General." A set of Captain's bars pointed to Smoke.

"Staff Sergeant Smokehouse?"

"Yes, sir."

"You did something very special the other day."

"Other day?"

The doctor added clarification for the general. "He's been out of it since the battle, sir."

"Of course." The General bent over slightly and spoke with a fatherly tone. "Son, you saved a lot of lives, and I came here to give you a shiny medal hooked on a colored ribbon. I wanted to do this personally, because I wanted to meet a real fucking hero."

"Hoorah." Felix was listening and couldn't help himself.

The captain put a blue box in the three star's hand.

The General opened the lid and took out a bright, shiny, silver star. "This is the highest honor I can give you in the field." He leaned over and pinned it on Smoke's hospital gown. "Now, it would be my great honor if you shook my hand."

Smoke's grip was weak but he accommodated the three-star's request.

The General looked to the doctor. "Does he know the extent of his injuries?"

The doctor shook his head.

"Tell him."

The doctor nodded and faced Smoke. "You took 7.62 rounds in the calf and in your side, suffered significant blood loss, but there was no damage to major organs. You will fully recover from those wounds. The not so good news is there is a lot of shrapnel in your back, most likely from a grenade. That explosion also broke two and cracked three vertebrae. We stabilized the area but additional surgeries will be necessary."

Smoke lay still.

"This will be a lengthy process and the extent of nerve damage will determine the length of your rehabilitation."

Smoke smacked his dry chapped lips. "I need to call Helen."

The General shouldered the doctor aside. "Everything back home is being taken care of. Right now, you need to focus on getting better. You're going to be shipped out tonight to our medical facilities in Japan."

Smoke nodded.

"I'm going to ask you to do something for me, soldier."

Smoke nodded again to the general.

"This is Captain Swenson. He needs to take a statement from you about what happened. No one witnessed what happened up there, only the results. I know it's tough soldier, but can you do that for me?"

"Yes, sir."

The General straightened up, clicked his heels, and snapped a West Point salute.

Smoke instinctively tried to return the honor but was restricted by the tubes running into both arms.

Captain Swenson stepped forward as the General and his staff left the room. He took out a notebook and pencil. "Start at the beginning, and be as detailed as you can."

Smoke began recounting the events as he was obligated to do in a de-briefing.

It was the last time he would ever talk about it.

Felix remained quiet, listening to every detail. At the story's end he was unable to speak, in awe of his friend's courage. Smoke had saved his life and the lives of his squad.

When Smoke finished, the captain closed the notebook, stood, saluted, did a parade about-face, and left the room.

After five surgeries at the U.S. Naval Hospital in Yokosuka, Japan, the surgeons, pleased with the results, sent Smoke to Tripler Army Medical Facility in Honolulu, Hawaii, for rehabilitation. After an evaluation, they told him that there would always be some stiffness and pain, but he would be almost a hundred percent.

Healing the body, however, proved easier than healing Smoke's mind.

He knew what happened.

They waited three weeks to tell him. And now he knew. Helen was dead, and the son he had never met was gone.

The hospital was a large pink building that smelled like antiseptic palm trees. His body was working, but his mind did not. He was stuck and couldn't get out.

A regular routine of exercise and pills got him walking and ready for discharge from the hospital and the army. Two days before he was to pack and return to Philadelphia, the three-star General he met in the Afghanistan hospital arrived at the hospital with his entourage, plus one.

A ceremony was arranged quickly. On the green grass, under a sparkling blue sky, the General presented Staff Sergeant Henry Smokehouse with the Distinguished Service Cross for bravery above and beyond the call of duty. At Smoke's side was the General's plus one. Actually, more like plus one and a half.

Former Sergeant Felix Grant hoped this moment would break through the fog that was clouding his friend's mind. He was also a little pissed off Smoke had not received the Congressional Medal of Honor. Apparently, an officer needed to witness the action for a CMH to be awarded, so Smoke's heroism received the second highest medal.

Smoke didn't care, but for much different reasons than Felix.

3

TWENTY YEARS LATER
NEW YORK CITY

A curious mix of automobiles lined up near the entrance to New York's Chelsea Pier on the Hudson River. Highly-polished stretch limousines were interspersed with Baby-on-Board, SUVs and other middle-class Fords, Chevys and Toyotas. The brand-name vehicles were driven to the event by Doctor Olivia Bennet's professional associates, a few select patients, and most of her contact list of friends. The waxed-bright limos held the celebs; Cyndi Lauper and Alicia Keys. Press cameras' flashes signaled the arrival of Joaquin Phoenix and Rooney Mara but the place really jumped when Johnny Depp pulled up in a 1967 Aston Martin convertible.

The event which drew this smorgasbord of Americana was the launch of the doctor's new book. Her first book was the only bestseller to ever be listed in the New York Times with two titles; *Sex and the Enlightened Mind* and *Release the Beast.* The title on the front of the book was the former and Bennet's preferred title. The latter was placed on the back by her publisher. He was right about the public appeal of the titillating title but she fired him for setting her up with someone who almost got her killed. The pre-orders for her new release, *Finding Satisfaction,* already placed it at number one on the list.

As the name Chelsea Pier suggests, the event was being held on what used to be a long pier built for incoming cargo ships on the Hudson River. It now housed a posh banquet hall that offered a spectacular view of the river. Positioned at the end of the jetty, a wide gathering space opened onto a deck with a glorious view of boats of every description navigating the waterway. The skyline of Jersey City provided a backdrop for the scene which featured a setting sun. A prism of colors reflected off the windows of the buildings and glimmered off the rising and falling crest of the changing tide. It was peaceful and calm.

The crowd inside was not.

Waitstaff dressed in white jackets carried hors d'oeuvres to people engaged in excited and boisterous conversations. Waiters carrying coconut shrimp and dim sum were very popular. Trays of red and white wines and fluted glasses of bubbling champagne also emptied quickly. But the staff carrying a chef's concoction of avocado, an unidentifiable red twig, and a chunk of walnut seemed lonely.

The civilian attendees were grateful for an invitation to the exclusive press event and were maxing out their iPhone memory with pictures. The celebrities had previously made the Doc's acquaintance, some through her professional services and others in a more social setting. Most were there because they respected her work but there was no denying that a few showed up for the photo op. Olivia Bennet's picture had appeared in every newspaper recently. The rags featured her on the front page while the more respectable, but still circulation-wise mainstream press, featured her in the entertainment sections. There was a lot of news coverage and this event would no doubt be a feature story somewhere in the morning papers.

There was one celebrity who had no ulterior motive. She could care less about the ink and was there only to support her friend.

"O, look at you. Jesus H. you look… fantastic." Cyndi Lauper was in full regalia— spiked pink hair, bright red lipstick, and a fit form tucked into long black Armani.

Dr. Olivia Bennet, standing in a corner just off the stage, turned and smiled brightly at the incoming rocket. "Hey Cyndi." O raised welcoming arms. "You're looking younger."

"Yeah, I'm always looking for something younger."

The two did a 'makeup respect' cheek kiss.

O pulled away grinning. "You, trolling for men… please. You've been happily married almost thirty years."

"Don't change the subject. I'm pretty pissed off at you."

"What subject?" O looked puzzled and hurt at the same time.

"You go unhooked until you're… mature… then write a book that makes you the most eligible woman… like anywhere… then… without the mandatory Monte Carlo nightlife, Bimbi yacht topless photo, dates with Clooney and DiCaprio… you go off and marry your bodyguard. You change the way a lot of people think about sexual freedom, and then… without one public scandal… you run off to Hawaii and marry your bodyguard… completely unacceptable. And… not only that, but how is it that I'm hearing about your questionable nuptials in the fucking tabloids? And where is this hunk of a man?" Her head began to pivot side to side.

"Wow, you got all that out in one breath. I'm impressed."

Cyndi immediately mugged a profile pose, one hand-on-hip and one finger pointed to her face. She then lifted her chin and breathed out, "Singer."

O laughed while scanning the room for Smoke. "Well, I'm not sure where to begin but it was all very, very spontaneous. Smoke asked me when we were in Hawaii." She stepped closer to her friend. "It was very romantic, ocean waves, sun, sand."

"I'm getting the picture. Okay that's the proposal but what about the party?"

"Neither one of us wanted it to be a circus, so when we got back to New York, I asked a judge I knew for a favor and he married us in the condo."

"Very disappointed. I get it... but again," Cyndi scrunched up her face. "Where is this... Smoke? And is that his real name?"

O finally spotted and waved at Henry 'Smoke' Smokehouse. He was standing alone near a potted tree and was pulling at the collar of the tuxedo shirt O had requested he wear. She saw him nod and start the long walk across the floor to where she knew he had to do what he truly hated to do—talk.

"Here he comes. You met him at the art auction a while back, remember?"

Smoke moved across the room and O smiled seeing her husband getting looks from the crowd. She knew he was uncomfortable wearing a tux but he sure looked good. The tailor earned his fee for fitting his wide shouldered, trim torso. His charcoaling hair spoke to his age but his stride denied it.

Cyndi eyed him with a Brooklyn squint then whispered, "I don't, but okay, I get it." The once over complete, she winked. "Damn girl."

"Smoke, this is Cynd—"

"Cyndi Lauper. Big fan." He reached out his hand. "Your performance at the White House concert for the Obamas was amazing."

She slapped the hand away and went for a hug she had to reach up on toes to get.

Two black suits with curly wires in their ears had been stationed behind the doctor like the potted trees. One of them stepped forward and politely said, "Doctor, they are about ready for you."

Cyndi punched Smoke in the chest. "I thought you were the bodyguard."

Smoke looked down at the pink head of hair. "Night off."

"My new publisher is paying for everything," O explained, "but I had to agree to a few promotional events. The publicity is good, I guess, but I... I mean we, have had some bad experiences lately."

"Stop… you don't need to go there, O. You don't need to re-live that shit for me. If I want the bits and pieces, I'll get the book like everybody else. But, listen girl, you can't have gone through that, without some damage, that all the shrink stuff... you know… doesn't cover. You're a bestselling author and celebrity. Those camera clickers won't leave you alone. You're their bread and butter till the next starlet gets caught with a Senator or a Senator's wife. And that won't change anytime soon… so if you're willing to take some advice from a performer like me, which, by the way, is what you are now... you need to take every event as a one off… a brand-new adventure. Get in, do your thing, then get out quick."

Smoke looked at O. "Wow, one breath."

"Singer." Cyndi smiled then punched him in the chest again.

O's laugh broke her tension.

Cyndi air-kissed her friend's cheek again and pointed to the stage. "Now, go perform."

O took Smoke's hand, and headed for the steps leading to the podium.

An elevated stage faced tables filled with the picture snappers. The celebrities looking for their New York Post photo op were seated in a different section to the right of the stage. The VIP area was gated with a low iron railing which didn't provide exclusivity, just suggested it.

Julian and Dominique were wrapping up their last song. The pair had been singing together for years and it wasn't talent that was keeping them from Carnegie Hall. Perhaps tonight they would catch the ear of the one who opened the door to fame but right now the crowd was loving their set, clapping and hooting at their last bars of a Motown tribute.

As the set ended, a short, balding man with a greying beard and a round jovial face came up the stairs from the other side of the stage and walked up to a podium positioned at its center.

He coughed nervously and stuttered out his opening. "Go…Good evening and welcome to Wright Publishing's launch party for the number one, best-selling author of the year, Doctor Olivia Bennet."

The crowd reacted with clapping and woo-wooing.

"You may not know this but—"

With a confident grin, Abe turned, looking off stage to where O was waiting.

O fearfully gripped Smoke's hand and whispered, "Oh Abe, don't do it."

He held the grin, faced the crowd and said, "I'm a writer too."

The crowd waited for a punchline.

"I wrote my name on the check for all this."

O winced.

The crowd mostly groaned but there were a few courtesy claps.

His grin disappeared.

Smoke shook his head. "Yeah, that was bad."

"Any whoo…" the publisher's forehead began to sweat, "you didn't come here for my bad jokes. You came to hear from the person of the hour, Doctor Olivia Bennet."

Abe held out his hand and O started up the stairs.

The crowd rose up.

A spotlight found her. It was blinding and she staggered a bit, her eyes adjusting. She felt awkward but looked fantastic. Isolated in front of a black curtain, the white light made the red satin dress shimmer and her alabaster skin glisten.

Smoke was behind her, stationed with a foot on the top step, admiring her walking away, a view just as appealing.

O came to the podium, smiled, and bent over slightly, kissing Abe's now red cheek.

He looked up sheepishly. "Sorry, that was a bad joke."

"You did fine. I appreciate all you've done for me."

He was healed and left the stage smiling.

The shaky spotlight became fixed on O and the audience became quiet.

"I want to thank you for coming tonight. And I would like you to thank Abe Filbert for this affair."

Polite applause went up and down quickly.

"Abe took me on when things were really up in the air for me. I was in a hospital... twice. Had to close my practice for almost a year, and I wrote a new book but had no publisher. Now, you should know that some of what you might have read in the papers was true but much was not." She paused a second. "There were, in fact, real life and death situations. Some of which could have ended very badly if not for the action of..." She turned and pointed to the steps, "My husband, Smoke."

He was caught off guard.

Applause came from everywhere along with a few hoots and hollers.

The spotlight swung from her to him. It danced around before it found him, but when it did, he waved once, then backed down the steps into the shadow.

The light swung back to the podium. "He's the quiet type."

O turned and faced the audience. "When I look around this room, I see many familiar faces, friends and colleagues, all of whom I treasure. I also see new faces that I've not had the pleasure to meet. So, for you, I feel I need to fill in a bit of my background."

She paused and looked around the audience, a reflective look setting her mood and tone. "My life so far has been an extraordinary journey. I came from a middle-class home and did very well in school, receiving a scholarship to the University of Virginia. My interest had always been psychology, and I was selected from many talented students by the FBI Behavioral Science Division in Quantico for an internship. The saga that followed has been widely covered by the press and is only somewhat accurate. The coverage was geared to the sensational... the film-at-eleven highlights, and didn't cover the background of a severe mental disorder in which thought and emotions are so impaired that contact is lost with external reality."

She took a sip of water then continued. "While I was interning for the FBI, I was asked to develop a random profile on someone I knew as a practice exercise. I chose a young man I had dated a few times, Hamilton Lighter. I did a lot of research, and when I put the pieces of his life together in the report, the head of the Unit determined that I had identified a possible serial killer. The Director brought in Lighter for an interview. Lighter came from a very wealthy family with excellent lawyers and was released immediately, however he became so enraged that in an act of vengeance against me, mistook my twin sister for me and murdered her."

Everyone was listening, even the waitstaff had stopped moving around.

"Lighter was sent to a hospital for the criminally insane but was released just seven years later. Still bent on revenge, he began a killing spree which resulted in the deaths of sixteen young women. I agreed to participate in a plan to capture him, and in spite of the unbelievable efforts of everyone to protect me, he still managed to kidnap and torture me for three days. I thought I was going to die and in fact I was just seconds away from death when I was rescued by my husband. Lighter was killed trying to escape."

She paused for a moment collecting her thoughts and to repress her rage. "Lighter was a monster. He killed more than twenty women including my sister. He was also insane."

Her voice cracked and her head lowered as she gulped back the pain. "I hated him... He tortured me... I wanted him, dead."

She looked up at the crowd. "But... I'm a doctor, a psychiatrist who took the oath of Hippocrates, which in part reads, 'I will respect the privacy of my patients, for their problems are not disclosed to me that the world may know. Most especially... must I tread with care in matters of life and death.'"

She looked at the audience and spoke slowly. " 'If it is given me to save a life, all thanks. But it may also be within my power to take a life; this awesome responsibility must be faced with great humbleness and awareness of my own frailty. Above all, I must not play at God.'"

Her voice changed; her delivery softer. "I believe the ancient Greek pointed to our need to protect our patients and society. We need to be ever vigilant and work with law enforcement when it is necessary to protect society from those who have become the monsters cloaked by insanity. It is the most difficult decision because doctors must, 'Above all, I must not play at God'."

The proverbial pin hitting the floor was ignored.

"Johnny Depp will be coming up here in a minute to read a few highlights from my book." She looked down. "I can't believe what I just said. A huge mega-movie star is going to read something I wrote." She shook her head in disbelief. "Mama, if you could only see me now."

Laughter and applause allowed her to let air build in her lungs.

Breathe like a singer.

She started slow. "But first… I am standing here tonight because of my husband. The FBI, local PD, even the native population of Hawaii all helped with my rescue but…he is why I'm alive and standing here tonight."

Heads were bobbing looking for the man hiding off stage.

Her voice became strong and determined. "It is not in my nature to retreat or hide. And to be clear I didn't marry my bodyguard." She looked to the faces and tilted her head. "I married my hero."

The audience cheered.

"*Finding Satisfaction* is my account of what happened in Hawaii. I assure you it has more detail and fewer moneymaker adjectives than the press versions. So now…" she shrugged, "I guess all there is left to say is…buy my book." A little red blush appeared on her cheeks.

The audience laughed and clapped.

A single voice rang out. "We want Smoke."

Then a chorus chimed in. "We want Smoke. We want Smoke. We want Smoke."

O took a few steps toward the shadow and held out her hand. The spotlight followed her.

Smoke didn't move.

She wiggled her outstretched fingers, and smiled the smile he always obeyed.

The spotlight spun to the steps.

Smoke started up, put a foot on the top step, and half-waved to the crowd.

O took another step toward him.

The spotlight swung back to O, then back to him.

She moved closer, halfway from the podium to the stairs. She took another step. The heel of her shoe caught in a gap between two sections of the stage floor. O stumbled and fell forward.

Smoke moved quickly and got his hands under her shoulders but couldn't stop her head from grazing the edge of a light stand.

The crowd gasped.

O's knees took the impact of the floor, her hands flat in front. Now on all fours, and Smoke's hands under her arms, she pushed herself up.

She yelled out, "I'm okay. I'm okay."

Smoke lifted her up like a child, her feet dangling limp, off the floor. He carefully set her down and looked into her eyes.

She felt dizzy but embarrassment began to overcome any physical discomfort.

A small bump began growing on her forehead. She reached up, felt it, then pulled a shaft of hair down to cover the injury.

She leaned on Smoke's arm for support, turned, and faced the crowd. "Really… shot, kidnapped, tortured and now… done-in by a high heeled shoe?" She smiled a brave smile. "No fucking way."

The crowd roared.

Smoke had his arm under hers.

She raised an arm to wave and her body listed, her feet not able to support her weight.

With an arm around her waist, Smoke half carried her out of the spotlight while O continued to wave into the shadows.

4

QUANTICO, VIRGINIA

The head of the FBI's Behavioral Science Unit, George DiSanto, looked down at a cleared-off space on his desk existing between tottering stacks of papers, reports, and folders. A legal-sized manila folder stamped FBI Tulsa, Oklahoma lay open. Clasped to one side was an incident report on a shooting that took place at the Arrowhead Casino in Medicine Hill, Oklahoma. The FBI special agent who filed the report, along with two field agents, responded to a crime-in-progress call involving a hostage. Like all Native American Indian casinos, Arrowhead was located on sovereign ground of the Odawa Tribe, which is federally protected and is not under local or state jurisdiction. The FBI, specifically the Indian Country Special Jurisdiction Unit, investigates the most serious crimes. While promoting cooperation with Tribal law enforcement, the ICSJU took control of the crime scene from the Odawa's understaffed Tribal Police.

DiSanto flipped over the cover page of the report. Underneath were pictures taken at the scene and information about the tribe.

The Arrowhead Casino, like many of the Indian gaming facilities in Oklahoma, was little more than a series of double-wide trailers bolted together. It housed 700 slot machines, a Keno parlor, eight card tables, a bar and an omnipresent cloud of cigarette smoke. The lack of health concern aside, they were new trailers illuminated with multi-colored LED lights and filled with echoing ringing bells of someone else's winning play.

On the night of the incident, the crowd was loud and only semi-behaved. Security consisted of the Tribe's only police officer and two guards, who were kept busy by the orderly disorder amongst the gamblers.

DiSanto flipped to the Special Agent's report. He read that once the call was received, it took fifty-five minutes for the Tulsa FBI team to reach the scene. Upon arrival, two men were dead. The report stated that the dead men had attempted to kidnap the Tribal Chairman in the parking lot, and when confronted by the three-man security team, the suspects opened fire with two semi-automatic handguns. The Odawa Tribal Police officer and the two licensed and bonded security guards returned fire, killing the suspects. Chairman Randle Two Horse was injured by friendly fire receiving a minor gunshot wound to his upper arm.

DiSanto flipped another page to the interview of the Chairman who said the men had accosted him when he was getting into his car. They demanded money from the casino. He told the agent he had never met the dead men before.

At the bottom of the page, the Special Agent had penciled a note speculating the Chairman was withholding information.

DiSanto then turned his attention to the other side of the folder, and the FBI's Medical Examiner's Report of a man identified from fingerprints as Taylor Bonsell, from Tulsa. He was twenty-seven years old, five foot ten and 152 pounds. There were two bullet wounds, both in the center of the chest. The body had tattoos on the back and arms, many of them appearing to be 'jailhouse' ink. The second page of the file documented a long criminal record, which included eight arrests with three convictions, the last for drug trafficking of ecstasy for which he served two and a half years of a five-year sentence in the Oklahoma State Penitentiary.

George then read the second man's ME report. He was approximately fifty-five to sixty years old, five foot nine, 175 pounds. He also had two bullet wounds, one in the center of the chest and one just above his right eye. He had several scars from previous injuries; three knife scars on the arms and back and a bullet wound in the shoulder. The body had no other markings or tattoos. Unlike the first dead man, there was no second page for this man. He had no ID on him, no driver's license or credit cards. There were no fingerprints or DNA matches in the National Crime Information Index or the FBI's CODIS database. The agent from Tulsa took an extra step, and sent requests for information to Interpol which were also fruitless.

The last database checked had a hit. The man's DNA was a 99% match to a sample taken at a crime scene that occurred in Philadelphia, Pennsylvania on March 2, 2002. The second dead man was the man who'd raped and murdered Helen Smokehouse and kidnapped a baby boy named Henry.

When DiSanto read the name, he sucked in air. It was a moment of shock for a professional who was rarely surprised. He closed the file and rested his hand on top. He looked at the phone then reached for the receiver.

He spun the wheel on his obsolete Rolodex to the letter S. He entered the number and heard it connect. There was a pause after the first ring followed by a series of quick buzzes which George recognized as a European phone connection. His call went unanswered and defaulted to voicemail.

A low-toned male voice gave an abrupt instruction. "I'm not around, leave a message."

"This is George DiSanto, FBI... wait, sorry, I get very official on these things. Of course, you know who I am. Smoke, please call me when you get this. I need to talk with you about something very important." DiSanto paused, scratched his head, and continued, his tone becoming a plea. "Please call me."

He sat for a while contemplating his options, then spun the Rolodex again, and found the contact number for the recently retired Philadelphia Police Lieutenant, Robert Aimer. He stared at the screen a second, hesitating, but then pushed the numbers.

The phone rang once. "Aimer."

"Lieutenant, this is George DiSanto of the FBI."

"George, I thought we dispensed with the formalities. I told you before to call me Bobby or Aimer or shithead but now...definitely not lieutenant. I'm retired."

"Yes, of course...Robert."

"To what do I owe the pleasure?"

"Ah…" George was revisiting the decision to involve someone other than Henry Smokehouse, but the FBI division chief was aware of Aimer's qualifications as a law enforcement officer and his familiarity with the case.

"Are you there?" Aimer's voice changed from friendly to serious.

"Yes, Robert. I'm here. I have… I mean something has happened… or rather something has been discovered—"

"George, I may be retired, but I'm still a cop, and you're stalling. What's up?"

"There was a shooting in an Oklahoma Indian casino parking lot, and two men were killed. Apparently, they tried to kidnap a tribal official and were shot by security. The FBI was called in, investigated, and the bodies transported to the morgue at Saint Francis Hospital in Tulsa."

George paused, then spoke quickly, like he was ripping off a bandage. "One of the men killed was the man who killed Helen Smokehouse and took her baby."

George had anticipated the long silence.

Aimer's voice broke when he spoke. "Name?"

"We don't have an ID. There was no trace of him anywhere in any active database system. However, we got a match from the DNA in cold-case files. It is still an open file because a child was kidnapped which is a federal crime and, as you know, kept the FBI as the lead investigator. This is the first new creditable piece of information we've had in years."

Aimer didn't respond.

"Robert, I tried to reach Smoke, but his phone went to voicemail."

"He took Olivia to Italy after the book signing accident. The doctors recommended she rest and stay away from any stress."

"What happened? Is she alright? Jesus. She's been through the ringer."

Aimer ran out the facts. "She fell and hit her head. It doesn't sound like a big thing, but it was the third concussion in two years. The first was at Smoke's cabin. You remember, right?"

"Sure, she was shot and was very lucky, the bullet just grazed her head."

"Correct, that was concussion number one. Six months ago in Hawaii, along with severe, almost fatal dehydration, three cracked ribs, and being beaten badly, she received a second concussion. The doctors told her to rest, but she didn't. Instead, as soon as she got back to New York, she went to warp-speed on the book about Hamilton Lighter, your outfit, and how Smoke rescued her. Smoke tried to get her to slow her roll, but she pushed through. She also drove herself to re-open her practice. Then two weeks ago, the publisher scheduled a big book release event and after giving a speech, she caught a heel, tripped and fell, and hit her head. Smoke took her to the ER at Mount Sinai, and the doctors said it was concussion number three."

"Jesus." George groaned.

"After seeing the CAT scans, she finally relented, and Smoke shut down her practice, cancelled all the book signing events, and flew her to a little town in northern Italy."

"How is she doing?"

Aimer sounded concerned. "I don't know. I call to check in, but he isn't answering my calls either."

"Should I keep trying to reach out to Smoke? I mean this is the first break in the case in almost twenty years."

Aimer considered his answer as a friend and a cop. "Since there's no ID and no leads, I vote to hold. He is taking care of the doc and, frankly, he could use a good rest too. O needs stress-free time to heal."

"That makes sense."

"She's in good hands, and this will keep until we get more information."

"Robert, I keep hearing you saying... we. Are you volunteering?"

"George, there's no way you could keep me out of this."

"Good." The FBI director was relieved. "In fact, your involvement is perfect timing. I am actually retiring myself... in two weeks."

"Congrats... but—"

"But the problem is every department in the agency is shorthanded and open cases keep building. This is an ice-cold case, and I think without me at the helm pushing, it will soon find the bottom of the pile."

"What can we do?"

"Robert, I want you to know, I looked into Smoke's background before I allowed him to get into the Lighter investigation. I looked at his war record, his association with the Philadelphia Police Department, and some of the private work he has done over the years. I also know you two were friends since childhood. I looked into your background, and I know your professional record is impeccable."

"That's good to know." Aimer sounded a little offended.

"I had to look, Robert. You know that."

"I get it. I guess."

"You were deeply involved in the case back then, and I can't imagine how hard it has been to not know what happened to Henry and who was responsible. However, this might be the break needed to find those answers."

"With both of us out of the game it will be uphill."

George spoke slowly with cold determination. "Robert, I assure you if you get into this, I will use every favor and every bit of leverage I've built in my thirty-five years with the Agency to find out what happened on March 2, 2002."

"What can I do?"

"I'll keep trying to get an ID on the John Doe but, in the meantime, we know the identity of the younger man, and that lead will be followed, but in reality, the FBI can be like an aircraft carrier in a pond... just too big to get information from the street on a guy like this. He appears to be a small-time hood who hasn't traveled anywhere outside of Oklahoma. We need to find out how these two men are connected. If we do, then we will find out who this John Doe is. Once we know who he is, we can build a profile and then... maybe... just maybe we'll find out why he was in Philadelphia in 2002, and why he took Henry."

George heard the voice of a cop on the end of the wire. "Send me everything you got and George—"

"Yes?"

"This will hit Smoke hard. It will change his life... again."

"I can keep him out of it until my retirement, but I won't have control over the case officer after I leave. We will have to tell him before then. But there is something else."

"What's that?"

"I left a voicemail for him."

"What did you say?"

"I didn't give details just told him it was important, and I asked him to call me back."

Aimer laughed. "He won't. He never checks voicemail, but if for some reason he does...don't answer the call."

"Will do."

"How long?"

"How long for what?"

"Before your last day?"

"We have thirteen days and four hours."

"Send your contact info with copies of the files."

Neither man broke the connection.

Aimer spoke in a low tone. "Is it possible… I mean do you think there's a chance the boy is—?"

"I don't know, Robert. I don't know… but what I can tell you is even after all my years chasing the most despicable wastes of oxygen… I still believe in hope."

5

STRESA, ITALY

The elevator opened to an extraordinary place. O held Smoke's hand and they walked side by side on a narrow path through a rock tunnel illuminated by soft purple light. The smell of lavender and jasmine reached them first, lemon grass and lotus flower saving their pleasures till they neared an arched wooden door.

Smoke pushed a brass plate, and they entered a primordial chamber that appeared to have been hollowed out of the mountain by a subterranean watercourse etched through solid rock. Inside the high-ceilinged cave, a pool of water rested quietly before completing its journey from the mountain top to Lake Maggiore. The winding stream was narrow where it entered and left the grotto, but it was wide and deep in the middle. One side was solid rock and rose straight up to the ceiling. On the other, small lagoons, hidden behind columns of rock, were lit with soft green and blue lights. Water trickled down from the ceiling on the walls and stone piers making a gentle babbling sound.

At the far end, grey mist beckoned from a small pool inside one of the alcoves. The hotel had added a heat source turning the pool into a hot tub, its water overflowing into the main pond changing the cool water to body temperature.

It was magical, even mystical, certainly heavenly. It was also a total surprise to the guests staying above it in the Hotel Regina Palace, an elegant, beautifully appointed structure that lived up to its name—Palace. Beautiful gardens surrounded a royal entrance and every room had a breathtaking view of the lake and the distant mountains near Switzerland. No one would suspect the Italian Renaissance architecture harbored such a primitive foundation.

O was in no rush and slipped into the water well after Smoke swam off to the far end of the pool. Tiny ripples created by her strokes made their way across the surface. O stretched her arms, ducked her head beneath the water, and took a graceful stroke, feeling the water touch every inch of her skin as it passed by. She lifted her head and glided, taking a long slow breath. When forward momentum stopped, she turned over on her back, suspended in weightless harmony. Beads of water from slicked back hair drizzled down over her cheeks. Her ears, covered by water, heard no sound. She was at peace. The pain in her head that kept her awake had been shut out. In that well-needed moment of relief, the throbbing was gone.

She knew Smoke was right to drag her out of New York over her strenuous objections and had apologized several times for her uncharacteristic behavior. She hadn't quite gotten to screaming and kicking, but came close. She knew the medical reason that caused her non-typical reaction but it didn't make her feel any better, and it was extremely depressing to possess the knowledge and understanding, but not the self-control.

A small bump on the head normally would be nothing more than a conversation starter. The CAT scan had revealed no bleeding, but her acuity exam confirmed that her brain had, for the third time, been bounced around inside her skull like a volleyball. Both doctors advised caution and careful monitoring but were divided on her leaving town. Doctor Carter was against it, stating if a slow bleed were to develop a New York hospital would be the best place to handle emergency surgery. Doctor Brightman, while not disagreeing with his counterpart, insisted it was vitally important to have at least thirty days of total relaxation. He supported whatever it took to remove all stress, including the publishing business, the medical practice, and all contact with the public. He contended isolation would be essential to achieve a full recovery. However, both doctors agreed that if any of the symptoms—headache, nausea, sleeplessness, or confusion persisted— she should get her ass back to NYC, ASAP.

The dizziness was gone as was nausea. There were periods of confusion and forgetfulness, and she still had sudden, crashing headaches. The thing that bothered her the most, however, was the bitchiness she directed at Smoke and Gia. It might be because of a lack of sleep but she knew it was also a symptom, confirming the injury had not yet healed.

She pulled her arms through the water, floating on her back, her legs rising to the surface. Her mind in a daytime dream— her life, her books… her Smoke. And the money—never in her wildest imagination did she believe she could afford to fly off to Italy in a private jet to recover from a bump on the head in a palace overlooking the crystal blue Lake Maggiore and the snow-covered peaks of the Italian Alps.

A ripple she didn't make broke her concentration.

"Hi."

O let her feet fall to the bottom, stood, blinked, then smiled. "Hi, yourself."

Even though they both whispered, their words sounded loud.

Smoke's mouth started to open, and she cut him off.

"I'm fine. The headache is almost gone, and I'm... believe it or not... hungry."

Concern changed to a smile. "That's good news. I won't have to eat by myself. I've been feeling guilty. You and Gia seem to be on a starvation diet... in food heaven, and I'm gaining pasta weight."

She was a few feet away, standing, water just above her navel, hair dripping down, eyes sparkling.

He was standing now too, motionless, hands at his side, a silly grin on his face.

She smiled. "If I told you I didn't like what you're doing right now, looking at me like a pastry on a serving tray... I'd be lying."

He reached out, grabbed her arm and pulled her close, then kissed her delicately.

"Ciao." Gia's voice broke the kiss and got their attention. She was across the pond greeting a young couple who had just entered the Spa.

The woman smiled and extended her hand. "Ciao."

"Il mio nome e Gia, qual e il tup?"

Smoke shrugged at O, puzzled.

O translated. "She asked their names."

Gia pointed the couple toward the lounge chairs. Smoke and O could see Gia was topless, which was not unusual.

Smoke grunted.

"Bothers you, doesn't it?"

"What?" he pretended.

"Gia's freedom, her nudity."

"Of course not," he grumbled.

"Such a liar."

He turned to her; his expression serious. "Can I be honest?"

She hit him. "Why do you ask such stupid questions?"

"Sorry."

She grinned. "Speak… neanderthal." The grin disappeared when she saw he was serious.

"I worry... which, basically, is my occupation. I worry about everything including," he pointed to her head, "your injury and your recovery."

"That's not it." She cocked her head. "What's bothering you?"

He hesitated but responded. "Okay, two things. First, you lost your best friend when Lo was killed, and at first, I thought the void would never be filled, but then Gia came along."

O lowered her head and moved her hands slowly back and forth, smoothing the water's surface as she listened.

"Gia was there and helped. It all seemed so natural. She began filling in at the office and with daily life but more importantly I watched you become very close to her, not like Lo… different but still very close."

O nodded, still smoothing.

"She stepped up when we were attacked at the cabin and you were shot." He pointed to her scar. "Then again in Hawaii, she was there for you. Both times she performed, way above and beyond. Then... her life, her livelihood, everything changed. COVID shuts down Broadway, so she's not dancing. Felix's club shuts down and the sexual surrogate stuff ends... she's out of work. She just assimilated into your... I mean... our lives."

She reached out and touched his arm. "No one could ever replace Lo, so I never was looking to fill a gap. Gia, Felix, David, Robert all have their own space and …" She looked up at him, her eyes demanding his. "You, my love... are my soul."

She kissed him and he kissed back but then O pushed on his shoulders. "Wait, you said two things. That was one, what is the second thing?"

He stammered. "Ah... umm."

"Spit it."

"Yesterday, I went for an early morning run. When I came back Gia was getting out of our bed. She was naked."

O nodded. "And?"

"And... did you... I mean did you and she …"

"Have sex?"

He was now bright red.

"I knew you needed to work out, and you were trying not to wake me when you left our room, but I had been awake for hours with a headache. It wasn't the mind numbing, head bashing kind. It was my usual all-day, all-night, pounding."

O went back to smoothing the water, head down. "I was worn out and feeling pretty sorry for myself. After you left for your run, I started to cry, sobbing really. Gia heard me from her room. She came in to see if she could help."

Smoke took her hands in his.

O looked up, tears welling. "I shook her off, saying no, but she laid down beside me anyway and hugged me. I had resisted but... it was exactly what I needed. I relaxed, closed my eyes, and fell asleep. That's what you saw when you came in."

"Oh."

She could see some doubt remained. She pointed to Gia who was laughing, standing almost naked in front of two total strangers. "Gia has always been, shall we say, clothing challenged, correct?"

"Ah huh."

"When you came in from running, was I naked?"

His face went to recall. "No... no you were wearing my undershirt. But you told me you two have… I mean in the past—"

"Smoke, I have different views about sex than you. I am a psychiatrist with a bestselling book about sexual freedom. It's my job." Her voice became softer. "I have a past and so do you."

Smoke ducked his head.

"But…" She waited for his eyes to come back to hers. "We, now, today… are together, married. I didn't take a vow or make a promise as much as recognized to you that we are spiritually one, and we will experience all that love and life has to offer, together."

She saw the understanding she was looking for.

He took her hand, and they walked toward the edge of the pool.

Abruptly, she tightened her grip and grinned. "But… about the sex... you did hear the part about... all life has to offer, right?"

He pushed her and she collapsed, laughing, into the water.

He reached down, also laughing, and helped her up and out of the pool.

She dried off with a thick white towel and put her hair up in a top knot.

She normally wore her hair down, hiding the gash in her forehead left by the bullet that hit her more than a year ago. The bump she got at the book signing was gone as well as the damage from the beating she took from Hamilton Lighter. The trauma, the horror, remained, hidden behind smiling eyes and a loving heart.

Gia sat, chatting with the couple in Italian.

Smoke whispered, "What are they saying?"

O whispered back, "Looks like she made new friends, and we'll be eating dinner alone tonight."

He reached for his robe. "I didn't say this before, but you look beautiful in that bikini."

"Why, thank you. It's nice to hear you're verbalizing your thoughts and feelings."

"Trying to grow." He grinned.

They started walking for the elevator.

"Ah ha." She went in for the kill. "I noticed you purchased a new swimsuit."

"Yeah, at the gift shop in the lobby."

"Hmmm. I guess you didn't try it on, huh?"

"No, the clerk…she said it would fit fine."

"She was Italian, yes?"

He looked puzzled. "Sure."

"Smoke. Dear. You are six foot two and weigh 220 pounds."

He stammered immediately. "I got an extra-large."

"I know, but its Italian and the material is very thin. It may be extra-large… my love but..." She reached over and pulled his robe open. "So is this."

He tried to recover. "That's your fault. You wore the bikini."

Smiling, she let go of his robe and he tied it tight.

The elevator door opened and they entered. Neither pushed the button, both smiling and facing forward.

He took the initiative. “You said you were hungry. So... is it back to the room or do we stop at the buffet?”

O pushed the button for their floor.

They held hands.

6

QUANTICO, VA.

The computer screen was the only light in the room. George DiSanto was seated in a comfortable chair but had been crouched over the keyboard too long. His back, frozen in a curve, started sending the message. Standing up would be difficult.

His index finger moved the cursor on the screen then clicked the tabs on the digital file, again and again.

I'm missing something.

He glanced at the time on the corner of the screen, 4:37 a.m.

Sighing in frustration, he clicked the first tab to review the information again, from the beginning.

He reread the summary of the Arrowhead Casino shooting. He reread the next page and the next. He poured over the medical examiner's and ballistics reports and examined every photo.

Nothing.

Pushing back on the chair, exasperated, George struggled to straighten up. He hobbled across his office to a small refrigerator and withdrew a bottle of water, unscrewed the cap, and downed its contents.

Gripping the plastic bottle by the neck, he tossed it into the air towards a trashcan near the door. It soared up, arching gracefully at midpoint of the distance, and fell back to earth landing, to his surprise, in the center of the opening. This feat might not be a big deal to the average person but to a man who possessed absolutely no athletic ability whatsoever, it was noteworthy.

His mood now slightly improved, he looked back to the computer and stepped toward its beckoning light. He stretched out, reaching his hands up and arching his back, trying to undo the knots.

Suddenly stopping cold, he turned to the trashcan, then toward the computer, then back to the trashcan.

"Center mass," he yelled. "Center fucking mass."

The steps he took seemed slow, but for him he was running. The cursor was moving before he fell back into the chair.

Center mass.

Tabs opened and closed, his eyes darting, searching for confirmation. He found what he was looking for halfway down the page on tab six and again on tab seven. Then, being a detail-oriented person, he pulled up the photos and matched up the information he had just read with the images.

Son of a bitch.

He picked up his cell phone, found Robert Aimer's number, and pushed the button.

"What?" A voice neither awake nor asleep answered.

"Robert, its George. I think I have discovered something very important."

"Who the fuck..." there was a rustling sound.

George looked at the time and thought for a moment Aimer would hang up.

"It's George. Don't hang up. This is important."

There was silence as the awake person overtook the sleeping person.

"I've spent hours reviewing the files looking for something that would get this case moving forward and I think I found it."

A raspy voice asked, "What did you find?"

"Center mass."

"Center mass?"

"Taylor Bonsell from Tulsa was hit dead center in the chest. Our John Doe took one in the chest but also was shot between the eyes. The odds of both men being killed like that in an open exchange of fire is astronomical. Shot patterns like that always indicate—"

"A professional hit."

George breathed a sigh. "Exactly. I think someone knew they were coming, someone set a perimeter, and when they arrived, they were executed."

"The file I read said the guards shot them."

"Uh huh." George waited to see if the retired cop came to the same conclusion. It only took a moment but he did.

Aimer's raspy voice now clearer, spoke. "The guards weren't who they said they were."

George almost shouted. "Exactly right. IDs were established from security licenses furnished at the site. They were not asked for any other form of identification."

"They weren't who they said they were." Aimer repeated himself.

"Robert, can you go to Tulsa and look into this?"

"Wait, what? I don't understand. Why me? Isn't your outfit in charge?"

"I'm not going to report it."

"Why?"

"I'm the head of the Behavioral Analysis Unit. I don't have jurisdiction or authority in the Investigation section… and also, I'm out in eleven days. That said, I know how it works here and you need to understand, this is not an indictment of the FBI, it's just reality. This is a twenty-year-old cold case that no one is going to reopen unless there is solid evidence. What I have found is not solid proof, it's conjecture. If there is an answer out there, we will have to find it, ourselves."

“Okay, I understand. So, what’s our next move?”

“Can you go to Tulsa?”

“Sounds like a country song.” Aimer laughed.

“Well, Oklahoma isn’t rock and roll, that’s for sure. For a city boy like you it can be like going to the moon.”

“I’ll survive.”

“Do you have backup? Can you get one of your retired cop friends to go with you?”

“The ones I trust are all working second jobs but frankly… I don’t want to put anyone I know with family in harm’s way.”

“I don’t think it’s wise to go alone. You need someone to watch your back.”

George heard a chuckle.

“I got somebody who will be perfect.”

“Keep in mind, it will be important that he fits in.”

“Don’t worry, he’s a big urban cowboy.”

7

STRESA, ITALY

A boat of highly polished mahogany, outfitted with perfect chrome fittings, seats for six, and an Italian flag flying on the stern, cut though the water using only half of the power it possessed. It was a Riva, which is like a Bentley or a Rolls on the lakes of northern Italy. O looked completely at ease, like she was Grace Kelly starring in a 1950's romance movie. Smoke, however, was not feeling Cary Grantish.

The lake limo was a necessary luxury. Even in this remote paradise, O's fame preceded her, and relying on the public ferry could be problematic. There hadn't been any real issues yet but Smoke preferred preventive measures rather than leaving things to chance. Isola del Pescatori, which means Island of Fishermen, was the first stop on the tour of the three islands in Lake Maggiore. They, actually O and Gia, had decided on having brunch on the island that harbored a small fishing village as well as tourist shops and two quiet restaurants.

"What a day." Gia, today sporting an outfit with both a top and a bottom, had her hands raised and was faced into the wind like a puppy hanging out a car window.

"It is, indeed." O sat next to Smoke smiling, bare legs crossed, a red scarf stretched straight out in the wind.

The boat captain turned and shouted over the engine. "Se stai cerando un pasto, dovresti provare Trattoria Imbarcadero. Il cibo e eccellente."

Smoke looked to O.

"He recommended a restaurant. Are you hungry?"

Smoke grinned. "I could eat."

O reached out and gently rubbed his belly. "Of course, you could."

Smoke put his hand on her knee and he could feel the warmth of the sun on her skin.

She pinched the fabric of his shorts feeling the quality of the material. "You look good in… I hesitate to say this…that outfit."

Smoke didn't respond, just nodded.

"I knew you would look good in Italian linen."

Gia piped up, "You'd look better if you got a little tan there, Philly."

Again, Smoke didn't respond. He was getting used to the tag teaming. It bothered him at first but he was enjoying it lately.

The engine roar lessened.

A small ferry carrying a couple of dozen tourists had arrived at the dock before them. Smoke moved forward and told the captain not to approach until the tourists offloaded.

The three passengers in the lake limo bobbed in the water taking in the beauty of the village. It might have been the same view one would have seen when the building at the center of the island was built in the ninth century. The white steeple of San Vittore rose above the red tile roofs of small shops, homes of the twenty-eight residents, and the shaded balconies of the restaurants. Stresa and this lake with its three tiny islands were peaceful, calm and so different than any place he had ever visited. The airport in Milan looked like JFK in New York, and its crowded streets like Any City, USA. But here, a place not frequented by tour buses or accessible by cruise ships, was where the Italians went for vacation. It was where viewing its wonders was free, and where one took long pauses between sips of wine.

The engine sputtered and the captain nudged the bow forward when the ferry backed out from shore. Smoke hung his hand over the side, testing the water. Fresh from its mountain home, it was crystal-clear and cold, unaffected by the sunny eighty-degree day. The seagulls flying overhead looking for a handout veered off when the engine gave the boat a sudden push forward toward the dock.

Gia got up first, and stumbled forward almost falling when the captain reversed the engine.

Smoke was next to stand; he braced and stuck a hand out to O.

She had her head back and he could tell, even behind her oversized sunglasses, her eyes were closed.

He waited patiently.

The boat jolted slightly as the mate on the dock tied the bow rope to a hitch.

O looked up, smiled, and took his hand.

"We should ask the captain for a recommendation for lunch, don't you think?"

Smoke didn't respond at first.

She didn't remember what the captain said.

O looked at him puzzled.

"Umm… I will." He pointed to the dock. "You go ahead, catch up with the dancer."

Gia was halfway to the steps leading to the flying flags, brightly colored awnings, and the cobblestone promenade. She was actually skipping.

O stepped off the boat and waved to her friend. "Hey, wait for me."

Smoke watched her walk, straight in the middle of the dock, no waver.

He tapped his back pocket feeling his wallet making sure it got off the boat when he did. He wasn't fond of shorts outside of a gym but he acquiesced to her wishes and agreed to a new look for this trip. She made an argument that dungarees and a t-shirt would make him stand out and draw unwanted attention. He didn't buy it, but like wearing a suit and tie and the occasional tuxedo in New York, he agreed.

He tapped the front pocket for his cell phone and for a second thought about returning George DiSanto's call. It had been three days since the FBI man left a message and he did say it was important. He tapped it again and decided.

Not now.

Smoke caught up to them at a shop selling everything touristy. Gia was holding a bracelet of multicolored stones up to the sun.

A small woman, whose age was hard to determine, stood close to her customers. "Thosea are da Seven Sacred Shapes of Balance and possess great powers. Th'ill will bring chakra healing, and…how you say… ah… balance to whomever wears it."

Gia looked to O for approval.

"It's beautiful. Let me get that for you." O turned to the woman with the long black hair. "How much?"

"Thirty-two euro… about forty dollars U.S."

Gia had a frown on her face. "I was buying it for you."

O was stumped for a moment. "I'm sorry… I didn't mean to—."

"The two of you could both use a lot of balance and that chakra stuff couldn't hurt." Smoke stepped up to the much, much smaller vendor. "I'll take two. One for each of the ladies."

He immediately received a double hug.

While paying, Smoke asked, "Where is the Tratt…a…oria Imbar…?"

"You mean the Trattoria Imbarcadero." The woman pointed, "On thisa side of da street, there are some a steps going up. The restaurant is at the top." She leaned closer and whispered, "Order the catch of the day. You wanta the fresha fish." She winked and handed Smoke the bag of chakra balance.

After buying a matching pair of sun hats from another store, they found the stairs going up in a narrow alley. There was no hand rail and the steps were definitely not handicap friendly. Gia went first of course, bounding up like a deer followed by a much slower O, with Smoke bringing up the rear.

O reached out several times, bracing herself on the walls as she ascended.

Smoke got up behind her, staying close, in case.

The sun hit their faces when they emerged from the alley, and, to their hungry delight, found the eatery door open in front of them.

A concierge smiled and beckoned them forward. "Ciao."

Gia responded quickly, "Ciao. Siamo molto affamati. Hai un tavolo co vista sul lago?"

O started to translate but Smoke held up his hand. "A table overlooking the lake, right?"

"What? How? Did you suddenly learn Italian?"

Smoke smiled and took her by the waist following behind Gia. "Nope, logic. A beautiful day, a beautiful view. She wasn't asking for a table near the fireplace."

They ordered the fish of the day. It was perch, fresh from the lake that morning and delicious, but the risotto was unforgettable. The waiter told them the creamy rice was invented in northern Italy. Going forward, any future orders would have to be held to this new standard. The dessert was Dolce Della Casa, a small tower of layers of cooked cream divided by sheets of dark chocolate.

Smoke pointed his fork to O's plate. "You didn't finish your Della... your chocolate thing."

"Too good. I'm savoring." O touched Smoke's hand. "Can you call the waiter? I'd like a glass of wine."

He winced. Alcohol was on the 'no list' but the headaches seemed to be lessening and her spirits were better. He gestured to the waiter.

A carafe of dark red wine appeared with three long-stemmed glasses.

The three tapped the crystal and sipped.

The sun was now lower in the sky and had slipped under the porch awning.

When O shaded her eyes, Gia went into her carry-all for O's sunglasses.

"Thank you," O said gratefully. "What would I do without the two of you?"

Smoke had an answer. "You'd be in your office with a patient and a headache."

O slipped on her sunglasses and didn't respond.

Smoke let the moment hang for a beat. "Excuse me, I need the bathroom."

He stood, pushed his chair in, and looked at O who was staring at the lake.

There was a small hallway leading to the restroom. He stopped and turned to look back.

Gia was reaching into her carry-all bag again. She took out a small white bottle, shook out a few pills and handed them to O.

O picked up her water glass and when she put the pills in her mouth and raised the glass to drink, Gia glanced up at Smoke, frowned, and shook her head once.

8

TULSA, OKLAHOMA

Robert Aimer had been a police officer for more than twenty-five years, serving the city where he was born and neighborhood where he was raised. He lived in a rowhouse three blocks over and two blocks down from where his parents brought him home from the hospital. His job and family kept him grounded and if one assumed he was not a world traveler they would be correct.

He had not lived his life entirely in Philadelphia. He'd flown before, several times to Florida visiting retired relatives, once each to Chicago, Atlanta, and Los Angeles to crime enforcement seminars, and a twenty-fifth wedding anniversary in Bermuda. There was also a trip to Las Vegas where 'What happens in Vegas stays in Vegas'. That is of course, unless one is a non-participant, and the pleasure seeker eventually becomes one's boss, in which case the secret becomes a bit of career leverage.

Nothing he had experienced in the past, however, prepared him for the trip to Tulsa. Looking for the cheapest flight, Aimer found there were no direct flights from Philadelphia. The one he chose had a three-hour layover in Houston before connecting to Oklahoma and the city on the edge of the Great Plains. The first flight was as expected but the second leg was a small commuter jet that had the same number of crew as seats across the aisle— four. It seemed old, a fact he assumed to be true, when he discovered the armrest came equipped with an ashtray whose lid had been welded shut. The plane had only ten rows of seats and about half of the seats were empty. He did not have enough facts to deduce if the plane was half full because of the Covid fears or because no one wanted to go to Tulsa.

The issues he had with the layovers and age of the plane paled when compared to the non-stop banter coming from his tattooed friend sitting next to him.

"Jesus H Christ on a scooter, will you give it a rest?"

Felix Upton Grant looked at Aimer, stunned. He turned away, a big meaty hand came up to his face, hiding his expression.

Aimer felt some regret. Felix didn't hesitate when Robert asked him to come along to watch his back. "I'm sorry… I mean… I'm not really sorry, but I really need you to shut up. I just didn't have to be a dick about it."

Felix spun back around with a big toothy grin plastered on his face. "Jesus H Christ on a scooter, that's a good one. Never heard that before. Very inventive."

The moment he thought his rudeness would cause Felix to stop talking passed.

Felix, undaunted, started in again about how Covid affected him and his business.

Aimer turned to look out the porthole window. Thankfully, he could see the airport. At first, he thought it wasn't Tulsa International because there were fighter planes lined up side-by- side next to a series of hangers. But then he saw a commercial jet in final approach and another taxiing to buildings on the opposite side of the runway.

The intercom speaker barked. "Looks like we lucked out here folks. We are in the landing pattern and will be coming around to runway two-six and should be touching down in about ten minutes."

The intercom broke off then crackled back on with information that no one needed. "We are landing just in front of a really bad frontal system moving in quickly from the west. It could be tornado time, so once we hit the tarmac, we will be hustling a bit faster than normal to the gate."

"Great." Aimer shook his head.

A flight attendant passed by and Felix grabbed his arm. "Did he say tornado?"

"He did, but don't worry about it, happens a lot this time of year. They hardly ever hit the ground."

Felix, dumfounded, responded, "Yeah, but we're not on the ground."

The attendant just smiled and headed off.

The plane suddenly hit turbulence, bounced through a banking turn, dropped quickly, landed, then did a Formula 1 racing sprint to the terminal.

They deplaned quickly and got their first view of what a tornado sky looked like through the plate-glass windows in the terminal. Huge black clouds expanding in height and width seemed to be tumbling towards the airport from the west. Above them, an almost stationary blanket of thick grey formed an impenetrable ceiling, pushing the rolling black energy back to the ground. The two forces dominated everything except for a sliver of daylight, just above the distant western horizon. The gap wasn't blue sky offering a hope of the passing of weather's violence, instead, it was filled with a lifeless yellow color that was streaked with grey and black. Neither Aimer or Felix had seen anything like it before.

A passenger from their flight wearing a well broken-in cowboy hat passed behind them. "Here she comes."

"A tornado?" Felix asked pensively.

"Don't think so," the man pointed, "see those clouds up there, twirling around? They're too high. If there's a twister...probably won't hit the ground."

Aimer exhaled a long breath. "That's good news, I guess."

The cowboy hat started away. "But then again, my wife says I'm wrong about everything."

Aimer and Felix looked at each other then back out the window.

A gust of wind hit the huge piece of glass hard causing it to pulsate rapidly. They backed up a step, fearing it would shatter.

Two men wearing ground crew vests suddenly abandoned a vehicle pulling a series of empty luggage carts and took off running full-out towards the lower level of the terminal.

A few drops of rain bounced off the glass.

There was a momentary pause, the howling wind ceased and the glass stopped moving.

In the next second, everything visible from the window was obliterated by sheets of rain. It came from every direction; horizontal, vertical, and what seemed like from the ground up.

The rest of the passengers were filing past without giving much notice to the violent weather just feet away. Aimer and Felix turned and followed them down the corridor under the sign that read *To Baggage Claim.*

Their first experience in Tulsa was memorable.

The area with the rolling belt and multicolored luggage did not have huge windows. They were surprised that by the time they retrieved their suitcases, and pushed through double doors to the access road, the storm had dissipated. However, it had filled the gutters to capacity and people crossing the access road stepped carefully to avoid the rushing water.

Felix looked up and down the sidewalk.

Aimer seemed concerned. "Are you sure we're to meet your friend here?"

"Yes and no. Yes here, but no, he's not my friend. The man we are meeting does some work with my David."

"Remind me please, I don't recall all the details."

Felix looked a little surprised. "Okay, a refresher. The love of my life, David, is a statistical analyst working with the capital investment arm of Goldman Sachs. Among the many ventures given to him by their customers for analysis are financing proposals for Native American Tribes. David tells me that they must be looked at very closely because the proposals while having the potential for high returns are extremely risky. If an offering gets past the initial stages, he calls Cliff Warford for local background information before finalizing his report. Cliff is who we are meeting."

A tall man with a ponytail wearing a long leather jacket came out of the parking lot and headed toward them. He was big, heavy-built and took long strides. He also was exactly what a white man from a big city would assume a Native American Indian looked like.

"You Felix Grant?"

"I am." Felix pointed, "This is Robert Aimer."

Cliff nodded. "I'm parked over there." He turned and started walking away.

The truck was a four passenger Ford with oversized tires, trails of dirt from the wheel wells, and spotted with the carcasses of several hundred bugs.

After they were seated, Cliff spoke. "You want to go to the casino?"

Aimer nodded. "That's the place to start."

Felix, sitting in the back, leaned forward. "That weather was pretty scary."

"Yep." Cliff turned the key.

An awkward silence followed.

Felix tried again. "So, Native American Indian, Native American, Indigenous People or that other one...First Nation, what do you prefer to be called?"

"Cliff."

The awkward silence built momentum but ended when Cliff broke into a belly laugh. "Wow, that never gets old. You big city fellows are so freaking gullible."

Cliff, after he stopped laughing, talked about the weather and how this time of year storms came up quickly and disappeared just as fast. He also talked about his background, growing up on the Keetoowah reservation, and his service in the Army which is where he met David.

"I got out after ten years and went to work for a fracking outfit. It was good for a while but I was very happy when David reached out a few years ago for background on his projects. The consulting fee really helps out with the truck payments."

"That reminds me, David didn't mention anything about how much…"

"No need," Cliff held up his hand. "David explained the situation. This one is on the house."

"Great, thanks. So, David filled you in then."

"Yep. I think it's best if I give you the broad strokes on the Odawa Tribe."

Aimer pulled out a notebook.

"It was recently recognized by the Bureau of Indian Affairs as a tribal nation which entitled it to have a sovereign property. That means along with tribal offices, a school and a clinic, it also has the right to a casino. They are among many tribes in Oklahoma that have them, about 140 casinos operated by 33, now 34, tribes."

"That seems like a lot," Felix said, surprised.

"Seems like it but most are small and they service the states that border Oklahoma. There are only a couple of casinos in the six surrounding states with Arkansas and Texas having the longest borders and the fewest casinos. The tribal casinos in Oklahoma are really drawing gamblers from all over the Midwest."

"And the newest one is the Arrowhead?"

"Uh-huh. It's a dozen double-wide trailers bolted together but they have all the bells and whistles. It's north, close to Kansas and Missouri and still only half an hour from the burbs of Tulsa."

Aimer shot the next question. "Anybody unhappy about the new competition?"

"The tribe met hard opposition in the BIA when it went in for recognition, but not from the government. It was the Cherokee. They threw all their lawyers at the problem but lost. They have ten facilities with the biggest and best, the Vegas style Hard Rock in Tulsa. And they hate losing market share to anyone."

Aimer, puzzled, asked, "One tribe fighting another? I don't get it."

"It's not about tribes or heritage or the First Nation's struggle for existence. It's about money."

Aimer wasn't satisfied. "But is this double-wide trailer casino really a big threat?"

Cliff was quiet for a moment. "The Odawa are a small tribe and the casino tiny compared to the hotel resort the Cherokee own and actually, no, not really. Just small-time action, a bunch of slots and a few table games, nothing big. I don't agree with what they did to this tribe, fighting to keep them from being recognized but this shooting—definitely not the Cherokee. I don't buy the parking lot-kidnapping story either... a gun battle with two dead... doesn't add up for me."

"You're right, Cliff," Aimer affirmed, "It doesn't."

A road sign for Route 281 north appeared out Felix's window. "I haven't seen anything but a few cows, wire fence, and a lot of empty road. How far till we get to a town and the casino?"

"Arrowhead is not far. About ten miles but it's not on this highway. It's back in a ways... and there is no town, just the casino."

Felix didn't hesitate. "Good thing we have an Indian guide."

Cliff whipped his head around to the backseat with a stern look on his face.

Felix froze for a second.

"Good one." Cliff laughed again and so did the boys.

9

STRESA, ITALY

The front doors of the hotel were tall, contained leaded glass, and were narrow compared to modern standards. However, the best of today's architects would be hard pressed to capture the same sense of arrival the Regina Palace offered. A paver sidewalk from the harbor lead to the entry, encircling a topiary garden displaying the hotel's name in yellow flowers and perfectly manicured shrubbery. Red flowers hung from the balconies of each room above the flag of Italy and the owner's family crest.

Smoke was returning after taking advantage of O's fatigue from the boat tour. While she napped in a darkened bedroom, he changed into gym shorts and a t-shirt, and went for a run. Favoring interval sprints followed by cool-down jogs, running kept his stamina up and his weight down. This small town built into a mountain proved more challenging than the streets of Philadelphia or New York. He had been out for an hour and the t-shirt had changed color with sweat.

Slowing to a walk, he turned off the only legitimate two-lane road in the town and came up the sidewalk split in two by the carefully manicured garden.

The cell phone in his pocket vibrated. The screen read Mt. Sinai Hospital.

He immediately pushed the button. “Hello.”

“Mr. Henry Smokehouse?”

Every time somebody called him Henry, he felt pain. “Yes.”

“Hold for Doctor Brightman.”

A click was followed by Muzak which also caused his ears to bleed. Smoke glanced at his screen; 3:30 p.m. here 9:30 a.m. there.

“Mr. Smokehouse.”

“Yes. Doctor Brightman?”

“I just finished rounds and got your message. What’s her condition?”

“She had a headache last night and again today. They seem to be less intense than before, but still happening. I also noticed she repeated herself… asking the same question a couple of times and then today, she had to steady herself going up a set of stairs.”

“Nausea?”

“Not much of an appetite, but no.”

“Any blood in the eyes or coming from the ears?”

“No.”

“Ringing in the ears, weakness of arms or legs?”

“She mentioned ringing but only once two days ago, and she hasn’t complained since.”

“Slurred speech, dizziness?”

“Just the stair thing today.”

Silence.

“Doctor?”

“Yes, I’m here. It’s, of course, impossible to draw accurate conclusions over the phone—”

“But?”

“But... I’m concerned the dizziness and headaches, even though they are less intense, are persisting.”

“Should we come back to New York?”

Another long pause.

Brightman answered with conviction. “No, I don’t think so. Not yet. I recommended isolation as the best way to remove stress from her life and I think we should stick to the plan.”

Smoke anticipated, “Is there a however?”

“Yes... however, I cannot emphasize how serious complications from a concussion could be. Granted, the last concussion was a small event compared to the other two, but the danger is still very real. Medical science has much to learn about the impact of multiple brain injuries. Concussion research is just ramping up, largely because of the press coverage of athletes.”

“I understand, but what should I be doing?”

“I know how it must feel thinking you’re helpless but you’re keeping her stress level down and, in my opinion, that is essential to her recovery.”

“How will I know if—”

“If she becomes confused, forgetful, dramatically changes her behavior, or overly fatigued, call me. If she passes out, get her to a hospital immediately. Don’t call first. Just go. And if that happens, if you take her to an emergency room, tell the attending physician I want an MRI stat. You have all my numbers. You can call me, anytime, day or night.”

“Got it.”

“Anything else, Mr. Smokehouse?”

“Ah... actually yes, one thing. I never asked you about sex?”

“Is this a post-facto question?”

“It is.”

“Did she seem relaxed and at ease during and after?”

“Yes.”

“Then yes, sex is okay but remember, everything in moderation.”

“Right, and thanks Doctor Brigh—”

“Bob. Please call me Bob.”

“Sure, and my name is Smoke.”

Smoke walked thru the lobby quickly and took the stairs because the antique elevator already smelled old and didn't need his lingering sweat adding to the bouquet. He ran up the first flight, and walked the next four. The hills in the town were enough of a workout.

The door to room 515 was in the center of the hall and the building. It opened into a living room that had a balcony overlooking the lake at its far end. Gold Italian Renaissance trim crowned the ceilings and framed period oil paintings on the walls. Upholstered furniture with thin wooden arms and legs had sustained wear and tear for decades, but he was careful assuming the chairs were not meant for his bulk.

The room was quiet and their bedroom door was closed. He stepped left and looked out the glass doors to the balcony and saw Gia's foot high in the air, keeping a beat.

She wore ear pods, sunglasses, and thankfully both pieces of her bikini.

Smoke gave a short attention-getting wave. "Hey."

Gia lifted her glasses and removed the earphones. "Hey back. Good run?"

"Yep. You should try it. The slopes are killers."

She leaned forward and whispered. "I saw you come up the walk from here… talking on the phone. New York?"

He nodded.

Gia asked reluctantly. "We headed home?"

"Nope."

She broke into a smile. "Good news then?"

"Okay, I guess, but we still need to keep all stress to a minimum." He walked over and sat next to her. "Any change? Did she seem dizzy? Or repeat herself?"

"No." She shook her head. "She went in and fell asleep pretty quick."

"Good."

"What did the doctor say we should be watching for?"

"Dizzy, disoriented, forgetful, and the headaches... if they persist or grow in intensity."

She gave an understanding nod. "I checked on her a couple of times. She woke up once, asked for some water then nodded off again."

He was relieved.

Gia stood and stretched. "I'm going to hit the gym then take a steam before dinner. Okay?"

"Sure, and Gia ...?"

She turned and looked at him.

"Thank you. I don't say it enough because I don't talk much, but I want you to know I really appreciate you."

Her face lit up then she kissed his cheek, and darted back inside.

When he heard the door to Gia's room close, he went inside, opened their bedroom door, and stood there. O was laying with her back to him covered by a pure white sheet.

Without turning over, she raised her arm up and over her body and tapped the bed beside her with her hand. "Take a shower before you come to bed. I think you need rest as much as I do."

10

OUTSIDE TULSA OKLAHOMA

The truck pulled onto a paved entrance road of the Arrowhead Casino. A low sign, labeled PARKING, had a long-feathered arrow directing traffic to the parking area. The lot wasn't full but it wasn't empty either. Since there were no painted lines, dozens of cars, trucks and vans were randomly parked. The ground surrounding the gravel lot mimicked the vast empty spaces they'd passed on the highway, flat, almost treeless, and surrounded at its perimeter with wire fence.

Aimer pushed open his door, noting the front of the truck was covered with grey dust. The heat made him wince. He adjusted his sunglasses as he surveyed the lot. "We are ten miles from anything. There are no gas stations or 7-11s and we passed maybe two houses, but at 3 o'clock on a hot Wednesday afternoon there are thirty cars in the lot."

"Twenty miles," corrected Cliff.

"In what direction?" questioned Felix.

"Every direction. The state line is north and there is a little town on the border. We just came from south; east isn't any different and to the west... might be more than thirty miles."

Turning back to the floor of the passenger side, Aimer picked up a manila file. He faced the lot, opened the FBI file, its contents secured with a metal clip. He flipped to a photo, then positioned himself to mirror the camera angle. He twisted the file to match the angle of each picture, looking at the difference between what was inside the borders of the image and what wasn't.

Felix was stretching but got curious and looked over Aimer's shoulder.

Aimer made his first comment. "This is interesting."

Cliff had joined them. "What did you see?"

"There are no cameras pointing toward the lot. There are two mounted on the roof, both aimed at the front door. I will assume there are others at the back and maybe a side exit, but nothing in the parking lot. Curious."

"Is that unusual?" Felix seemed bored.

Aimer didn't answer and instead flipped the file to a long shot photo of one of the bodies. The photographer must have had his back to the casino and was facing the fence line. "What do you see?"

Both Cliff and Felix looked but did not see.

"I give up." Felix went from being bored back to hot and uncomfortable.

Aimer put a finger on the background of the photo. "See it now?"

Cliff bent closer, examined the photo, then looked out to the fence line. "Son of a gun."

Felix's boredom became frustration. "What? I don't see anything different."

"There was a pole with a camera right there." He held up the file and pointed toward the fence. "The pole and the camera in the picture are gone."

Felix scratched his head. "Damn."

Aimer closed the file, tossed it into the truck, and the men headed to the casino entrance, Cliff in front. The three walked single-file up a wooden ramp leading to a sign with three red arrowheads arranged in an arch which was fastened over a solid double door.

Felix commented from the back of the line. "Not exactly the fountains at Caesars."

Cliff opened the door and the heat and sunlight changed to air conditioning and cool darkness. Their relief was momentary and spoiled by ringing bells, country music, and a lungful of cigarette smoke.

"Oh my god," Felix exclaimed, "this smoke is crazy."

Cliff coughed a little. "Low ceilings on the trailers. There are smoke arresters and the air conditioners run non-stop but this is like most of the small casinos. Smoking restrictions don't apply on sovereign ground and most people just get used to it."

Cliff continued inside with the two men in tow.

They passed slot machines with players in almost every row. At the end of a line of tall, noisy, progressive slots, a gray-haired woman in a summer smock wearing sneakers had taken up residence. On the seat to her right were a giant handbag and a water bottle. On her left was a pull cart with a portable oxygen tank and clear plastic tubes running to her nose. Her eyes were fixed on the flying wheels, her right hand ready to push the red play button again. Her left hand held a half empty cup of beer and a lit cigarette.

The three arrived at a bar near the back, next to a small slightly elevated stage. It was empty save for a set of drums and a microphone stand.

Felix broke off from the procession and got the attention of a woman pouring beer from a tap. "Can I get a cold water please?"

You would think he'd asked her to change the music to Rock and Roll. "Water…just water. Nothing in it?"

Aimer raised his hand. "Make that two please. Wait. Cliff, you want one?"

Cliff pretended he didn't know them.

The barmaid shook her head, poked around in a cooler of ice, and pulled out two bottles of water. "Eight bucks."

Aimer stepped in front of Felix, who looked like he was about to complain, and put a ten on the bar. "Keep the change."

Cliff gave a direction with a head nod and both men followed.

A man in a western shirt, black jeans, and black boots had his back against a wall next to a steel door under a red exit sign.

Cliff approached and stood right in front of him. "Lieutenant Eyota, he here?"

The man, young, stocky, and several inches shorter than Cliff, looked up. "Who wants to know?"

Cliff paused then said slowly, "I do."

The man hesitated. His eyes darted back and forth but then said, "I'll check."

Cliff fixed a stare on the man walking away and spoke softly to Aimer. "When the Lieutenant gets here, identify yourself and why we're here. He will tell us to leave. He will never talk where he could be overheard. If he follows us out, he'll talk. If he doesn't, he won't and nothing will change that."

A long five minutes went by before the Lieutenant appeared. He was tall, thin, and young, maybe thirty. He had a long pony tail, a uniform, a badge, and a gun.

"What can I do for you gentlemen?"

Aimer took the lead. "My name is Robert Aimer. This is my associate Felix Grant and a friend, Cliff Warford."

The tribal officer addressed Cliff. "I know you…Keetoowah band of Cherokee?"

Cliff nodded.

Aimer spoke quickly, like a cop. "I am investigating the shooting that took place in the parking lot."

Lieutenant Eyota's expression didn't change.

"I would like to ask you a few questions."

Eyota took a beat, looked at Cliff, then Felix, then back to Aimer. "No."

Aimer objected, “We have come a long way and I only have a couple—”

“I said no and let me show you the exit.” Lieutenant Eyota nodded towards the front.

Cliff put his hand on Aimer’s shoulder. “Let’s go.”

The shock of the light caused hands to shade eyes and locate sunglasses quickly.

When they reached the bottom of the ramp, Lieutenant Eyota spoke in a low voice. “Keep walking, and don’t turn around. People are watching. Cliff Warford is known to be standup and he is the only reason this is happening. You have time for two questions.”

Aimer walking and facing forward, responded quickly. “The two bodies…we know one, Taylor Bonsell, from Tulsa. We don’t have an ID on the other. Do you know who he was?”

“Don’t know either one. I ran them out of here twice for selling cocaine and ecstasy. Question two?”

Aimer paused, calculating the next question’s value. “Both men were shot, by your guards, center mass, two shots each.”

“Not my guards.”

Aimer started to turn around but Cliff put a hand on his shoulder and gave him a nudge foreword.

“What? What does that mean, not my guards?”

“That’s three questions. You only had two.” Lieutenant Eyota stopped walking as they approached Cliff’s truck.

Aimer and Felix got in, but when Cliff walked past Eyota to the driver’s side, the Lieutenant lowered his head and spoke to the ground. “Some people said the guy with no name had a funny foreign accent.”

Cliff continued on without acknowledging Eyota. As he was getting into the truck, he saw four men standing on the ramp.

Eyota yelled to them as they pulled out. “Don’t come back.”

Felix leaned forward over the front seat. “Gee, he wasn’t very nice.”

Cliff turned the truck back toward Tulsa. “Did you see the guys watching us leave?”

"Yep," Aimer nodded, "they didn't look like they belonged. They looked like me and Felix…like they were from a big city."

When the truck paused at the exit, Cliff turned and faced Aimer. "Before I got in the truck, Eyota told me the guy we were looking for had a funny accent."

Aimer nodded again then looked out the window as the endless fence passed by and spoke low, almost a whisper. "Center mass…center mass."

The hum of the wheels was hypnotic. The hot afternoon sun overwhelmed the truck's minimal air conditioning. The small space of the crew cab caused Felix to get jostled around as he tried to fold his six-foot-four frame sideways on the seat.

The truck hit a bump and Felix's head bounced off the window he was using as a headrest. "Damn," he exclaimed, rubbing the back of his head, "how come I got stuck back here?"

Still in thought, Aimer didn't turn around. "I paid for the tickets."

Cliff chuckled for the first time. "And it's my truck."

Felix grunted but apparently accepted his current lot.

Cliff had a deep voice and when he spoke, which wasn't often, his words came slow, commanding attention. "Center mass is a term used in training, military, police."

It wasn't a question but Aimer answered. "Yes, not something usually found in a shootout in a parking lot. Multiple bullet impacts would be in evidence, dug out of walls, cars, and the bodies…rounds fired by both sides."

"Both sides?" Cliff asked.

Aimer turned away from the window. "The ME… I mean the Medical…"

"Medical Examiner, I watch CSI." Cliff didn't look over.

"Right. The ME report contained information on four bullets, all from the dead bodies. The bullets matched the weapons taken from the guards. None matched ballistics from the gun carried by Lieutenant

Eyota. His weapon had been fired recently but there was no evidence proving the weapon had been fired at the scene."

Felix weighed in. "What about the Chief? He got shot. Wouldn't that be five rounds?"

Cliff corrected Felix. "Chairman, not chief."

"Huh?"

"The title chief implies one person with ultimate authority. Almost every tribe has a chairman with decisions made by a committee."

"The chairman," Aimer continued, "was wounded in the upper arm with a thru and thru. No bullet, no fragments. He was grazed, a clean wound, impossible to determine with certainty a bullet caliber."

"Hmmm." Felix followed the thought to the next level, seemingly pleased with his deduction. "So, what you're saying is there were five shots fired, two each at the dead guys and one hitting the...chairman."

"Actually, no."

"Again, huh?"

"The guards had Glocks with only one shell missing from the clip. So, one of the bullets was in the chamber and the other one came from the clip. Four casings were recovered from the scene."

Felix continued his line of questioning. "Which means they carried a pistol with a round in the chamber? Not the way I was trained."

"A Glock has a safety making the weapon virtually impossible to fire accidently."

"And?" Cliff turned to Aimer, now also looking puzzled.

"The shooter from Tulsa had a 38 revolver, all rounds fired. The other had a 45 automatic with an empty clip."

Felix put his paw on the seat and leaned forward. "Which means?"

Aimer looked back out the window.

Cliff was patient.

Felix not so much. "Come on, man, don't leave us hangin."

"I think the dead guys didn't see it coming. I think they never drew their weapons. I think they were killed and their guns fired afterwards to make it look like the guards acted in self-defense. I think that is what Lieutenant Eyota was trying to tell us. When I said your guards shot two men, he immediately said, 'Not my guards.'"

Cliff blew out a stream of air. "Which means?"

"Four shots from the two guards' guns with a fifth shot wounding the chairman, indicates he wasn't hit during the gunfight. The chairman was shot afterwards with one of the dead guy's guns."

Cliff drew in a stream of air.

Aimer looked at Cliff who was staring out the windshield. "It also indicates the chairman is involved."

Quiet ensued.

Felix pushed back into the crew cab seat.

11

STRESA, ITALY

The mirror fixed to the lobby wall accurately reflected a man in desperate need of a shave and a haircut. Smoke checked his watch, scratched his stubble, and looked at the mirror again. Reluctantly, he pushed the door leading into the Hotel's Salon and entered like he was walking into the ladies room.

"Oh mio dio, guardati." A very thin man with jet black hair had both his hands on his cheeks and a look of shock on his face.

"Umm... Can I get a haircut here?" Smoke made a cutting scissors motion.

The man, who looked like he could have been thirty, forty, or perhaps even fifty, glided forward. "Please excuse my rudeness. Americano, yes?"

Smoke nodded uncomfortably, surveying the room for anything masculine or sports related, but found none.

"Carlo, please call me Carlo... Mister?"

"Smoke."

"Ah, Mr. Smoke, you are a guest with us?"

The uncut hair nodded and Carlo guided Mr. Smoke to a chair and another mirror.

A young woman with eyes outlined in black and hair dyed platinum blond, appeared and stood close to Carlo.

Carlo made a tsk tsk sound, then spoke to his assistant. "Mio dio cosa dovremmo fare con questo mocio?"

Smoke looked at Carlo's reflection in the mirror sternly, like he understood what had been said.

"Sorry, Mr. Smoke, but I don't know where to start... you're so... overgrown."

"I get that a lot."

Carlo smiled, revealing unbelievably white teeth. "Gloria will shampoo you then I will work my magic. But first can I interest you in a very close shave?"

Smoke scratched his face again. "Why not?"

"Eccellente."

Carlo spun the chair around, away from the mirror so Smoke could not see what was going on. The hair master looked at his client. "Trust me."

Smoke shrugged acceptance, thinking, worst case, it'll grow back in four weeks.

Smoke's phone buzzed an incoming message just as Carlo exclaimed, "Ecco." He raised his hands in celebration then explained. "That means ta-da in English."

The phone came out of his pocket as Smoke looked in the mirror for the first time in an hour.

"Hmmm. I look... human. Thanks, Carlo."

"You're very welcome, Mr. Smoke."

The text read: *Getting in elevator. Meet you in lobby.*

Smoke, with his new do and Italian linen shirt, arrived near the front door just as Gia and O exited the lift.

A couple in a corner stopped talking and stared at the two women. A single man coming from the dining room almost tripped over the stairs going up to the next level.

They were showstoppers.

Gia wore a red top and bottom, naturally both skimpy, that fit her form perfectly.

O, next to Gia, seemed more conservative. Her white summer dress had a scoop neckline with a hem showing off legs that went all the way up.

"Do you like it?" Gia approached, gleaming. "O bought this outfit for me. Isn't it wonderful?" She spun as only a dancer could.

"Beautiful."

O looked at him. "Hi handsome, you live around here?"

Smoke remembered his new hair. "Oh that. Yeah well, I just let Carlo—

"Carlo... I can't wait to tell Felix you have a stylist named Carlo."

Smoke tried, unsuccessfully, to fend off the remark and sputtered, "Are we going out for a walk or what?"

Gia fake punched him. "Don't be so sensitive. You look... great... almost, kinda—"

"Human?" he finished her thought.

"No, butt-head. I was going to say, almost presentable." She winked, then bolted past them. "Bye-bye. Have a good time."

O took him by the arm and started for the door. "Gia isn't coming with us; she's meeting a new friend for lunch."

They left the Palace and ambled along the Corsa Umberto and the seawall near the lake. They weren't talking, just walking.

The buildings, houses, stores, churches, all had foundations going back centuries but like any town the cityscape had changed over time. The Chiesa Santi Ambrogio e Theodolo was untouched by progress, weather, or purpose. Some other structures remained as built, but many, over time, changed their outerwear along the way; swapping out original function for current need. Progress happened but in Stresa, Italy, it happened very, very slowly.

"You hungry?"

"I could eat."

She laughed. "You always say that."

From the walkway near the harbor, O spotted a sign hanging out from a stone wall midway up an alley. "That looks interesting, let's go there."

"I wonder if the food is good?"

She started up the street. "Don't be silly, of course it is."

The road was narrow, paved with cobblestones and lined on either side by three-and four-story buildings each with long windows, and multi-colored wood shutters. It was more an alley than a road, built for horse-drawn carts and foot traffic, not automobiles.

The sign O had seen was for a small neighborhood restaurant. It had two rooms. One had five round tables each with four chairs. The other was a smaller area with ornately framed black and white photos of the generations of the owners, and a glass display case. It was filled with blocks of cheese, trays of olives, and dried meats bound tight with string, and looked photo ready for a gourmet magazine cover.

Two old men with grey scraggly beards, busy concentrating on a game of chess, paid them no mind.

O and Smoke sat at a table next to the window.

A short, stout man wearing a white apron appeared. "Ciao."

O took over. "Ciao, Come stai oggi?"

"Bene e tu?"

"Bene, bene."

"C'e un menu?" The man tilted his head, giving it a short shake. "Americana, yes?"

"Si, we are Americans."

"No menu but please, allowa me to bring my besta to you, bella signora."

O smiled and nodded to the man then looked to Smoke. "Understand all that?"

"All I needed too... he's bringing food, correct?"

"You're a bit of a barbarian."

"Indeed, but like Popeye says, I ams what I am."

The man reappeared, interrupting Smoke's scholarly repartee, carrying a large tray of... everything, two long-stemmed glasses, and a carafe of red wine.

Smoke looked longingly at the tray and with concern at the wine.

"It would be a very grave insult to turn down the wine." O shrugged off his apprehension and poured.

The bread crust snapped when he broke off a piece. Every chunk of cheese was a different color and it was an arrestable crime if eaten quickly, but the wine... the wine... beyond description.

Three games of chess passed by on the old men's table; two carafes of wine on the American's.

"Enough." O called out first and pushed away from the table. "Oh my God. I won't eat for a week."

Smoke nodded while finishing off the end of a loaf of bread and draining the last of the wine from his glass.

"I have to pee." O stood and walked away. Both old men, the waiter, and Smoke watched.

He motioned to the man in the apron and he arrived with a check anticipating their departure. "It's a been a ..." he stumbled searching for the English word, "... piaceren... a... a ..." he suddenly grinned, "pleasure."

"Believe me, it's all mine." Smoke opened the leather folder.

Twenty-two euros? That can't be right.

"Ready?" O arrived at his side.

"Am I reading this right, that's like only, what, twenty-five bucks?"

"Actually, about twenty-seven." She patted his shoulder and winked. "Leave a big tip."

Smoke stuck a fifty euro note in the folder.

O frowned a little. "A bit much?"

"Just doing our part in dispelling the Ugly American thing."

The afternoon sun was warm and a gentle breeze drifted up the alley from the lake.

"Which way do you want to go?"

O looked up and down the cobblestone path. "Don't want to go back the way we came. Let's see what's up there."

The path went from the harbor to the foot of the mountain about three blocks up from where they exited the trattoria. They walked past a dress shop, a tailor, a lawyer's office, a bakery, and an old bookstore; all of them closed.

"I wonder why these places aren't open. Siesta?"

"Probably, but in Italy it's called a Riposo."

Their pace slowed dramatically as the slope got steeper.

A red arched church door on a stone building facing them became their goal and they trudged on.

"We can walk along the road at the top before heading down to the Hotel. The view should be pretty good from there." Smoke looked down and saw O struggling. "You need to take a break?"

"Nope, just too much to eat. I need to walk it off."

It took several minutes to reach the steps leading up to the chapel and a few more to climb them. Smoke pushed open a small door that was cut into one side of the two huge twelve-foot arched doors. Anywhere in the U.S., someone would be selling admission tickets to look at what was inside but in Italy it was just another chapel.

While Smoke was looking at the wooded arches supporting the roof, O plopped into a yellow oak pew.

Smoke stepped to her and took her hand. "You really need to take a break. Let's rest a while before we head out, okay?"

Her usually expressive face was blank and her eyelids drooped.

He sat beside her.

"Headache?"

She nodded.

Too much.

"Can you see if there is any water?"

He jumped up and hurried off—to where he didn't know. He spotted a door off the altar in the front of the church.

It was locked. He knocked, then banged.

A priest in a black cassock opened the door, looking a little upset. "Posso aiutarla?"

Smoke held up his hands. "I don't understand Italian."

The priest shook his head, "No englash, no englash."

"Agua, no wait... I mean acqua. You know, water... water." Smoke pointed toward the back of the church without looking.

The priest looked where he was pointing then back to him and shrugged his shoulders, confused.

Smoke whipped around.

O was gone.

Smoke sprinted.

He found her laying over on the pew.

Her face was white, eyes closed.

Smoke turned and yelled out. "Call an ambulance."

The priest seemed frozen in place.

"Doctor... a doctor... call a fucking doctor."

In spite of the priest's inability to speak English, he grasped the gravity of the situation. He hurried down the aisle and saw O in the pew. "We need to take." He used the universal two- handed, pick up and carry gesture.

With the priest leading, they carried O out the front door and down a short street to where a white rectangular sign with a green cross in the center hung over a door in the middle of the block. It was this small-town's combination pharmacy and emergency care center. It was certainly the nearest, and perhaps the only, health care facility for miles. The front room of the narrow storefront held crystal clear glass display cases in front of shelves filled with large and small plastic bottles, all appearing to be prescription stock and all labeled in Italian. On the backwall a floor-to-ceiling curtain separated the pharmacy from a treatment room.

The two men placed O, who had been bounced back to semi-conscious by the trip, on the examination table.

Smoke took her hand and time seemed to stop. She was looking at him with wide eyes and white skin, pale and fragile. She was scared.

At the doctor's insistence, Smoke walked to a corner and called Gia.

Ten minutes later the front door banged open and Gia stood, huffing and puffing. "Is she okay?"

The curtain was open and Smoke beckoned her forward.

O was sitting up on the examination table drinking a glass of water. She nodded at Gia and waved her in.

On one side of the table, a middle-aged woman wearing a doctor's white coat was talking on the phone. On the other side an elderly woman wearing an apron sat in a metal chair and was holding O's free hand.

Smoke was standing in the far corner. He looked relieved but only a short distance from full panic.

Gia crossed the room and stood at Smoke's side. "What happened? Is she alright?"

He pointed to the doctor talking on the phone. "I gave her Dr. Brightman's number. My cell isn't getting a signal here and she's calling on a landline. I told her what happened and asked her to call New York immediately. She understood but didn't say much so I don't know how good her English is. You may have to translate."

"Doctor Robert Brightman?" The woman turned to Smoke and gave a thumbs up.

Gia looked at Smoke. "I think she understands."

"A patient was brought into my treatment center in Stresa, Italy, and her husband gave me your number. He asked me to call you before I begin treatment."

O had finished and gave the glass to the old lady. "Grazie."

"Prego."

Gia's attention turned from Smoke to O. She motioned to the old lady who rose for the incoming replacement hand holder.

The doctor was listening intently to the voice on the phone. "Of course, I understand. I did undergraduate at Sapieza University in Rome and received an MD at University of Milan. I also interned at Medical Park in Berlin."

There was a pause and she added, "Again, I completely understand, I would ask as well."

Smoke couldn't hear what was being said but she gave an answer to what his next question would have been.

The doctor smiled. "My mother. I was born here. My mother lives here and refuses to move. So, I opened—"

There was another pause as she was interrupted. "Yes, of course, sorry. The patient arrived about twenty minutes ago. She was awake but dazed, rapid heartbeat, 92, BP 145 over 85, temp 99. She had mild chills and a headache but did not exhibit any signs of confusion. She had recently eaten lunch, drank wine, then walked three blocks, uphill, sat down to rest then fainted."

Smoke watched as the doctor listened.

"Yes, her husband was with her. He said she was unconscious about a minute or less."

More listening then, "I didn't notice anything in my preliminary examination, but hold on, I'll check again."

The doctor placed the phone down and walked to O. "Doctor Brightman asked me to look for any bruising or contusions where your head might have hit the pew. Which side?"

O pointed.

A slow minute passed as everyone watched the doctor reexamine O's head, and returned to the phone.

"Doctor." She paused for the response. "No, nothing. No indication of an impact of any kind. One would assume she fell onto her shoulder when she passed out."

O sighed relief.

Smoke watched as the doctor nodded in agreement with the voice on the phone. "I will relay your advice."

O, Smoke, and Gia had eyes fixed on the doctor as she hung up the phone.

"Dr. Brightman and I agree, you probably tried to do too much, too soon. You are still in recovery and perhaps the larger than normal meal and maybe an extra glass of wine or two proved too much for your condition. He recommended you stay down for the rest of the day and drink plenty of fluids."

Gia nodded furiously.

Smoke was stiff.

"So..." The doctor smiled reassuringly, "no worries."

Smoke instinctually knew there was something else.

The doctor opened a drawer and removed a card. "Here is my cell phone, please call me anytime." She walked to O and dropped the professional attitude for a moment. "Big fan of your books. Best sellers here, too."

O smiled.

Smoke walked over and took both O's hands in his, then looked to the doctor for permission.

"Yes, yes." The doctor pointed to the door. "Remember anytime."

"Ready to go?"

She nodded and Smoke pulled up on her hands.

The three amigos walked out into the late afternoon sun, Smoke on one side and Gia on the other. O's feet were barely on the ground.

"Are we going to get past this? I mean... I can walk on my own."

Neither of them listened.

Boats were bobbing gently on the lake. The sun, slowly disappearing behind the mountains, caused the tall masts and poles holding multi-colored flags to reflect long shadows on its surface. Gulls looking for their evening repast added a soundtrack to the echoes of their footsteps on the cobblestone street.

When they reached the walkway up to the hotel, O said, “I know you’re not going to believe this... but.”

Smoke and Gia both swiveled their heads with immediate concern.

O smiled. “I’m hungry.”

Gia laughed.

O elbowed Smoke in the side. “How about you?”

“I could eat.”

12

OUTSIDE TULSA OKLAHOMA

A whirlwind about three feet high appeared, then disappeared, quickly. The furious miniature tornado left a small cloud of brown dust hanging mid-air, without a purpose. It settled quietly back to earth.

"Damn, its 70 at breakfast, 90 at lunch, and hot as hell by sundown." Felix, his butt parked on the tailgate of Cliff's truck, stated the obvious.

"But… it's a dry heat." Cliff's joke caught Aimer and Felix off guard.

Aimer adjusted the sunglasses under his red Phillies baseball cap. "You might like the man we are trying to help. He has the same sense of humor you do."

Cliff sat next to Felix, hands in his lap, fingers laced and tapping. He wore a cowboy hat but no sunglasses.

Felix pushed off the tailgate impatiently looking at his watch, "He's late."

Cliff cocked his head slightly. "Is that Mickey Mouse?"

Felix grinned and extended his arm. "Best watch ever, my pride and joy. Cool, huh?"

Cliff shook his head, looked down, and started tapping his fingers again.

Aimer paced a bit while looking up and down the road. Heat waves emanated from the tar causing the wide, flat, empty terrain to look distorted and moon-like. "You think he's coming?"

"Yep."

"You sure?" Felix cross-examined the witness.

"Yep."

A few more minutes passed and Felix impatiently checked Mickey again.

Aimer pointed to a disturbance on the road, off in the distance. "Is that him?"

Without looking, Cliff said, "Yep."

"How do you know that?" Felix half mocked.

"It's him. He's late on purpose. He needs to be sure he's not followed. He can't be seen with us."

Aimer looked around. "Nothing for miles, pretty sure we're safe here."

"He can't be just... pretty sure."

The dark speck grew and became a black Cadillac Escalade.

Cliff pushed off the tailgate and the three men stood side by side as Chairman Randle Two Horse pulled off the road and opened his door. He was alone.

"Warford?"

"Yep."

They shook hands.

Cliff pointed. "Lieutenant Robert Aimer, Philadelphia Police retired, and Felix Grant his associate."

The chairman, a large portly man in his late fifties, didn't offer his hand. "What do you want from me?"

"Two men were killed and you were wounded in a shooting at the Arrowhead Casino. We attempted to speak with the tribal police officer in charge but he refused to talk to us."

The chairman's eyes were darting around nervously. "And?"

"And… we need to know who the two men were and what they were doing that caused them to be shot and killed."

"They grabbed me—"

"Stop… that's not true." Aimer cut him off. "They probably never even got near you. They were shot before they drew their weapons."

Two Horse, now stonefaced, turned and stared at Cliff. "Why should I answer any questions? You are known amongst us, Keetoowah. You have standing and you bring white men to me expecting answers."

Cliff stepped forward. "This isn't us. It isn't government. Its personal. One of the dead men in the parking lot raped and killed their friend's wife and took his son."

The chairman looked at Aimer for a long minute. "Your problem, not mine." He spun and started back to his car.

"I can make it yours."

Two Horse stopped, turned, and again stone-faced Cliff.

"He can."

Aimer held out his phone. "This has a satellite connection. Use the internet, look up the FBI in Quantico, Virginia, then call and ask for Director George DiSanto. Tell whomever answers Robert Aimer is calling."

Two Horse didn't take it.

Aimer stretched out his arm and shook the phone back and forth. "Director DiSanto is this man's friend as well. But he thinks if the FBI gets involved things will get very messy. He only wants what we want… the identity of the man who committed these heinous crimes. He sent us instead of suits from Washington to get answers." He shook the phone once more. "Go ahead, call."

The chairman's façade broke. "You don't understand. This involves very bad people. If I'm seen talking to you, if I tell you something no one else but me knows, they will find out and I will be dead."

"We're not looking to damage them, or whatever they have going on, or looking to put you in harm's way. Cliff agreed to help us only after we gave those assurances. Any trouble you have put yourself or your tribe in, is yours, and yours alone."

Two Horse glanced at Cliff who was now stone-facing him.

"What do you want to know?"

Aimer stepped toward Cliff's truck. "Have a seat."

Two Horse sat on the tailgate and Felix plopped down beside him, making the chairman a little nervous again.

"Why were the men killed?"

"Drugs. They were trying to make the casino a drugstore— cocaine and ecstasy. We ran them out a couple of times but we are understaffed and they kept coming back. Several other tribal casinos had the same problem with them. The money guys didn't want that kind of trouble or attention in their… I mean our… casino."

"That's half a story."

Two Horse started to get up but Felix put a hand on his shoulder and shook his head no.

"We are a new tribe, just recognized by the Bureau of Indian Affairs. It took years and a lot of money. We had to look for financial help."

Aimer pressed. "Who?"

"A group from Kansas City… capitol investors. They lent us two million dollars."

"You want us to believe that a bunch of bankers put a hit on a couple of drug dealers?"

Two Horse lowered his head. "Not bankers."

Felix expressed instant sarcastic shock. "Really?"

"No, they aren't bankers but they aren't the mob guys like in the movies, either. They look like bankers, act like bankers, but they are tough, ruthless, and will do anything to protect their investment."

Aimer shook his head. "Okay, but there were no drugs on them or in their car. Their guns were fired but not by them." He held up his hands, palms open and fingers spread. "No residue on their hands. I think these two guys showed up looking for a meeting, maybe a meeting you set up."

The chairman's face got white. "I told you, ruthless."

Aimer pondered a minute. "So, you want me to believe that the imported muscle killed these guys instead of breaking bones? Why?"

"It's about the money, lots and lots of money." He took a long breath. "We agreed… I mean, I agreed… when the casino opened, credit accounts would be set up for them. Money would be wired in and we would then transfer it to offshore banks." Two Horse looked at Aimer, almost pleading. "They figured there would be an investigation but it would happen on casino property, sovereign ground. When was the last time you read about a robbery or a murder on Indian turf? There are 147 casinos in Oklahoma and about a dozen agents. If it wasn't for your friend in Quantico, this would have been case closed."

Aimer stood quiet.

Felix let Two Horse get up and walk around. "It's money laundering. But…" The chairman was emphatic in defense of his decision. "It was supposed to only be for a year or two, then we would get clear of the loan and them."

"How much so far?"

"A lot," he lowered his voice and his eyes. "More than five million."

Aimer had to get him off answers that didn't help with what he needed to know. "Forget about the money." He took a beat. "The guards we met inside the casino yesterday didn't seem to be in the employ of Kansas City… bankers."

"They weren't our guards. We only have by-the-hour ex-football players, and barroom bouncers, not killers. They sent a couple of men in from somewhere east, like Chicago or New York… I'm not sure. They took over security for a couple of days, killed those men, then left."

Aimer was surprised. "They had licenses. A security agency out of Tulsa."

"We hire locals. They told us to send our guys home till they dealt with the problem. They made us hire the agency. Check them out, you'll see."

"And you don't know who the two dead guys were? Do the men from Kansas City know?"

Two Horse shook his head. "I guess you'll have to ask them."

"Where are they located? Do you have an address, a number?"

The chairman answered, frustrated, "I have no idea. About two years ago, I put out feelers for a loan through an attorney who knew somebody, who knew somebody. I got a phone call and they came to me… I mean the tribe. I met them once and from then on, I dealt with a lawyer, named Shore... Gerry Shore."

There was silence before Aimer decided he had gotten all he could get. "Chairman, Cliff is responsible for us meeting and that's it. We are leaving but he will still be here. We have no intention of harming you, the tribe, or the casino in any way. If you or Kansas City create any trouble for him, I can assure you our friend in the FBI will rain fire on you and your tribe. Understand?"

The chairman nodded, head down.

Aimer raised his voice for the first time. "Look at me and say you understand."

Shocked, Two Horse sputtered, "Yes, I understand."

Aimer's voice went back to normal. "Thank you for your cooperation."

The chairman almost sprinted to his car, the tires raising twin spirals of dust as it sped off on the heat distorted asphalt.

Felix looked at Aimer, puzzled. "Really... a satellite phone? That thing doesn't get a signal when you're standing downtown."

"Yeah well... he didn't know that."

Cliff started pushed up his tailgate. "Think I'm done now, right?"

Felix smiled. "Yep."

Cliff shook his head then looked to Aimer. "I know a good steak place on the way back. Nothing fancy but …" he looked back to Felix, "They serve everybody, even men with funny watches."

"Sounds like my kinda place." Felix smiled and snapped up the tailgate.

They bumped back onto the road, the over matched air-conditioner a welcome relief.

Aimer was quiet.

Felix wasn't. "What are you thinking?"

Aimer checked his phone for signal, nothing.

"I'll need to get DiSanto to run down the guard agency, which is probably a PO Box but more importantly we need information on Gerry Shore, Esquire, before we—"

"Wait." Felix shouted. "Don't do it, please. Let me."

Aimer looked down, shaking his head. Felix began to bellow,

"I'm going to Kansas City.
Kansas City, here I come.
I'm going to Kansas City.
Kansas City, here I come."

Cliff looked over at Aimer. "When will you white people stop abusing Indians?"

13

KANSAS CITY, MISSOURI

Robert and Felix sat side-by-side in plastic bucket seats at Gate 9. Their flight, United 1216, used to be on Mesa Airlines when Tulsa and Kansas City were 279 miles apart and an hour's flight time. Today however, post-pandemic, the surviving airline companies readjusted service and routes, so the distance by air, between the two cities, expanded to 1,296 miles. The flight time including a lay-over was now seven and a half hours. The original non-stop flight became 700 miles west to Denver before returning about six hundred miles east to KC. Aimer had considered a rental car but found it would have been cheaper to buy a car and abandon it on the street in Kansas City. Post-Covid travel was a bitch.

The two men shared one side of a single set of headphones plugged into a laptop inserted into one of their ears. It was awkward, the chairs uncomfortable, and their heads, bent sideways, were an inch apart.

On the computer screen, George DiSanto was looking down at his desk and peeling back pages from a file folder. "Ahhh… here it is. Kansas City…yes." He looked up. "I asked the local office for all available information on Mr. Shore and who he represents. I also requested a brief on organized crime and money laundering."

Felix started humming *Going to Kansas City* and Aimer punched his leg.

"Owww."

"Big baby." Aimer scolded the hulk sitting beside him.

"Gentlemen, this is serious." DiSanto chastised them both. "You are walking into a very dangerous situation."

"Really, Kansas City?" Felix chuckled and Aimer hit him again.

"Yes, really. Our statistics show it is the fifth most violent city in the country. Hard to believe, I understand, but it is number five in the country for violent crimes per capita."

Felix became semi-interested. "I never would have guessed. Drive-bys, drugs, pillaging?"

"All of the above. However," DiSanto turned a page and looked down, "it is also because of organized crime."

"You mean the five families, like in the Godfather. I thought that was all done." Felix's comment was as serious as he could muster.

"Reality is not the movies, Felix, and much of the public knowledge of the mob is pure fiction. Most is dramatized for movie screenplays but there are some elements of truth. Kansas City has connections to the infamous New York mobs but it was always, even back in the day, an open city. Currently, there are some elements of 'connected people' that still deal in loan sharking, gambling, and prostitution. And those people have lawyers. Good ones. And one of them is the attorney Mr. Two Horse said set up the loan for the tribe."

"I take it you have a brief on him as well?"

"I do and you have an appointment to see him at his office this afternoon."

Aimer grinned into the computer camera. "Now I'm impressed. How did you arrange that?"

"I made him an offer he couldn't refuse."

Both Aimer and Felix looked at each other dumbfounded.

DiSanto laughed. "Now, that's funny."

Felix leaned over closer to the screen. "George, we definitely need to hang out together."

Aimer pushed Felix back off camera. "Will he talk? What did you threaten him with?"

"Absolutely nothing. I just identified myself as a director in the FBI, and asked if he wanted to talk to you two in his office, or would he prefer me to send a couple of agents to bring him downtown and start a full investigation into his business dealings in Indian Country."

"So, he opted for an unofficial conversation?"

"Yes Robert, but we call it a... private interview."

"Your research gives you a hint about who is involved?"

"Nope, but Gerry Shore has represented a building company called Premier Drywall in the past."

Aimer started taking notes.

Felix yawned.

"The company is owned by Frank Simon, a cousin of Nick Miramonte, who was a capo in the old KC Italian mafia. His company sells drywall to construction companies in five states cheaper than any other supplier. It has been alleged that once they get involved with a contractor or a developer, they find a weakness, lend more money then, after the companies' default, take over the assets in bankruptcy. Shore is Frank Simon's court executioner. They are also into gambling and extortion but they haven't hit any radar screens at the DEA."

"No investigations underway with Drug Enforcement but how about the FBI?" Aimer asked curiously.

DiSanto smiled. "Looking at them, but there are no witnesses and no direct evidence—"

"But..."

"But our attorney friend doesn't know that." DiSanto lowered his voice. "Robert, do you play poker?"

Aimer nodded. "Uh huh."

"Can you bluff?"

"George, how many times do I have to remind you… I'm a cop."

"Good, then you'll know how to play this interview, correct?"

"Flight 1214 to Denver now boarding, all passengers."

"We got this, and that's our flight, George. Gotta run."

He started to close the lid of the computer.

"Robert, you still there?"

Aimer pushed the screen up. "Yes."

"One more thing… any more thoughts on talking to Smoke about this?"

"After Kansas City. We'll tell him, together, after this meeting."

"Sounds like a plan."

Aimer closed his screen.

"What plan?" Felix now looked hurt.

"I hear there is Smashburger in the Denver airport."

"Really?"

The yellow cab was new, clean, and the driver drove directly to City Center Square, a high-rise office building in downtown. After paying, Felix and Aimer retrieved their carry-on bags from the trunk and the driver took off like he was late for dinner. They walked up concrete steps to the concrete building. The sturdy material used in construction was its best feature.

They took the elevator to the eighteenth floor and found Eric Shore's name affixed to a door halfway down a long windowless corridor.

A secretary looked at them when they entered. She was seated behind a black walnut reception desk, had a phone to her ear, gum in her mouth, and 'a wait a minute' finger in the air.

Aimer and Felix looked around the waiting room. Four chairs, three magazines on a coffee table, and no coffee. Reproduction landscapes with matching frames on white painted walls did not resemble a downtown New York office.

"I don't care, honey. He's not here." She popped the gum and reapplied the finger. "I'll tell him you called, again." Red painted fingernails dropped the phone from about a foot from the receiver.

"Asshole." She gave them a blank stare. "Oh... not you, her. She's an asshole."

Aimer responded quickly. "And how would you know I'm... we're not assholes, too?"

She gave Robert a quick glance then gave Felix a long once over. "Believe me, honey. I can tell. Especially you." The finger arose again, this time pointing at Felix.

Felix waved his hand. "Thanks, but... wrong flavor."

"What?" Her eyes blinked rapidly. Wit apparently made her confused.

Striking while the iron was hot, Aimer said, "Robert Aimer, Felix Grant to see Mr. Shore. We have an appointment."

She sputtered something unintelligible, then looked down at papers on her desk. "Just a sec."

The finger pointed to the chairs but they remained standing.

She picked up the receiver. "Mr. Aimer and Mr. Grant are here to—"

Apparently cut off, she dropped the phone from about the same height as before then pointed again. "Through that door."

Gerry Shore wore a dark, pinstriped suit and was seated at the end of a small conference table. On the wall behind him, and directly above his head, hung his Harvard diploma. He had a round face with no facial hair, short jet-black hair—too black for his age— and appeared to be in his forties. "Have a seat gentleman. Did Angel offer to get you coffee?"

Aimer took the closest seat to the attorney. "No."

The attorney leaned back in the chair and put his arms behind his head, framing the diploma with his elbows. "Well then, what can I do to assist the FBI?"

Aimer stared at Shore. "Coffee would be nice."

There was a power pause, but reluctantly Shore rose, walked to his desk, and picked up the phone. "Coffee."

He returned and plopped into his power chair. "Now, what do you want?"

"Just sugar no cream." Felix grinned.

Harvard didn't respond.

They waited in silence until Angel arrived carrying a tray with coffee and three cups.

Aimer slowly poured a cup while Angel beat a retreat. He started pouring a second cup for Felix then without looking up said, "There was a shooting at the Arrowhead Casino two weeks ago Friday."

Shore shrugged his shoulders. "And?"

"And two men were killed."

Another shrug, this time accompanied with a 'what the fuck' look.

Aimer reached for the sugar. "The FBI cannot identify one of the dead men and we were hoping you could help us out with that."

Shore did the angry lawyer table-banging thing, slapping his hands flat on the table. "I have no idea what you're referring to. I had nothing to do with a shooting in a casino parking lot and you're wasting my time."

Aimer glanced at Harvard. "I didn't say anything about a parking lot." Aimer looked at Felix, "Did you say cream or sugar?"

Felix raised a pinky. "Just sugar."

Shore started to get up.

"Sit… the… fuck… down." Felix's voice was low and meaningful.

Shore froze, then dropped back into his chair.

Aimer stirred his coffee. "We know you arranged for financing for the Odawa Tribe. The company that funded them has, as a part of their deal, laundered five million dollars through the casino. We know two men, trying to move ecstasy and cocaine at the casino, were set up, then executed…in the parking lot."

Shore's face was white, sweat beaded on his forehead. "I had nothing…"

"Wait for it." Felix pointed a finger, stopping Shore mid-sentence.

Aimer nodded a thank you to Felix. “The men were executed on property under federal jurisdiction.”

Shore’s voice changed, trying to regain footing. “If you believe me or my clients had anything to do with this alleged incident, there would be men with handcuffs here.” He seemed pleased with his comeback and crossed his arms.

“Accurate.” Aimer turned to Felix. “He’s smarter than he looks.”

Felix tapped the table, shaking his head. “Not that smart. He’s going to jail for a very long time and he’s still dancing.”

“Oh…yeah.” A weak gulping sound came from the lawyer.

Felix looked at Aimer. “See, what’d I say, not that smart.”

“I’m going to try again.”

“Okay but I still don’t think he’ll get how deep this shit pile is.”

Aimer leaned toward Shore. “There are no men here with handcuffs, yet. There is no official investigation, yet. Neither you, nor your client are implicated…yet. Because the man from the FBI who called you has an ongoing investigation that might be related to those dead men. And he sent us instead of men with handcuffs.”

Shore reacted to the opening. “So, hypothetically… if certain information was available, what then?”

“If the information has value,” Aimer looked at Felix who shrugged. “In that case, there may be a favorable window of opportunity for you, and the people you represent.”

“That is very vague.” Harvard was attempting to act firm.

“You have already checked out who George DiSanto is so you know he is a very important man. I can assure you he wouldn’t have sent us here unless there was a case against you and your associates.” Aimer pushed back in his chair, “But he sent us for a private interview… informal… no official record.”

“Which means?”

Aimer took another sip. “If what you tell us helps his other case, the investigation into the murder of two known drug pushers in a casino parking lot might get stalled because of a missing file.”

Shore shook his head again and crossed his arms defiantly. "Not near enough."

Aimer stared blankly at the lawyer. "What time is our flight, Felix?"

"Ninety minutes."

Still staring, "If we leave empty handed, I will immediately make a call and every resource in the FBI and their friends at the IRS will climb up your ass. You and every client you have will be the subject of exhaustive investigations… and even if they find nothing, after a year or two—"

"Probably two," Felix added.

"You'll be broke, have no clients left, and selling used cars to buy that hair dye."

Felix was examining his fingernails. "Ouch, that was harsh."

"Okay, okay." Shore unfolded his arms, smoothed his hair, and took a breath. "Hypothetically, let's say I have a client. And they lend money to people—"

"Cut the bullshit. You're out of time." Aimer slapped the table doing the lawyer thing.

Harvard lowered his voice. "Hypothetically… I mean… well."

"Tic… tic." Felix started to get up.

"The two men… they were from Penose."

"What is that?" Aimer was legitimately confused.

"It's an organization out of the Netherlands called Penose. They're like the Italian mafia only not as well-known. However, they are the biggest supplier of ecstasy in the world. They work out of New York but move their product in a number of states. They tried to establish a distribution route through the Midwest in Indian Country. They've had success with some of the other tribes and tried to muscle into Arrowhead. They wanted to use it as a drop for shipments to local dealers." He looked up and weakly uttered, "Hypothetically."

"Right, hypothetically."

Shore then tried earnest. "There isn't any local or state law enforcement in Indian Country and you guys, I mean the FBI, are short staffed, so once the Penose guys bribed the right people, drugs could be moved with almost no interference."

"Why did your guys give a shit? Are they competition?"

"Absolutely not. We are not drug dealers." He was indignant.

"Hypothetically," Felix added quickly.

Aimer pressed. "Why not take a cut?"

"Because… they didn't want any attention drawn to their money… thing." His eyes were darting back and forth and sweat beaded on his forehead. "Those two men were told to stop but they kept coming back. My client, the people with the money at stake, is old school and they handled it old school." Shore shrugged. "They sent a message. Don't come back."

"If they were so concerned about attention, why there? Why in the parking lot?"

"Because, like I said, you guys are short staffed." He waved his hands. "It would have worked too. We had a good story, believable witnesses, and if you really had proof, I'd be in handcuffs, right?" His face gave away his last attempt at lawyering.

Aimer didn't blink. "Who were the men killed in the parking lot?"

Shore raised both hands now slightly pleading. "They don't know. I swear they don't know. You gotta ask the guys from Penose. The guys in New York who sent them."

Aimer and Felix sat quiet.

Suddenly, Aimer got up and started for the door. Felix followed.

"Do we have a deal?" Shore yelled at their backs.

Felix spun around. "Forgive their startup debt, get out of Arrowhead, and you have a deal."

Aimer looked at Felix, blankly.

Felix opened the door and gestured to Aimer. "Don't want to miss the flight."

They walked past the gum-popping secretary and out the door.

Felix pushed the elevator call button. “We back to square one?”

“Yep. No name but we still have a lead.”

“What about Smoke? Are we going to tell him?”

Aimer shrugged. “Let’s talk to George and decide.”

The door opened and they walked into an empty elevator.

Aimer looked up at Felix. “Forgive the debt? Where did that come from?”

“DiSanto told us to bluff, didn’t he?”

Aimer just shook his head in amazement.

“See, I was listening.” Felix pushed the down button.

The door closed, Aimer shaking his head.

14

STRESA, ITALY

It was a different kind of silence. An occasional car drove by. Soft conversation from couples strolling along the harbor and a melody from a distant violin traveled through the night air. Smoke sat alone on the balcony, feet up, eyes closed. It was a small city but still a city with people and cars moving about, but somehow, it was different. In Stresa, Italy, on this lake, with the Italian Alps framing the view, even the sound of a city night was subdued and easy.

Then there was the smell.

Smoke had no idea what flowers combined to scent the air but he easily identified the smell of the morning's bread being baked in the hotel kitchen. The combination was intoxicating and could only be completely enjoyed in this city's brand of night.

He took a long deep breath. O was asleep, finally. Her attitude and restlessness had worsened since the fainting episode and it was only after he insisted that she agreed to take a sleeping pill. The headaches had returned but were sporadic and varied in intensity. Tonight was the worst, lasting for two hours and leaving her in tears. Sleep would be welcome. Deep restful sleep would be a gift.

He heard the handle of the balcony door turn and reluctantly opened his eyes.

"You awake?"

Smoke turned to Gia. "Yep. Is she still asleep?"

"Uh huh, she started to stir when I got up. She's gotten five solid hours. I think she should stay down for at least another hour or two."

"You look tired."

"I'm okay but after I hook you up with this call, I'm going to crash in my room. I'll leave her door open. If you hear her stir, come and get me."

"Did you get the car set up for tomorrow?"

"Eleven a.m. Straight to Milan. Our flight leaves at midnight so I booked a room at the Sheraton in the airport so she could have dinner and then rest before we have to endure airport security."

"You have any trouble with this zoom thing?"

Gia giggled. "Easy peasy." She walked back into the room, returning with an open laptop. "It's all set. When you hear it ring, tap the touch-pad and you're in. Felix will be in New York and George in Virginia."

She placed the computer on the table and then bent over and kissed him on the forehead. "You're a good man Charlie Brown."

"That's a pretty old reference for a millennial."

"Huge Schroeder fan. The whole unexpected greatness thing." She spun and disappeared back inside before he could respond.

He spoke to her shadow. "You are all of that."

He checked his watch. *2 a.m. here— 9 p.m. there.*

He closed his eyes again, listening for the distant violin. It wasn't there.

The screen lit up when the call came in. Reaching for the laptop he saw it was almost three.

A whooshing sound effect announced the two participant's arrival. Felix's blond spiked head on the left and a somber looking FBI director on the right.

"How's O?" Felix's voice echoed loudly. Smoke clumsily banged on the volume button.

"She's okay. Not great but okay. We are leaving the hotel tomorrow and are on a redeye Emirates flight to JFK."

"You need me to pick you up? I just got to New York but I can be there."

"Thank you but no. Gia arranged a car."

"Glad you're headed back." George DiSanto hadn't changed his expression.

A brief moment of silence ensued.

"George, I'm sorry it took so long to get back to you."

"No problem."

Again, there was awkward silence.

George cleared his throat. "My boy, a case has been brought to my attention that has a connection to you."

Smoke sucked in a breath.

George did as well then spoke quickly. "A shooting occurred in Oklahoma that resulted in two fatalities. One of the men killed was the man who murdered Helen."

Smoke's eyes drifted off the screen, up and out to the dark sky over the lake.

"We were able to draw that conclusion because of DNA. However, the identity of the man remains a mystery. I enlisted your friend Robert and he, accompanied by Felix, traveled to Tulsa, Oklahoma to investigate. They followed a lead to Kansas City, but the man is still unidentified."

Felix spoke. "The only thing we have to go on is that he was sent to Tulsa to open a drug route for the Penose, a syndicate operating out of Amsterdam."

"Felix is correct. My sources tell me that Penose infiltrated cities in the U.S. and set up individual networks all controlled from a single source in Amsterdam. We suspect the unidentified dead man was living in the U.S. and had a connection to the Netherlands. We believe he hired backup from Tulsa and both were killed by a group out of Kansas City whose territory these men infringed upon."

Smoke was stone-faced.

"I know this is a big shock...after all this time. We waited to tell you until we had more to go on about who he was and what happened—"

Smoke closed the lid of the computer.

The silence of the night returned. He was numb to sound, light, smell. It was blurry at the corners of his sight. The black night his only view.

Her hand touched his shoulder.

Smoke turned his head slowly.

"My love... my love. I'm here for you." Tears were streaming down her cheeks, eyes red, her face bearing sadness he had never seen before.

He put the laptop on the table and stood. She stood, her hands raised up, his safe harbor.

He went to her. He pulled her to him— his head lowered to her shoulder. He sobbed from his soul.

She gently stroked his head. "I know, I know."

He took in a lungful of air and let out years of sorrow.

"You will find him."

15

MILAN, ITALY

George called Felix's cell phone the moment Smoke ended the zoom meeting.

Felix answered on the first chime and began talking without a greeting. "I think we wait till it's morning in Italy then get Gia to set up another computer call. Robert will be back by then and can join."

George was upset. "It's my fault. I could have told him… differently. I said it too fast and didn't give him a chance to digest the news."

Felix responded knowingly. "Stop. Not your fault. And I would have done it the same way. There was no way to sugarcoat it. You said it fast, didn't patronize, and gave him the bare bone facts. He'll appreciate that, eventually, believe me."

George paused. "I guess you're right, but one would think after all the time I've spent in the FBI I'd be better at this sort of thing."

"Really, George? When was the last time you did a family notification?"

"Many, many years. The last time... I was about as old as the victim. She was a mother of three and only thirty-two."

Felix took a beat and changed direction. "I think once he hears the rest of what we learned, he'll gear up."

"Thanks Felix. Why don't we try to get some rest? You'll get to Gia and set up the next zoom call and let Robert know, yes?"

"Of course."

George looked at his watch. "Robert's flight should be arriving in Philadelphia about now so he can plug in as well."

"If there's a problem, I'll get back to you, but figure about 3 a.m."

"I'll be up." He paused, his voice becoming fatherly. "Honestly Felix, I've been doing this work for thirty-five years and I've seen it all. Everything you can possibly imagine and more. But... this case... Smoke's pain, what he's been through, and what he will now have to relive. It has me at my core. I need to make a difference, now, for him."

"George, listen. I have mad respect and admiration for this man. He risked his life to save me, which sounds cliché... but he did. Bullets flying, bombs going off, death a millimeter away. We were pinned down, outflanked, with no support. Then this man, a civilian at heart, who had a baby son he'd never seen, put it all on the line to save my sorry ass. And... in all the years since, and after all the pain he's been through from the wounds he suffered...never once talked about it again. I know, to him, it was just something he had to do. As far as I'm concerned, every day I have lived since has been a bonus. Me and a couple of dozen other grunts should be pushing daisies. I'm in. Whatever it takes. George. I mean it... whatever it takes. Robert, me, you, we need to find out if Smoke's son is still alive."

The limo was comfortable and quiet. Gia sat facing O and Smoke who were sitting opposite on the bench seat in the back of the car. No one had spoken since they left the hotel in Stresa.

Gia's iPods were implanted, the white tails looking like dangling earrings, were dancing to a beat only she could hear.

Smoke stared out the window.

O laid her head back, hands in her lap, breathing slowly, trying to relax. Occasionally, through tired eyes, she peeked at her husband, awaiting his return to this time and place.

The Duomo di Milano appeared outside Smoke's window, its ancient spires towering high above the modern buildings in the center of Milan. Somehow, the destruction visited on the city during WWII missed the massive church, leaving the structure virtually intact. Its survival was a calculated miracle, neither the Germans nor the Allies wanted the unforgivable act of the ruin of one of the most iconic structures outside of Rome to follow them into history.

The sites had no effect on Smoke. It could have been Istanbul or Peking or Cleveland for all that Smoke cared. He was deep in thought. Too deep to be reached. The rage he had driven deep into the darkest, deepest part of his soul was burning down the barriers he had needed to survive. His conscious mind knew that anger, hate, or revenge did not lead anywhere. He knew he had to beat the demons.

The dead man's identity was the key to unlocking the door that had been barred shut for twenty years. One stupid move, one miscalculation and it would be sealed tight gain. Information needed to be finessed, tactics needed to be skillful, deliberate, efficient. Tipping his hand, just once, could mean this last bit of hope could be lost, forever.

The limo came to a stop and the driver popped open the door. The sounds of the streets of Milan rushed in.

Gia bolted and assisted the driver in removing the luggage from the trunk.

Smoke sat still, transfixed, motionless.

O slid across the seat and kissed him on his cheek. “We’re here.”

Smoke turned and saw her looking up at him. Her face strained and drawn from lack of sleep.

Her face inches away from his, her body leaning against his, brought him back, out of his head and close to his O.

He popped the handle, slid out, and turned to help her get out.

A bellman, fitted with a tight red jacket, pulled a dolly up to the luggage. “Checking in?”

Gia stepped up and took over.

Smoke was not all there, yet.

O took his hand and led him into the lobby. Gia who had left with the bellman returned with room keys. The elevator took them to their floor and within minutes of the arrival they were comfortably behind closed doors.

Gia walked surreptitiously to where O was seated on the bed and bent to her ear. “It’s almost time. He okay for another call?”

O nodded and waved her off politely.

Smoke was at the double glass doors leading to the balcony.

O got up and put her hand on his arm. “The call will be coming through shortly. You ready?”

Smoke turned and looked at her.

She smiled.

His eyes became focused and determined. “Absolutely.”

He saw Gia standing with the laptop open and nodded.

Smoke walked to a table near the window and invited O to sit opposite.

Gia set the computer down and a few keystrokes later she spun it to face Smoke. “Same as before. Wait for the tone then—”

“Hit the keypad.” He looked up at her. “Thank you.”

Gia sat on the bed and put her hands in her lap.

The computer made the whooshing sound as the screen lit up.

Felix popped up first. "Smoke, you okay?"

"Yep."

The screen split and Robert Aimer appeared. "Hey buddy, sorry I wasn't on the call last night. I was in the air coming back to Philly from KC."

George appeared in another box on the screen.

Robert continued. "How is O?"

She leaned into the camera's range. "I'm fine. We'll be in New York tomorrow and headed to Sinai to see Doctor Brightman."

Felix responded authoritatively. "I'll be there to pick you up."

"I'd say it wasn't necessary but I know that's useless." She blew a kiss then backed out of the screen shot.

There was a moment as the three men just stared at Smoke long distance.

"What?" Smoke queried.

George coughed then took control. "We should bring you up to date."

Smoke listened silently as George replayed the events from his first seeing the file on the shooting in Oklahoma through Robert and Felix's meeting with Gerald Shore in Kansas City.

Smoke didn't take long to digest the facts. "You're certain this Kansas City outfit doesn't know who this man is?"

Robert responded. "Yes, I'm certain. What Felix and I heard made sense and we believe what they told us. Based on the information we got from the tribe, it made logical sense. The dead guy worked for the Penose organization."

Smoke wanted more. "George, I assume you have information on this Penose gang."

"Indeed. But not a gang, it's a criminal organization operating out of Amsterdam."

Smoke appeared confused. "Amsterdam— the Netherlands?"

"Yes. I reached out to a contact in Interpol last night. She gave me a brief background on Penose and sent a dozen files via email. I haven't gone through all of them yet, but this is what I know so far."

Loud static, like crinkling paper, disrupted the conversation. Felix had stepped out of his frame and when he came back his cheeks were bulging. He mumbled barely intelligible, "Sorry, I'm hungry."

"Anyway," George shook his head and continued. "Penose is a tightly run outfit, and is responsible for about ninety percent of the Methylenedioxymethamphamine smuggled into the U.S. A drug that is more commonly known as ecstasy or molly."

"Ninety percent? Interpol is telling you that one organization has a monopoly on a major drug business?"

"They say it's accurate, because it's not easy to manufacture. It is made from chemicals derived from sassafras trees and thus it is geographically specific. The Penose limits their exposure by maintaining tight control of shipping and distribution. Unlike other drug smugglers, they set up dealers in different cities that report directly to them in Amsterdam so there is no middleman. Also, not much competition because it is not a high profit drug. Small time dealers of heroin can make big money fast. Ecstasy is thought of as a recreational drug with short term effects and has a lower profile in the drug wars. But, Penose controls the market and X is still big money."

"What about the risk? Without a middleman the trail leads right to the top." Robert questioned.

George had the answer. "Technically yes, but there have only been a few arrests, all at the distribution level and no one has flipped because convictions usually result in short sentences."

"So why the shooting in Oklahoma?" Smoke asked.

"I believe the attorney Felix and Robert talked to was telling the truth. The men killed in the parking lot were there representing the Penose, and were trying to set up a new distribution point. They accidentally happened into a money laundering scheme that created a conflict with the Kansas City people which resulted in, basically, a rival gang shootout."

Three camera images went quiet waiting for Smoke to speak.

"George." Smoke's voice was raspy, emotions held in check. "What is the FBI's position in this shooting?"

"It's an open file but the agency's investigation has been slow so far, and as I told Robert; my retirement may stall it completely. I have kept our inquiries unofficial and off the books. The good news is while Kansas City didn't give us answers we have a new lead."

Smoke filled in the blank. "Amsterdam."

"Yes, the Netherlands. My Interpol contact is in The Hague, about an hour from Amsterdam and has agreed to meet...unofficially...and share information."

Smoke leaned forward. "Meet with whom?"

"You." The voice wasn't from the computer. O put her hand on his shoulder. "You need to go...today. The next flight. As soon as possible."

Smoke put his hand on hers and without turning to look at her said, "No. Absolutely no."

O's voice became equally as determined. "Yes. Absolutely yes."

Smoke turned and saw the determination on her face.

"And don't give me that, 'I have to take care of you' crap. Gia will get us on the plane and Felix will pick us up at JFK."

Felix coughed and started to speak but stopped.

Smoke stared at O, making up his mind.

She nodded.

He faced the screen again. "Okay. I'll send the flight schedule when—"

"Leaving in two hours, arriving 7:30 p.m. at Amsterdam Airport Schiphol." Gia stood with her cell phone in hand.

George chimed in. "I'll call now and text the time and place for the meeting."

Another reality pause followed the conversation of progress.

Smoke broke the ice. "Thank you."

Felix rattled cellophane again. "Gia sent me your arrival time. I'll be in baggage claim with bells on."

O leaned forward. "The last time you said that to me you showed up with actual bells on."

Smoke recentered the screen. "I'll be in touch and thanks." Then he closed the lid.

He looked at O.

"Don't say it," she warned.

"But."

"Stop." She held up her hand. "Order room service. The food here is way, way better than in the Netherlands." She smiled.

Smoke leaned forwarded and whispered. "I love you."

16

AMSTERDAM, NETHERLANDS

The phone call had taken him back in time. A place he had put into a box. A lid he kept sealed, never to be opened. Since that call, Smoke hadn't been able to sleep. He couldn't focus. He couldn't concentrate on what needed to happen next. His eyes were closed and his head back but the half inch the seat reclined wasn't helping him rest.

The plane touched down at 1 a.m. at Amsterdam Airport Schiphol. It was a short flight, just under two hours but the entire trip, including security, took four.

"Ladies and Gentlemen, we are taxiing to gate B4. Luggage will be available at baggage claim 26. We hope you enjoyed your flight on KLM Royal Dutch Airlines and we hope you choose to fly with us again."

People in the front seats began to rise when a single chime announced the plane's arrival at the gate. The exodus of the sleepy passengers was orderly and quiet.

Smoke remained seated, staring out the window, even when it was his turn to exit. A few minutes went by and the last of the passengers moved past his seat.

"Are you okay, sir? Do you require some assistance?" A very pretty blond in a pale blue uniform and matching scarf interrupted his trance.

He spun around and looked up apologetically, and sputtered, "Um, no... no, thank you."

She smiled a million-dollar, 1 a.m. smile, and stepped back, but stayed in the aisle near his seat.

He looked to the back of the plane and realized he was the last passenger. "Oh, sorry. I'm holding you up."

She tilted her head, still smiling, and held an open palm towards the exit.

He stepped into the aisle, pulled a gym bag from the overhead and, ducking his head, made his way to the front, then out onto the jetway.

The gate area in the terminal was void of passengers or employees, except for a janitor riding atop a floor polishing machine. Smoke passed the closed food court and newspaper/book store. The corridor opened into a spacious lobby which got his attention. He walked past a full-sized KLM jet engine connected to a full-sized landing gear sticking out of a wall, to get to the exit. The odd decorating diverted his concentration momentarily, his mind still fighting to focus on the task at hand.

Before walking out of the terminal, he sent a text to O. She was still in the air but it would be on her phone when she and Gia arrived in New York. *In Amsterdam. Text me when you arrive NYC.*

He leaned against the wall near the exit doors and looked at his watch, 1:45 a.m. It was 6:45 in the morning at Quantico.

He texted George, next. *Arrived. Call me when u r available.*

Smoke pulled his notebook from an inside jacket pocket and tried to pronounce the name of the meeting place— a restaurant named Omelegg–de Pijp. After two stuttering and stumbling attempts, he decided to just show the notepad to the taxi driver.

In spite of the hour, taxis were lined up outside Arrivals. He jumped into the first in line, flashed the name he couldn't pronounce, and thirty minutes later he was dropped off in the commercial district of Amsterdam. He looked up and down the street. Streetlights cast yellow circles of light on a deserted sidewalk. The restaurant had a red and white striped awning and, like every other storefront on the block, was closed. There were a couple of tables made from thick cuts of trees with matching workbench seats for outside dining. Smoke dropped the gym bag on a table and sat. He put his elbows on his knees, palms on his face and rubbed. Sleeplessness had caught up and every muscle was aching.

He pulled out the notebook. The last entry was the Interpol contact's name.

Bram Visser.

Smoke looked at his watch again. 2:52.

He turned sideways on the bench seat, put his feet up, and crossed his arms on his chest. Yawning, he leaned back against the glass and ducked his chin to his chest.

The phone rang. He bolted upright and picked it up off the table. The LED read GEORGE.

Smoke pushed the icon. "Yeah."

"I just got the text. Sorry for the delay in my response. I actually managed to sleep a bit."

Smoke looked at the time, 4:34. "I guess I slept too."

"Where are you?"

"Sitting in front of the meet."

"What? Why? Didn't you get a room?"

"Not yet. The plane was late getting in. I didn't want to spend time looking for an open hotel so I came here instead. George, it's alright. I've gotten use to sleeping sitting up on stakeouts."

George intervened. “I’ll get you a place when I get off our call and text you the address.”

“Thanks.”

“Okay, back to business. I have information for you.”

“Shoot.”

“Bram Visser is the chief superintendent of Criminal Investigation, a similar position to mine at the FBI. I’ve occasionally consulted with him on a few cases over the years. Have you ever heard of ‘The Beast of Harkstede’?”

“Can’t say I have.”

“Grizzly business. Serial killing. Anyway, the Dutch police hit a dead end in the investigation and asked the Interpol desk in The Hague for help. Interpol is based in the Netherlands and is responsible for international police cooperation and also charged to assist the county and surrounding region. Visser reached out to me to help him build a profile on the suspect. I did and it led to an arrest and conviction. Made all the papers over there and the resolution of the case helped Bram’s advancement at Interpol.”

“So, he owes you big time.”

“Humph.” George sounded a little embarrassed. “Yes, in short, yes, I guess he owes me. And now I’m cashing in. But don’t be influenced by that story. Beyond the professional relationship, we are friends, but he is a ridgid by-the-book man. In the past, there were boundaries he wouldn’t cross.”

“In the past?”

“Yes, I think I’ve convinced him this situation is different, and he agreed, reluctantly, to help you... I mean us... in any way he can.”

“Even cross professional lines?”

There was a bit of a pause and the tone of George’s response surprised him. “If he doesn’t give you what you need the first time you ask... call me, immediately.”

“George, your FBI persona is cracking.”

"Ten days eight hours."

"Huh?"

"I'm FBI for ten more days... so I guess I'm trying to get used to being a civilian."

Smoke actually chuckled. "George, there is no chance you'll ever be a civilian again, but you have the makings of becoming a damn fine ex-cop."

Smoke pushed the end button and resumed his position, his arms crossed on his knees and his head resting back against the window. He started numbering his questions about Penose. He needed to know only one thing, who was the dead man they sent to Oklahoma?

"Sergeant Henry Smokehouse, Sergeant Smokehouse."

He heard a voice he'd heard before.

"Smokehouse. Phone call in Communications in five. Get there now."

He drifted through a blurry haze. Walls were leaning and the floor was soft. The receiver was thick and black and wired to a box lighted with dials and buttons.

"Smoke... Smoke. Are you there?"

"Helen?"

"Yes, darling its me." Her voice was distant.

"Helen, I was asleep."

"You have to know."

His stomach tightened. "I know."

"No, you don't."

"Sure I do."

"Henry!"

His back straightened.

"Wait, what don't I know?" The haze started moving.

"I'm pregnant."

"Pregnant?"

"It's a boy."

"A boy?"

"You're a father."

"Helen?"

"He'll be here before you get back."

"Helen?"

"You're dreaming."

"I am?"

"I'm still mad at you."

"We needed the money."

"You didn't have to go back."

"I made a mistake."

He heard her laugh through the darkness. "You did and there will be retribution."

Light was sneaking in under his eyelids. He tried to keep them closed but couldn't.

"Retribution, Smoke. I'm naming him Henry."

"Nooooo."

She laughed.

He could almost see her. "Helen."

Her voice drifted away. It was a whisper. "His name is Henry."

"Henry Smokehouse?"

The voice was loud and foreign.

"Mr. Smokehouse?"

A face was surrounded by light.

Smoke's eyes blinked open. He shaded his eyes and straightened up.

The face moved out of the streetlight.

Smoke's neck and back sent a pain alarm to his brain that brought him back to Amsterdam. "Uh... yes, and please just call me Smoke." He unfolded his legs and slung them down to the ground.

"I'm Visser from Interpol." The man wore a grey tweed suit accented with a brass buttoned vest. He had a hand resting on the top of a walking stick and a curious look on his face.

"Mr. Visser. Thank you for meeting with me. Should I call you Director Visser?"

The man smiled politely and shook his head. "No, Bram, please. May I sit?"

Smoke felt at ease and pointed. "Of course."

Bram sat on the bench across the table from Smoke. "How can I be of help to you?"

"George said you would help me understand how the Penose runs its operation."

Bram nodded again. "Indeed."

Smoke heard an accent that was familiar but not easily identifiable, almost English but not. "Did George explain why I need to know about them?"

"Yes, he did. And might I say, I hope that what I may contribute to your investigation helps lead to a successful conclusion."

"Thank you."

"Right, Penose." Bram set the cane on the table and folded his hands. "It's actually not a single group. It's more like your U.S. version of the Mafia. It's a group of smaller crime groups that have an... arrangement."

"I'm specifically interested in the shipment of ecstasy. I've been told that this Penose controls the entire market."

"That's true. Difficulties in manufacturing and the low profit margin has left the lowest profit illegal drug without much competition. One enterprising group has perfected its production and distribution and has a de-facto worldwide stranglehold on the drug."

"George gave you the background, so I'll cut to the chase."

"Yes, of course. You need the most probable source for this fellow from Oklahoma's employer."

Smoke nodded.

"Anton Gurds is most likely the person you're looking for."

Smoke searched for his notepad.

"No need for notes, I've taken the liberty of bringing copies of his file's summaries." Bram withdrew an envelope from an inside jacket pocket. "He is a careful criminal who has legitimate business, pays taxes promptly, and maintains an extremely low profile. There is a fully staffed office downtown and a factory in the country that deals in manufacturing of soap and bath products. He has never been arrested or even detained; however, he is known to be the kingpin of most of the ecstasy trade. It is true that the drug isn't as profitable as cocaine or heroin, even marijuana, but it is rumored the exported product realizes more than thirty million euros... beg pardon... almost forty million U.S. dollars a year."

"Serious money." Smoke changed the line of questions. "What's he like, I mean is he ambitious, looking to expand?"

"Right question." Bram smiled. "No, he's not. Interpol has been helping with tracking this man for more than ten years and no one, not the Dutch nor any country that receives the drugs has gotten enough to make a case... how do you Americans say it…?" He pointed and smiled. "Stick."

Bram rolled the cane over so the brass headpiece tapped the table. "He's almost seventy, in failing health, and has been forced into letting his son take the reins."

"The son?"

"Quinten... Quinten Gurds." Bram lowered his head. "This is a bad man. He's forty-four and his father had held him in low level positions because he drew so much attention to himself. He thinks he's a rock star, spends a lot of money, always in trouble, trashing hotels and restaurants, a few alleged sexual assaults but, never a charge. It is rumored that he is backing the move to expand in the U.S. He is the ambitious one in the group and thinks the United States is an underdeveloped market."

"Thus, the expansion." Smoke scratched his day-old beard.

"Indeed. There is another rumor." Bram leaned forward conveying a look of urgency. "This drug is historically recreational. It contains no addictive elements and other than it is illegal almost everywhere, causes little damage physically or economically."

"You said historically."

"It is rumored that Quinten has formulated a new drug, only this one is more potent and... as addictive as cocaine."

Smoke straightened his back. "How good is the information?"

"Good. But, that's all we have, no details. We don't know how or when."

"I appreciate the background, it is helpful, but I need a name. I need to know who was sent to Oklahoma. Is Quinten the guy who can tell me what I need to know and, if so, how do I get to him?"

Bram put both hands on the table. "I believe he is or in the alternative he knows who will know. To get the name you'll have to make him talk."

"Is there a weakness? Something I can probe?"

Bram nodded. "Mr. Quinten Gurds likes his own product. He does the drug often, which has gotten the attention of the press and police before. This behavior threatened his father's belief in the son's ability to take over the business. So, to please his father, he is maintaining a lower profile and has been avoiding the civilian population. But to entertain himself, he has taken to the professionals in the nightclubs of our Red-Light District. Are you familiar?"

"Familiar no, aware yes."

"As I mentioned, Anton Gurds is in failing health and undergoes treatments on Tuesday and Friday. The son, out from the father's watchful eye, reverts to his bad habits. One of which is a fondness for a pair of performers appearing on stage at the Theater Casa Rosso."

"Casa Rosea."

"Casa Rosso," corrected Bram, "a nightclub and bar. The stage show is performance sex."

"Bodyguards?"

"One, a former boxer, tough, and loyal to Quinten, so no fallout with the father." Bram had a concerned look on his face. "He'll be a problem if confronted."

Smoke shrugged.

"Do you have a plan?"

"Not yet. Surveillance first. I'll need to watch and learn."

Bram smiled then got up. "George said I should have confidence in your abilities but if you need assistance," he withdrew a business card, "anytime, day or night."

Smoke took the card and put it away without looking at it. "Thanks, hopefully I won't bother you again."

Bram saluted by tilting the tip of his cane. "No bother. Anytime."

Smoke leaned back against the window and watched the Interpol man walk away twirling his cane. Bram Visser, unlike him, had no worries.

17

NEW YORK CITY

Mount Sinai hospital was cold. O, chilled, crossed arms and pulled her shoulders tight together. A shiver went up her spine.

Felix, attentive as usual, pulled his windbreaker off and slung it through the air like a matador's cape, surrounding O in New York Jets green and white. The jacket hung to the floor making it hard for her to walk, but appreciative and warmer.

"Thank you, Felix."

"Walter Raleigh without the mud." He bent slightly at the waist and made the sweeping arm gesture. "Follow me."

She kept her head down, Gia by her side, and both fell in behind Felix as he snowplowed through the busy lobby. The fluorescent bulbs were adding to her discomfort, their light seemed to be pulsating. She glanced up then winced, her eyes beginning to water.

Gia, who also watched her every move, pulled a tissue and forced it into O's hand.

The trio walked quickly toward where a woman, fiftyish with grey hair and BEA lettered on a brass name tag, sat behind a glass screen at the admittance desk.

Felix leaned over and spoke into a round hole in the glass.

Bea, who was typing, reluctantly pulled her eyes away from the computer screen, gave Felix a once over, and said, "May I help you?"

Gia gave Felix a push and stepped in front. "We are here to see Doctor Brightman. Can you direct us to his office, please?"

The woman was slow to respond, giving the three a long New York once over. The only thing missing from the character from central casting was chewing gum. She had Brooklyn cold. "I could, but I won't."

"Listen, honey—"

Gia elbowed him. "We have an appointment and don't know where to go."

The woman was still staring at Felix, giving him a more effective stare down than a left hook.

O was looking at the floor, the light still affecting her.

Bea looked back to Gia. "I'll call up but you'll have to wait here until they come for you." She picked up the phone, pushed a few buttons, and waited with the receiver on her ear. In the silent moment, she diverted her gaze to O. Her subway tough expression changed as did her voice. "New rules, honey. Not up to me. I'll tell them you're here but, in the meantime, there are some comfortable chairs through the door behind me." She then winked. "I'll get someone down here stat."

"Thank you. You're very kind." O's voice was weak but the words were genuine.

The woman glared at Felix and pointed to the door. "You too." As O walked past her, she whispered, "Loved your book, honey. Couldn't put it down."

O nodded as her cohorts took her arms, guiding her to the private room. It was painted some shade of green not on any color chart and had carpeting that must have coordinated, once. But it was quiet and the light was from table lamps. She plopped into a chair and sighed. It had been a long flight where sleep only came in bits. Her head was pounding and the tension from the lack of rest and the pain was written all over her face.

Gia reached into her carry bag searching for the prescription.

Felix observed and held up a finger. “Should that wait till after the Doc sees her?”

O, her eyes closed and head back, stuck out an open palm. “Give.”

Gia obeyed.

Felix shrugged.

Five minutes went by before the door opened and a young man wearing a white jacket, and sporting the profession-identifying stethoscope around his neck, entered. “Dr. Bennet, I’m Dr. Brightman’s PA. I’m going to take you to the examination room and I’d like to ask you a few questions on the way up to the fifth floor. Will that be, okay?”

“VIP treatment. Nice.” Felix seemed impressed.

The PA shook his head. “Not really, new rules. No one goes above the lobby unless they’re escorted.” He then added quickly, “But you are a VIP Dr. Bennet.”

“Too late, bucko.” Felix almost picked O off the chair.

The elevator was close, and the ride short, but long enough to answer the perfunctory identification questions.

Gia small talked. “So, Doc, I’m curious. Why does everyone ask for a birthday? Doesn’t seem like a real security question.”

“Isn’t,” the door opened, “two people with the same name never have the same birthday.”

“Ohhh.” Felix and Gia both nodded when a question for the ages was finally answered.

O wasn’t paying attention.

The PA escorted them to an examination room where he seated O and escorted Felix and Gia out, closing the door behind him.

O sat back in the chair, exhaling deeply into the quiet air.

Her phone vibrated, she looked then answered quickly. “Hi.”

“Where are you?”

“Waiting for Dr. Brightman. Where are you?” She tried to sound normal.

"George got me a hotel and I'm going to try to get some sleep. How are you?"

"Don't worry about me. My two bodyguards are watching every move I make, but you're alone, there by yourself, with no one to help."

"Okay, stop. I'm fine but if you can't get past this, I'll jump the next plane back to New York."

"No... don't do that." She paused. "I'm just not used to you being away. We haven't been apart since —"

"Your last concussion."

"Funny."

"I miss you too."

The door opened and Dr. Brightman came in with the PA and a nurse.

O nodded to the team and spoke quickly to Smoke. "I'll have to call you back. The doctor just came in. Love you."

"You too."

She pushed the button and looked up.

Dr. Brightman stood with his arms crossed and a concerned look on his face.

"There's a look I've seen before." O felt small.

"Father?"

"Mother."

"Ah huh, you did act childishly. I told you to rest and relax. Stress-free, remember?"

"It was. Quiet, peaceful and very relaxing. Mostly."

"Except when you had too much to drink and passed out in a church."

The nurse rolled her eyes.

O gave her a stare which was effective. "Yeah, well, there was that."

Brightman started the trip debriefing and she answered every question honestly and completely. It took a few minutes—the nurse transcribing the questions and answers.

"Okay, just a couple more. Which side did you fall on?"

O thought for a second then pointed to her right shoulder.

Brightman beckoned to the PA who stepped forward and began a careful examination of O's head, parting her hair section by section.

"Are you certain you didn't bang your head in the pew when you collapsed?"

"I don't think so." She paused a second. "Actually, I can't answer that. I did black out, but there was no swelling and no pain other than the persistent headache."

The PA, holding a section of hair apart, looked at Brightman.

Dr. Brightman looked at the spot on her head then did another complete examination.

"Olivia, there is a four-centimeter contusion on the right parietal. It's discolored, indicating that injury coincides with the event in the church. It is small, and would have been easily missed during the exam in Italy, but given your history I am admitting you today for observation and a few tests."

Her face went pale.

He smiled reassuringly and patted her shoulder. "Observation, Olivia. I'm just being cautious."

The PA and nurse were nodding like bobbleheads.

"Does that work often?" O didn't look convinced.

Brightman answered quickly. "Almost always."

"The, almost always, part of that saying is still appropriate."

He chuckled. "Don't worry, it's probably nothing. I'll come to see you after you settle in."

The nurse opened the door for the Doctor and PA, then turned to O. "I'll see you to your room."

Felix had flown in when the medical duo left and heard the nurse. "They're keeping you?"

"Yes, observation." O had her head down and was speaking to the floor.

Gia was a step behind and heard the answer. "Okay then. I'll get back to the car, head over to the condo, drop the luggage, and get what you need for the stay. Felix, you got this?"

"Why would you ask me that? Piece of cake. Of course, I got this."

The nurse rolled her eyes again and this time, O let it go without retaliation.

"It should take about an hour." Gia glanced at her watch. "Did you talk to Smoke? Or do you want me to call him?"

O instantly became angry. "No, absolutely not. Neither of you are to call him. He has important work to do, and I don't want him to worry about any of this bullshit. Understood?"

The pair were stunned to silence.

"Understood?" O repeated it slowly.

"Yes." Both answered meekly.

"Okay, good." O put her hands flat on the table and started to get up. "He is all alone in Italy and doesn't need any distractions."

"Amster—" Gia started to correct O but Felix grabbed her arm and shook his head.

Felix stared at Gia but spoke to O. "No problem, if he calls... you're sleeping, and you'll call him back. Okay?"

O looked at Gia and her voice changed again, softer. "Are you going to the condo? I'll need some fresh clothes."

"Yes, right now." Gia's expression was blank.

Felix moved to O and took her arms, helping her to her feet. "I got you honey, I got ya."

The nurse came back in the room, her mouth open and at the ready.

Gia, moving fast, grabbed her arm and persuaded her to exit.

Felix put an arm under O's and lifted. "Don't you worry about a thing, darlin."

"I know." O leaned her head against his shoulder. "You got my six."

"And your two and your eight and your twelve... we got you covered. Every time you look up one of us will always be there."

"Almost all of you... almost."

18

AMSTERDAM, NETHERLANDS

It was culture shock even to a seasoned city-slicker like Smoke. The number of bicycles; streaming, flowing, flooding the sidewalk was ridiculous. There was a road in the middle for cars, of which there were only a few, the occasional taxi, and the trolley running on train tracks. Both sides of the narrow strip of roadway were filled with a wall of thin tires attached to metal rails flying by the hotel door.

It was so out of Smoke's wheelhouse of comprehension that after exiting the Volkshotel, he backed up against the wall. He needed to observe and get the rhythm before plunging into the path of Amsterdam's commuters. A few minutes before, while drinking coffee in the café, he'd read some tourist brochures in an attempt to put a virtual map of the city in his head. Compass directions from this hotel— ground zero— train stations, proximity to the Red-Light District, police station, hospital. He also absorbed local facts like more than eighty percent of the Dutch citizens owned bikes and more than sixty percent used them every day. From what he could see fifty-nine percent of the sixty were on the street in front of him.

The buildings, the road, and the sidewalk were all made of brick. The road in a herringbone pattern, the walking sidewalk in wide stacked pavers and the brick in the bike path, laid lengthwise in the direction of the traveler. While descriptively individual, the road, bike-path, and sidewalk were visually inseparable. They were placed side by side with no curb or borders. The only attempt to define the areas was a change of color— darker brown to lighter brown. If a tourist on the paver walking area should happen to look up and step into the bike lane they would be instantly swept away, disappearing into a world of spandex and polite bell ringing not to be seen again till a dyke broke.

Smoke had seen many crazy things but the efficiency of the people in the parade was inspiring. As fast as it was moving, people were still texting or talking on phones. Riders were moving like schools of fish, all veering at an obstacle as one organism, flowing in and out, splitting at corners and reforming in other groups moving in different directions. It was actually kind of beautiful, assuming one had the genetic structure to participate. Smoke theorized the only way the system worked was Amsterdam's human herd had been thinned to a point where the Dutch were born with bike commuting immunity.

Smoke stepped forward; confident he had the rhythm. He was wrong. There was an unaccounted-for video game, psycho, bad guy— the motor scooter. This death machine appeared from nowhere, approaching, somehow virtually silent, at twice the speed of bicycle. A black helmet with a black visor on the head of a man suited in black flew under Smoke's arm just inside the bike lane.

"Mother..." Smoke bit off the second half of the word because the driver had already disappeared.

"They are not required to drive in the road with the trolleys and cars. They can, of course, but some like to ride in the bike lanes." A blond woman, wearing a smile and huge sunglasses, looked up from her diminutive height.

"They are dangerous." Smoke nodded and pointed to where the motor scooter used to be.

"Yes, they are. Only supposed to be able to go about 25 kilo... sorry," she hesitated and then pointed at him, "Americano, yes?"

He nodded.

"Fifteen miles per hour but most go much faster. Some even double that."

"Seems odd they're allowed to go that fast."

"Indeed, especially since they account for so many accidents. We just hope they all crash into the channel... which is more likely than getting everyone to agree to change the law."

A male voice came from behind Smoke. "Very liberal here, in case you haven't noticed. Very conscious of the rights of the individual."

Smoke didn't turn around. He just lowered his head and shook it side to side.

The little woman peeked around Smoke. Robert Aimer was shorter, but looked equally as American.

"Making new friends, I see." Aimer put a hand on Smoke's shoulder as he came around.

"This nice lady just explained local custom."

Aimer stuck out his hand to her. "Hej, hvordan gar det."

The woman put the smile back under the sunglasses. "Jeg er god dig."

Smoke was stunned. "You speak Danish?"

"Nahh," Aimer laughed. "Nope, just 'hi, how are you.' That's it. I'm not working twenty hours a day anymore. I'm retired and started watching a Danish detective series called *The Bridge*."

Her smile widened. "Yah, *The Bridge*. Very good."

Aimer tipped a fake hat to the lady. "Madam, nice to meet you but this man and I have business."

She started walking away but turned for a last look.

"I see you still got it," Aimer said, noticing her over-the-shoulder check out.

"Got what?"

"For a guy who sees everything, you're as blind as a bat."

"Whatever. Eat?"

"Yes, starving."

Smoke and Aimer carefully stayed clear of the bicycle lane and began walking toward an outdoor cafe. The avenue, bordered with four-story brick houses, split into two one-way streets. The median between the two roads was a restaurant with a curved glass front and white cloth covered tables and black iron railings. An awning hung over colorful plates and napkins with brass rings being served by waiters with black and white uniforms. In Philadelphia a diner was the neighborhood norm. A place where the staff was gruff but the food predictability good. Here the servers had white towels on their arms and moved like skaters, quickly with trays of food raised above their heads. It seemed too formal to Smoke, but without alternatives, it was close and the smell of coffee dismissed any objection.

"I have to admit, I'm surprised you're here," Smoke said after they'd been seated.

"But happy to see me, yes?" Aimer grinned.

A waiter arrived, and not waiting for instruction, poured water and coffee into waiting receptacles and placed a plate of fresh baked Danish in front of them. He handed off a menu and disappeared.

The two men were silent as they read, made decisions, and emptied the plate of pastry.

Their orders came out quickly but the men ate slow enjoying the time, both knowing from long years of manning stakeouts that this might be the last hot meal they ate in a long time.

Over breakfast, Smoke shared the file Bram Visser gave him with Aimer and brought him up to speed on Anton and Quinton Gurds. The file was thick and had profiles, pictures, and newspaper articles on both of the men.

Smoke pushed his plate to the side. "I want to focus on the son. He seems to be the weakest link, and given our limitations on manpower and supplies, I think posting up outside the office will be fruitless."

"Why the kid? He's not in charge."

"Visser said the father is sick, but more than that he said the father doesn't have a number two, there's no one to handle day-to-day. He said Interpol profiled Quinton, who is the hopeful if not natural successor, as ruthless and ambitious. Bram assumes that the kid is using his old man's sickness to expand into places his father doesn't want to go."

"Possible or likely? And why? They already control 90% of the market."

"Bram says likely. And think about it. It's not about more market share, it's about more market."

Aimer pondered over another sip of coffee.

"Exactly. I told Bram we would do some background on this putz and turn over anything we get to Interpol."

"Sure, but why can't he do this? Why us? I mean he is the man at the largest criminal investigative organization in Europe, right?"

"One of them, yes, but you know why, Lieutenant." Smoke gave his friend a disappointed look.

"Probable cause."

"Gurds runs a squeaky-clean outfit, operating for years without one charge being brought against them. There is only rumor and suspicion. He also suspects that Gurds and the Penose are receiving protection from the local police and being tipped when any inquiry gets close."

Aimer smiled the I got it look. "Okay. So, the old man is smart. How—?"

"We set up on Quinton. He's our in."

Aimer drank the rest of his coffee and mused over the situation. He put the cup back in the saucer, clasped his fingers together and looked at Smoke. "Where do we start?"

"We mark Quinton and tail him till we find something we can use to get a name." Smoke flipped open a map of the city and pointed to a red circle. "The office is a waste of time. It will be too hard to get in and, even if we did, where would we start looking? No, we need to tail Quinton when he's on his own, out for the night. The sheet on him reads, he's forty, no children, never married. He used to be a brawler, drove drunk, and there were a bunch of quashed arrests including sexual battery but—"

"No witnesses would testify." Aimer finished the sentence.

Smoke pointed a 'correct' finger at Aimer. "Exactly, bought off. Typical MO. Boy finds girl, boy beats girl, dad buys silence."

"Prick."

"Worse but…Bram said that he's changed his roll since the old man got sick. He's been a good boy for a while, no brawls, no bad press. Interpol is guessing, but they think Quinton is trying to stay in the old man's good graces, hoping his father promotes him before he croaks."

"Makes sense. Where do we start?" Aimer suddenly yawned.

"First, you need to get some sleep. I need you at full speed. Bram says Quinton has been hanging at a club in the Red-Light District."

"When?"

"Tonight." Smoke looked at his watch. "Check into your room, get a couple of hours shuteye. We'll get there at eight, do a one-inside-one-out rotation and hope we get lucky."

"First night on stakeout." Aimer shook his head doubtfully. "That would be lucky."

Smoke paused before answering. "Bobby, I want to get a name and get back to O as fast as possible."

Aimer pulled back. "Right, of course. Of course, sorry." Aimer stared at his friend with a serious look on his face. "You're right, but we are here now, and there's nothing you can do in New York. I think we stay in touch with Felix, work this for a day or two and like you said maybe we'll get lucky." He looked at his friend. "Smoke, we can jump whenever you say. I'm in, no matter what."

"I know, I know." Smoke looked down the street and said softly, "A couple of days."

Aimer tried to change the focus. "What are we going to be looking for?"

"Leverage."

19

NEW YORK CITY

Doctor Brightman, his PA on his right and his RN on his left, stood side-by-side in the hall outside of O's hospital room. They were talking, or rather Brightman was talking and his loyal assistants were sync-nodding, to a man who apparently was of similar professional stature as Brightman. The two doctors wore the same white coat made of the same heavy cotton, were perfectly groomed, but the giveaway was they both wore designer dress shoes. Brightman's shoes adorned with gold buckles countered the other doctor's brass snaps.

Felix had been chased from O's room by floor nurses who were changing sheets and attending to O's personal needs. He plopped into a plastic chair in the hall just before Brightman's group came down the corridor. They too halted in the hall outside the door, where Felix could overhear their confab about his girl. He understood only a few of the words they used. It was doctor speak and unintelligible to common folk.

A few minutes went by, the doctors looking at hand-held computer screens, pointing, faces concentrating. Eventually, the two doctors nodded, apparently reaching agreement. The consulting doctor shook Brightman's hand but ignored the staff, and turned to leave while pulling a cell phone from his jacket pocket. Brightman spoke to the PA directly and the RN leaned forward, listening intently.

The huddle broke.

Brightman headed for Felix who rose causing the chair to sigh in relief.

"The CAT scan showed a small spot that concerns me," Brightman began without formalities. "It is in the proximity of the contusion which apparently occurred when she passed out in the church."

Felix stared at the doctor waiting for part two.

"I'm keeping her another few days. We'll continue to monitor her vitals and mental acuity and I have issued an order for another scan tomorrow afternoon."

Felix remained quiet.

Brightman seemed, as most men did when Felix was serious, uncomfortable.

The doctor's tone changed. "Don't worry, I'm sure everything will be fine. We're just taking every precaution."

There was a moment of silence, then the nurse who was nodding like a bobblehead doll, spoke. "Doctor is the best."

"I thought your name was Bob?" Felix's expression hadn't changed.

"Excuse me?" The doctor inched back a half step.

"She said, Doctor is the best. No article of speech just Doctor. She didn't say, the Doctor, or Doctor Brightman, or Bob … just Doctor is the best. What's up with that?"

The nurse moved back a bit further, a step behind the doctor.

"And as far as concern goes, here's my deal." Felix inched forward closing the distance between him and the nervous medical professionals. "If I think that any of what you're doing is a self-serving publicity grab or if a single paparazzi gets near her, all of you will answer to me."

A voice came up from behind, cold watering the situation. "That's enough." O stood in the open door of her room.

All heads turned.

"I heard what you said, a few days. Okay, I get that, but I don't appreciate people talking about me when I'm ... right...fucking ... here."

Felix blew past the group of three before they could take their next breath. He literally swept O off her feet with one giant swing of his arm and lifted her, like a groom crossing a threshold.

"Put me down, you big oaf." She playfully hit him in the chest which did nothing.

"The food here must be working for you."

She hit him again. "Why?"

"Losing all the Italy weight."

She was laughing too hard to hit him again.

He placed her back into her bed and pulled up the blanket.

The RN stepped in.

Felix growled at her and she backed out quickly.

"Stop that. She means well."

Felix tucked her sheet. "They all mean to do well, and I'm here to make sure they... do...do."

They both laughed.

"What's going on?"

Gia walked in with a shopping bag and a cooler.

"Food." Felix shouted and started for her with his arms outstretched.

"Get away you animal." She brushed past the sulking hulk. "This is for our girl. I got Caprese and Pasta Primavera from Patsy's."

"You're killing me." Felix grumbled. "I'm starving."

"Then go eat." Gia pointed to the door then walked over, stood up on her toes, and kissed his cheek. "I got this watch."

Felix mumbled but ducked his head and started to leave. "If you need anything—"

O did a haunted house impersonation. "Get outttt."

Gia slid O's bedside tray around, pulled up a chair, and unloaded her treasure.

O patted Gia's hand and inhaled the aroma. "I love you."

Gia smiled. "What happened with your team of medical minds?"

"They're keeping me for more tests."

Gia's hand hesitated a second. "Really, how come?"

O reached for a fork. "Just more tests. No biggy."

Gia turned from the bed to get a bottle of water from the cooler. She was also trying to wipe the concern from her face.

O exclaimed gleefully. "Hmmm. This is awesome."

"Good," was all Gia could manage.

"Do me a favor."

"Anything."

O finished another bite. "Don't tell Smoke yet. He'll just worry."

"Whatever you want. When he calls, I'll tell him you're leaving tomorrow morning and deal with tomorrow, tomorrow."

"Thanks. You want some?" O held up her plate.

"No... God no... I ate while I was waiting for this dinner. I'm full."

O waggled her fork. "Sure?"

"Certain." Gia changed the subject. "How's the headache?"

"Not bad. I actually forgot about it for a bit. I guess that's good."

Gia nodded then looked at her watch. "Did they give you the meds? It's after four."

"It's four o'clock? You sure? Doesn't feel like it."

"Yes, I'm sure. Did they give you your meds?"

O's eyes drifted up. "Ah... I don't remember." She looked puzzled for a second then lit up with recognition. "Wait. Yes, I took them, I'm certain. The nurse came in when Smoke was here a little while ago." She took another bite, smiled, and shook her fork at Gia. "Best in the city."

Gia turned her head around so as to not give away her emotions, and pulled a long baguette from a brown paper bag then put it on the tray. She picked up the remote and turned on the TV. "We should see what's happening in the world these days."

The local news anchors were droning on about something or other. Gia didn't hear. She wasn't watching or listening. It wasn't good news.

20

AMSTERDAM, NETHERLANDS

The sign bolted to the roof of the building featured a pink elephant dressed in a tuxedo waving hello. The venue's name, Theater Casa Rosso, like the pachyderm, also seemed innocuous— almost like a sign above a kid's playhouse. If it wasn't for the triple x's on the tie around the elephant's neck, a tourist looking for adult entertainment might walk right past the most popular live sex nightclub in Amsterdam.

The infamous Red-Light District draws hundreds of thousands of curiosity seekers every year. Their interests are diverse, some wanting just to walk on the sidewalks and gasp as they look through the windows into what they had been taught to be the next level of hell. Others strap on their courage and step inside the museums, galleries, and sex toy shops. The really adventurous gird their loins and buy a ticket to a live sex show like teenagers sneaking into an X- rated movie. Most enter to be titillated, to veer from the norm, and to observe, live and in person, what is forbidden in every other major city. In Amsterdam, sex is a commodity for sale in public, like clothes in a mall or tools at Home Depot. Endless selections and products to fit every need. The district is promoted around the world, advertised in magazines, and of course, online. Hourly tours put thousands of people every hour onto the sidewalks and into the stores, sitting in theater seats and sometimes inside storefront brothels where entrepreneurial women conduct a service business. It's legal and has, at least for the recent past, existed without sex trafficking, organized crime bosses, or other crimes against humanity.

One might expect the pleasure-seeking customers visiting the Theater Casa Rosso to be single men. However, amongst the expected are couples, some single women, and of course, boisterous bachelor and bachelorette parties.

Smoke and Aimer arrived early and sat on a stone wall three doors down from the theater that Bram Visser from Interpol said Gurds would visit that evening.

The people filing by on the sidewalk were not paying any attention to them. They were walking slow and taking in the sights. There were no vehicles and no damn bikes, just people all moving slow and talking low.

Smoke pointed to the expanse of water behind them separating the opposing lanes of the street. "If we sit here much longer somebody is going to notice."

"We are exposed, but is anybody looking?" Aimer countered, looking up and down the street unconcerned.

"Maybe not, but we need to be cautious. Quinton is trying to stay under his father's radar. He might be looking for a tail his father hired. We can't afford to be spotted. When I confront him, it has to be a complete surprise. I'll get only one shot and it has to be unexpected. We need to find something I can use if I'm going to be able to get a name."

"Tell me again why you think he knows the name of a guy killed in a parking lot in Oklahoma."

Smoke ducked his head and said slowly. "They didn't set up like the mob or the cartels. There are no middlemen only local suppliers. They ship to small independent dealers. Quintin is expanding his father's business and Oklahoma was an expansion."

Aimer nodded. "Right, we got that from Kansas City. The guys were sent from the east."

"Right, and that was the exception."

"Okay that's where I lost you."

"George said one of the dead guys was local, hired help, right?"

"Yep."

"Okay, who hired him?"

"The other dead guy."

"Right, and who hired him?"

Aimer smiled. "The guy expanding the turf."

Both said, "Quinton Gurds."

Aimer nodded. "Okay, makes sense. How we going to work this tonight?"

Smoke pointed. "See the alley next to the theater?"

Aimer looked where Smoke was pointing.

"It probably leads to a stage door in back of the building. If things don't go well, if trouble starts, that's my emergency out— if I don't come back out the front. I'll look for that exit from inside."

Aimer pointed to the ironwork on the opposite side of the building. "Look up there. There's a fire escape."

"Okay. Good. If the stage door is blocked, I'll go up and out a window— that'll be my second out."

"Overthinking this?" Aimer puzzled.

"Seriously." Smoke looked at his friend. "You forget all the cop shit, already?"

Aimer was a little embarrassed. "Escape routes are not cop shit. We're more about catching than getting away. Anyway, what are you expecting?"

Smoke took a beat. He pushed off the wall, stood and stretched but his eyes continued searching the passing crowd for anyone who was out of place. “I don’t know what to expect, so I prepare for everything. I anticipate him coming with a bodyguard, probably one, maybe two. This guy isn’t John Gotti but he isn’t Mr. Rogers either. Their gang doesn’t operate on street corners, and there aren’t bodies in car trunks, but they run a multi-million-dollar drug business. They have enemies. He’s young and inexperienced but maybe just smart enough to see us coming.”

“And the bodyguard—”

“My guess… probably young, big, gym muscles, and most likely hasn’t seen much action.”

“That’s a lot of maybes, buddy.”

“Well, that’s my plan and if I’m wrong…” he cracked his knuckles, “that’s why I have three exits, front, back, and thanks to you, up.”

Aimer looked at the theater. “What’s the layout inside the club?”

“I looked at the website. Narrow entrance, long rectangle with a stage and a bar in the back. I’ll go in, get a drink, and put my back against the wall and wait. Text when you see him. One for just him, two for a him and a bodyguard.”

Aimer nodded.

Smoke started toward the ticket booth then stopped and turned to his friend.

“What?” Aimer looked puzzled.

“He’ll go in with the bodyguard. You’ll watch for a tail from the father, you will spot them easily, if they’re there.”

“But?” Aimer tilted his head.

“It’s possible our friend, Bram, has got Interpol in this, too. They will be harder to spot.”

“Just Interpol?”

Smoke thought for a moment, then shrugged. “Make it simple, if you see anybody other than just suits with shiny shoes, text me to get out.”

Aimer nodded and Smoke turned and walked toward the theater.

21

NEW YORK CITY

The sun was shining on O through her room's eighth floor window. It had risen high enough to pass over the roof of another wing of the enormous campus of Columbia Hospital. A solid beam of light crept across her bed taking a bit of the chill off the sanitized air conditioning. O closed her eyes, angling her face to receive the welcome guest. For a moment, the warmth made her relax and gave her, if for only this moment, a sense of normal.

She kept her eyes closed in spite of a loud clatter emanating from the hall. The banging was accompanied by a recognizable voice. She opened her eyes, blinking in the light but not moving her head.

"Hi gorgeous." Felix, who was gripping two handles on paper bags, entered the room sideways because of the girth of his body and the baggage he carried.

"Hi yourself. What in God's name have you got there?" O reluctantly moved from the light.

Gia, who had been hidden behind the wide body, stepped forward and walked to O's bedside. "How are you feeling?" Gia reached up and brushed a wayward lock of O's hair off her forehead.

Felix had paused to answer O's inquiring question with a demonstration of his wares. He rummaged a bit, then removed a red and white checkered tablecloth, silverware, and a vase complete with a red rose.

"Oh my." O sighed in surprise, a hand instinctively covering her mouth.

Felix reached into the second bag, withdrew an insulated case, unzipped it, and removed several cardboard food containers, placing them on O's roll-up table.

O started to reach.

Felix scolded her. "No … wait … there's more."

He reached back in and took out a ceramic cup and saucer, a silver teapot, and a thermos.

Felix pointed to a chair near the bed. "Come on you, out, put your butt over here."

O complied with a grin and giggle.

Gia grabbed a blanket and tucked it in over O's objections.

Felix pushed the cart close. "Ta da." He pulled back the cardboard covers. Inside were plates filled with two works of food art.

"What … Oh my, what did you two do?"

Gia arranged the knife and fork. "This is from Norma's at Le Parker Meridien Hotel."

Felix pointed a finger. "This is their specialty, an egg frittata with lobster and Sevruga caviar and in case you don't like that, we have eggs Benedict with artichoke and porcini-truffle sauce." His grin was as big as one of the plates.

O was overwhelmed and speechless.

Gia pulled a small container and a glass from one of the bags and poured a creamy drink. "Strawberry, papaya, and pineapple smoothie."

"And," Felix opened the thermos and poured hot water through a strainer into the silver pot. "Organic jade pearl green tea."

"This is just too much." O's face was beaming.

"You've been through the ringer and deserve something special." Gia tucked again.

"Come on, eat up." Felix chided.

O took a forkful and rolled her eyes with delight. "This is fantastic, but there's no way on earth I can eat all of this."

"God, I'm glad you said that." Felix grabbed one of the bags and took out two more plates and silverware.

O reached up, grabbed his arm, and pulled. "Come here."

Felix received her kiss with a blushed face.

O put her arm out to Gia who responded with a two-arm hug.

After dividing the bounty, the three sat without conversation just making yummy sounds.

"That was absolutely wonderful but how much—"

"Don't you dare ask." Felix shook a finger.

"But Norma's is the most expensiv—"

"What did I just tell you? Don't ask."

"You two..."

Gia got up and got busy cleaning up. "You want to jump in the shower? The doctor should be making rounds soon."

"That's a good idea. Yes, a shower sounds good."

Gia jumped up to help.

Felix began leafing through a magazine. "Any news on when they're going to kick you out of here?"

O shook her head. "Not yet but I'm hoping today."

"Hear from Smoke?" Felix paused on a page.

"Not this morning. I talked to him last night. He was waiting for George's contact from Interpol."

"Bobby should be there by now. I'll call him later. What time is it there again?"

From the bathroom Gia yelled out, "Six hours ahead. Ten a.m. here, four p.m. there."

"Don't bother them, Felix. If you start calling, Smoke will just start worrying. He'll call when he can."

O stood up and started for the bathroom. As she fastened her robe she listed and quickstepped, trying to regain her balance.

Felix practically flew out of the chair and grabbed her arm.

"I'm fine, honey. Just took a bad step."

Felix wasn't convinced.

Gia who was in the bathroom doorway wasn't either. Her face was drawn tight. "Come on, your shower is ready. I'll give you a hand."

O started to protest. "I don't need any—"

Gia took Felix's place at her arm. "Exactly how fucking far do you think that is going to get you? I'm helping and that's it."

O nodded. "Okay."

When the door closed, Felix headed to the hallway to look for a nurse and/or a doctor concerned about O's misstep. His head was on a swivel, rotating up and down the aisle, in and out of rooms. The nurse's floor station was around the corner and across from the elevator. Nurses were hustling around behind the glass enclosure preparing forms, getting supplies and tapping on keyboards. With his quarry now in sight he quickened his pace.

The person who stepped out of the elevator stopped him in his tracks.

"Jesus H Christ on a scooter." Felix stood staring, frozen in place.

The woman who just exited the lift couldn't help but be taken aback by the hulk who seemed transfixed in front of her. "Uh … are you alright?"

Felix stuttered his reply. “Sorry, I just, I mean … you are … I mean.”

The woman backed up a couple of steps. “Are you a patient here?”

“No, no.” Felix stammered. “Wow, you look exactly like someone I used to know.”

Her face became red and indignant. “Sir, this isn’t a bar and that’s a very bad pick-up line.”

“No… no. I apologize. Please, this’s a real thing. A friend of mine, who looked exactly, and I mean exactly like you, was killed a while back and seeing you startled me. I apologize.”

The woman’s face softened immediately. “Your friend’s name was Loretta?”

Felix sucked in air. “Yes.”

“I’m her sister, Lauren.”

Felix actually staggered a bit before reacting then darted forward.

Lauren was too slow and almost panicked.

Felix wrapped both arms around her and lifted her off her feet. “You’re Lo’s sister. Oh dear one, Oh, I miss her so.”

He put her down and pushed her to arm’s length without letting go.

“I do too.” A tear was falling down Lauren’s cheek.

“I’m Felix Grant and I’m guessing, now, you’re here to see Olivia Bennet.”

“Indeed. You’re a friend of Doctor Bennet, I’m guessing.”

“Uh huh, I’m, she’s a very good friend.”

“At the funeral she insisted that if I ever got to New York, I was to look her up. I’m starting classes at NYU in a few weeks and, of course, I heard about her condition in the papers so I decided to come and visit her in the hospital. I hope that’s okay?”

“Certainly.” Felix grinned. “You may be just the thing to help her out of a difficult situation. She loved your sister so, and misses her something terrible. Come on, she’s just down the hall.” Felix took her hand and they walked down the aisle.

Gia stood close while O dressed into fresh flannel pajamas.

"I hope I can get back into real clothes and get out of here today," O said, looking into a mirror and running her fingers through her wet hair.

"Me too. Grab a seat on the john." Gia reached for a hair dryer and began blowing O out.

O didn't like Gia doing this but accepted the help. Her hands shook a bit when she tried to do it by herself and she didn't want to show the vulnerability. The noise from the dryer was loud and echoed off the tile bathroom walls. She closed her eyes and let herself drift into the comfort of warm air.

Gia clicked off the dryer and puffed O's hair with her fingers. "All done."

"Thank you, honey." O patted Gia's cheek.

Felix's voice broke the moment. "Hey, look who's here."

"Wait one." Gia yelled out through the partially opened door.

O turned and whispered, "You two have another surprise?"

Gia shrugged her shoulders. "Not me."

O stood up from her seat on the toilet top and stepped toward the door. On the second step her foot went numb, the third her arm, and on the fourth her knees buckled.

Gia was there, her arm went under O's and she lifted her slumping friend erect.

The dizzy spell lasted only a few seconds.

They stepped through the door opening together.

Felix was on the other side with arms outstretched. "You ready for a huge surprise?"

O looked up as Felix stepped aside.

A tall, short-haired blond woman stood looking a little uneasy. Her deep blue eyes reflected hesitation apparently unsure that her presence was welcome.

O let out a gasp, her hands went to her face and she started walking forward quickly.

Gia didn't anticipate her move.

"Where have you been Lo? I need you here with me."

Felix and Gia both were stunned into non-action.

Lauren was mystified. "I'm Lo's sister. We met at her funeral, remember?"

O's arms were up as she advanced. "Lo, we have to cancel the appoint..." Two steps away from her past, O came back to the present.

Gia caught up and took O's arm.

"I don't understand." Lauren looked at Felix, puzzled.

He came up beside the sister and the four were now standing a step away from each other.

Felix looked at O. "This is Lauren, Lo's sister. She's studying at NYU and stopped by to see how you're doing."

O, now recovered from her momentary delusion, smiled. "Yes ... of course ... Lauren, it's so good to see you and I'm glad you found the time to visit me. And..." she paused and tilted her head. "You look exactly like Lo."

"I get that a lot." Lauren smiled weakly.

New people entering stopped the reunion cold.

"Good news." Dr. Brightman came through the door flanked by an intern and an RN. "You're going home today."

The four turned and stared at the doctor.

There was a long pause and then the doctor said, "What? Did I miss something?"

Felix recognized Lauren was totally confused and feeling like leaving was her best option. After briefing the doctor on O's breakdown, he hustled her to the waiting room to explain.

"O... I mean Dr. Bennet, is suffering from a serious concussion, actually three concussions. She's being carefully watched but, as you just witnessed, has moments that cause us all great concern. The doctor was ready to let her go home but he's ordered another CAT scan."

"I feel like I did something wrong."

"Oh my God, no, honey. You didn't do anything and there is no predicting when or what will affect her. But..." He took her hand, "you look so much like Lo. I mean you really could be her twin. I did mention that O was crushed when she was ... I mean when she died. I think she still feels responsible."

"Responsible? How? She was shot by someone who broke into her office. Dr. Bennet wasn't even there. I don't understand." Tears from old wounds began to flow.

"They were breaking in to get some files on one of the doctor's patients. In fact, Smoke... You met him too, yes?"

Lauren nodded.

"Well, Lo was in the hall while the men were inside the office. He was on the phone with Lo and told her to wait till he got there. She didn't, for what I'm sure was a good reason but of course we will never know what the reason was. I think that is what haunts both Dr. Bennet and Smoke. Why Lo went in alone."

"She was always a badass. Never afraid of anything. It was just like her to ignore the warning and charge in."

Felix smiled and nodded knowingly. "Yeah, she was badass. Almost as badass as me."

Lauren chuckled and wiped the last tear from her cheek.

Felix patted her knee. "Come on Kiddo. I'll buy you a coffee while we wait for O to be brought back to the room. I have a lot of Lo stories to tell you."

22

AMSTERDAM, NETHERLANDS

Smoke had to duck in the narrow passage leading from the ticket booth to a set of red velvet curtains. A barrel-chested man, wearing the same triple-x tie as the elephant on the roof, pushed the curtains apart, then stepped back to let Smoke pass. The man was much wider but several inches shorter. Smoke thought about how long a quick exit out the front would take, and added a minute or two to get past this guy.

A long bar with stools stretched across the back wall of the long, wide theater. A bartender was busy washing glasses and doing what bartenders do between serving customers. A center aisle split rows of about a hundred theater seats down the middle. The floor had the typical slant that allowed the audience, of about fifty, an uninterrupted view of a stage as wide as the room.

To Smoke's surprise, it was clean—no trash on the floor, no foul smells. Smoke assumed the odor of urine or something worse would make him cringe. Instead, there was the smell of disinfectant from a diligent post-Covid cleaning team, an odor being countered by a pleasant mist of flowered air freshener coming from the air-conditioning vents. Smoke stood for a moment doing a quick recon, then walked to the last stool at the bar against the far wall. He took a seat, and signaled to the over-bleached, blond woman who was tending bar.

She acknowledged him with a head nod as she continued to work previous orders. She was busy at the other end of the bar handling patrons who entered and stopped at the bar to order some liquid fortitude before going down the aisle to fantasyland. It took a minute but she took his beer order and she delivered a tall glass of ice-cold German beer which, again, exceeded expectations.

Smoke looked at a poster hanging behind the bar promoting the acts performing that night. It had the act name in black bold print, a brief description, and the exact time it began and ended. The show was four acts and lasted one hour, repeating every hour on the hour till closing. Smoke thought it to be clever. There was no first act. No plot to miss. The audience would arrive at various times and would leave when the act they saw was repeated. The turnover occurred every fifteen minutes, so there was constant movement in the aisle. Customers would enter randomly, most staying for the entire hour, leaving only when the performers they had seen first returned to the stage. NO CELL PHONES NO PHOTOS was printed on the bottom of the poster in wide threatening letters.

It was clever, no waiting crowds and a constant turnover of the audience. Great for the owners but not ideal for surveillance. People were always moving about in the aisles, especially between acts. It was possible, even from this vantage point, to miss someone coming or going.

He pulled the phone from his pocket, held it low, and clicked it to vibrate then texted Aimer. *In position.*

The lights dimmed, but only slightly. Enough remained to keep the aisle and the audience visible. People standing found their seats. Down in front, two men emerged from behind the curtain and took up stations at either side of the stage. It wasn't hard to figure their purpose, they were the only two people in the place facing the crowd. Smoke judged them to be seasoned bouncers and alert for bad behavior.

There was no curtain on the empty stage. A motor whined and a backdrop painted with a scene of an average looking bedroom lowered from the rigging. The huge canvas was professionally done and seemed odd for a crowd who would have been expecting something untamed and wild rather than a suburban middle-class bedroom. From stage right, a man rolled out a bed with a black-iron headboard. From stage left, another man pushed a dresser and lamp completing the limited set decoration. Both men disappeared off stage quickly. A moment passed then a circular spotlight lit a spot on the stage. Without introduction or fanfare, a woman stepped into the center of the light and stood silent. She had short blond hair, was maybe late forties and seemed to have an athletic shape. She wore a simple flowered print sundress and flat black shoes. The light followed her as she crossed the stage appearing completely relaxed and, although the crowd was restless and getting noisy, acted as if she was in her own room, completely alone. She stopped to whisk away some dust from the dresser, walked to the bed, fluffed the pillows and pulled the bedcover taunt. She then turned and faced the audience, still pretending solitude, and kicked off her shoes.

The chatter diminished slightly.

The woman turned to face the long mirror over the dresser. She centered her image then using both hands smoothed the fabric of the dress, pulling it tight, the shape of her hips and waist now more evident. She raised her arms slowly toward the ceiling. When fully stretched, she shook her hands rapidly, threw her head back, and let out a loud sigh.

People moving about in the aisle found a seat.

She pivoted on one foot, then slowly extended a leg, thigh high, knee bent, toe pointed then took one step. Then another. Each step beginning with the pointed toe. A soft saxophone came up. It took eight steps to center stage where she stopped. Still in profile, she raised her left hand to the right strap of the sundress, pushing it off her shoulder. She spun around, her profile now stage left, and pushed off the other strap. The fabric fell, but halted against the crest of her breasts.

Smoke's phone screen lit and he saw Aimer's code appear— *2.* He looked to the entrance and saw no one coming into the theater, and no one moving in the aisle. He shifted the barstool so he could see the entrance and the stage door.

The blond woman turned to face the crowd, her expression now focused and intense. She raised her hands over her head and held them there, motionless. The saxophone got a little louder. As the music rose her fingers began to twirl. Faster and faster. Her dress slipped down a bit more but magically resisted gravity.

The crowd was now completely silent.

Her fingers stopped keeping time and she looked up to the ceiling now making a come-to-me gesture. Two thick black straps began to drop down, stopping when they reached her waist. She pushed her hands forward, separated the straps and stepped in between them.

Form the corner of his eye, Smoke saw a man and woman come in from the entrance and begin to walk down the aisle. The woman seemed uneasy and tried to sit in the back, but he pulled her down the aisle toward the front.

On the stage, two men dressed in black appeared from the shadows, stopping on either side of the blond woman, who was still staring straight ahead as if no one was in the room. Each man took one of the straps and pulled them apart revealing connecting straps making the contraption resemble a playground swing. They held it steady, then stood at attention next to her. She took a step backward, crossed her hands across her chest and flicked the fabric of her dress. It fell to her hips. She paused a second, then shimmied, and the dress fell to the floor.

Smoke couldn't help but register a bit of surprise.

Her body was near perfect; fit, mature and shapely. There was a single spotlight framing her, as she stood... posing... like a model would have for Van Gogh or Toulouse Lautrec. The men were there beside her, but they were props, like the bed, or the dresser, or the swing hanging from the ceiling. In that moment, standing naked in the spotlight, she had completely captured the audience, each alone in their seats, and she alone on the stage, all seeming at ease and natural.

She raised her hands again, and the men, on cue, pulled the straps taunt as she backed up. She sat on one belt and leaned back on the other. The men bent over, picked up a loop at the strap's end, and slipped a loop over each foot.

She leaned her head back. A motor began to whine. The contraption began to rise, as did the woman in the swing.

A group of giggling girls came down the aisle, annoying the crowd who shushed them. They quietly hurried to a row of empty seats.

When the swing rose a few feet and stopped, the blond woman broke her solitary stare and looked at the two men for the first time. She let go of the straps and reached out stoking their chests then slowly dropped her hands down between their legs.

Smoke looked down at the phone screen. No message.

Where was Quinton Gurds?

The blond woman slowly looked at both men again, then pointed to the man on the left. He immediately positioned himself in front of her, the other moving behind. The man in front pushed the straps apart and swung the entire rig sideways, her body now in profile to the audience. The spotlight shifted and narrowed to highlight only her form. The two men were shadowed in front and back. The man in front stepped to her. She let go of the straps, and in an expertly executed move, pulled off his breakaway black outfit. His face was still hidden in a shadow. His body now in the light, the audience could see that most of him was average, but not all.

She reached up and grabbed both straps. Her head fell back, her mouth slightly open and eyes closed.

The man stepped forward, between her legs.

It was her face, her expression, that was the most erotic thing happening on the stage. She moaned and the audience knew without seeing it happen, exactly when the man entered her.

Her expression was hypnotic.

Her head thrashed side to side.

The man in front grabbed her by the waist and pulled her forward. The man at her back pushing her forwards. They began to move like a unified pulse which began matching the rhythm of the saxophone, beat for beat.

Her eyes were closed, her body writhing. Beads of sweat rolled down her face, her body glistening, reflecting like dew on a flower.

The music intensified and the audience was soundless. They could hear every sound she made.

Suddenly, she let go of the straps and lifted her hips, reaching back with both hands, grabbing the arms of the man behind her. She pulled hard. The swing stopped. The man in front pushed up on his toes lifting her off the straps.

She moaned, then yelled out. Her head and back rose up and down on the swing. The man in front anchored against her thrust.

She screamed, once, then again, and then again, louder than the previous two, shattering the silence of the audience. Her body arched, shuddered, then sagged down into the swing. Her head was back and mouth open.

The men stepped back and she lay, alone in the light. She shuddered again.

Smoke guessed that this performance was a prime example of what O was talking about when she told him they needed to enjoy all that life has to offer.

A minute of silence went by. The two men stood motionless. The blond woman swung gently back and forth.

Then the stage light came up and the blond woman quickly dismounted. One of the men immediately helped her put on a robe. Now, out of the character, she stepped forward and bowed to the crowd.

A single clap turned into a raucous audience response. Clapping, cheering, and woo-wooing got loud as the lighting got brighter and the players on stage positioned for another bow. The men left and, left alone on the stage, the blond woman, in a silk robe, gracefully bowed then exited stage left.

There was movement in the aisle and at the entrance. Smoke saw several people who appeared to have been stopped by a bouncer during the climax of the blonde's performance start down the aisle.

Two couples came down first, heads bobbing like typical tourists. Then another pair, but the last was a man in a suit. He was thin, tall, had short sandy hair and a well-groomed goatee.

That's him.

Gurds strolled slowly, with an air of confidence. If this was an old English movie, he would have been carrying a long ivory cigarette holder. The suit was European, a look Smoke recognized but didn't get. It was shiny and fit like it belonged to a younger, thinner brother. What really didn't make any sense was Smoke knew how much this ill-fitting fashion statement cost.

Smoke watched him closely while still keeping an eye on the entrance. A second man, heavy set with no beard dressed in black pants, black t-shirt, and black suit coat came in next but stood next to the entryway, arms crossed.

Bodyguard.

Gurds took a front row seat just as the lights dimmed slightly again and a new backdrop fell, followed by a silver pole that lowered to center stage. A disco light appeared from the ceiling next, and rays of light began twirling. The setting was supposed to be something on the order of a nightclub, or strip-bar, but neither effect was being achieved. From stage right two girls, maybe women, it was hard to tell their age under the makeup, emerged. They ran, ungracefully, to center stage, and the pole. A soundtrack of some barely recognizable disco beat came up and the two began a dirty pole dance routine. Both seemed drunk, or high. They stumbled a bit and were relying on a rehearsed, humdrum, striptease choreography. Their pretend lesbian dance routine was painful to watch. The lackluster performance continued until one of them spotted Gurds. She whispered to her partner whose head snapped around looking through the stage light to the front row. Both became energized, demeanors changing from lethargic to passionate and directed. They forgot the rest of the audience and began dancing for one— Quinton Gurds.

Gurds sat relaxed, king-like, observing the subjects of his domain.

Smoke looked down to where Gurds was being entertained by the dancers whose only interest was the man in the first row. Smoke knew this was a weakness that was exploitable.

Smoke's phone screen lit up.

Another tail. Two bad guys. Look Middle Eastern.

Smoke raised the phone screen and tapped a message to Aimer.

Take pictures. We need faces.

Smoke put the phone back in his pocket and stood to leave. Gurds has another problem; these bad guys are not a tail hired by a suspicious father.

This might have gotten a little easier.

23

AMSTERDAM, NETHERLANDS

Aimer was easy to spot, sitting on the wall where Smoke left him. He held a paper cup emanating steam from what, presumably, was coffee. Envy struck him as he was tired and needed a lift.

The former cop had assumed a stakeout mode, and appeared to be just waiting for someone's arrival. He was good at it. The act was well practiced from years of beat duty and actually having to wait for his friend to arrive.

Smoke caught his attention with a small wave and Aimer acknowledged by dismounting.

"They're over my right shoulder, other side of the canal. Two, one tall, one short, dark hair, facing the club."

Smoke continued to look at Aimer but peripherally spotted Quinton Gurds' tail. "How long?"

"They showed up about fifteen minutes ago, ten minutes after he went in."

They turned and Smoke did a tourist point. "We need pictures."

"Got them. I walked over to the café behind them and bought this coffee."

"Yeah, nice, just one. Always thinking of me."

"Oh … fuck you. I'm out here chilling my ass on a stone wall and you're in there watching God knows what."

"Believe me when I tell you, God's never been in that joint."

"Really?" Aimer's face gave away uncharacteristic boyish curiosity.

Smoke passed on trash talk. "What do you make of the tail?"

"Middle Eastern, the tall guy is the point and the short guy is the muscle. Check out the small guy."

Smoke turned away as if deciding which way to walk. The men were leaning against the stone wall bordering the canal, thirty yards opposite them. The tall guy was maybe thirty, slim, fit, with black hair and a stubble of black beard. The short one Smoke knew immediately could be trouble. He was stocky, maybe five inches shorter and twenty pounds heavier. He also was at least twenty years younger. Normally, size didn't matter and Smoke's experience overcame youthful enthusiasm every time, but this guy stood like a wrestler and had a face to match.

"Hmmm. I need a closer look."

"We worried about losing Gurds?"

"Nope." Smoke looked at his watch. "He's being entertained for another ten minutes."

"Right. We should walk over to the café. You get coffee and I'll take a leak."

The bridge was stone and arched over a surprising clean waterway. If this were New York or Venice the canal would look and perhaps smell much different. Yellow lights lit a peaceful and calm backdrop to a teeming mass of hedonistic humanity. The café was under an awning and twenty feet from the two Quinton Gurds stalkers.

Smoke ordered coffee and Robert went inside.

The two men stood focused and wordless. It was very odd behavior and they stood out from the rest of the crowd. Both apparently bought their tourist disguises at the airport. The tall man wore a brand-new soccer jersey over creased dungarees. The problem child wore sweatpants and a red hoodie. Both had on well-worn brown leather sandals. Neither had paid any attention to Smoke.

Smoke thought about a picture but they were turned away and a back-of-the-head shot was hard to identify.

"Next?" Aimer showed up wiping his hands on his jeans. "Out of paper towels."

"You have a zoom on your phone camera?"

Aimer nodded.

"We walk back over the bridge; I'll stop and you fake taking a picture of me. Zoom as best you can on their faces."

"Then pick up on Gurds?"

"Maybe."

"That's clear as mud."

Smoke chuckled. "Sorry, I don't know yet. We'll have to see who he's with when he leaves."

The pictures only took a minute. More than that might have been obvious. They walked back to the theater and took up a spot near a tree where they could remain partially hidden from the two stalkers while keeping an eye on the front door and the alley beside the theater.

"You hear from New York?"

Smoke shook his head. "No news is good news."

"True that."

"I'll call when this is done."

"Where are we with this?"

Smoke finished his coffee. "I only need leverage to get a name. That's it. We have two possibilities now. Gurds needs to keep his image away from the father's attention and now the Middle East connection. We stay on both until one bears fruit."

The two girls from the stage show were draped on Gurds' arms when he emerged from the alley's shadows. His bodyguard followed two steps behind.

"Jesus, you could make a fortune over here. A bodyguard walking behind?"

"Maybe the bad guys are bad at it as well."

Gurds was standing tall, like a primped-up rooster. The girls, whose ages were still undeterminable, were laughing hysterically and struggling with balance, obviously drugged and/or drunk.

The group turned toward Smoke and Aimer.

"Shit." Aimer whispered. "We can't follow until the tail makes their move."

Smoke was already concentrating on the men across the bridge. "Gurds will be easy to spot."

The Middle Eastern men started walking quickly but stayed on the other side of the canal.

"Good," said Smoke. "We split up here. I'll take the stalkers, you take Gurds. He's probably headed to a hotel. Get more pictures if you can pull that off without being spotted by Gurds or the tail."

Aimer nodded.

Smoke took off, walking quickly back to the bridge then hustled to get thirty feet behind the two men. They were focused on Gurds paying no attention to being followed themselves, a detail Smoke thought odd. They walked with no hesitations and no effort given to stealth.

The journey was short. Gurds and his girls traveled only a few blocks before entering the Sofitel Legend Hotel. Even with limited travel experience Smoke could readily see it was an expensive five-star hotel. Aimer wisely strode past the entrance and took up a post at the nearest street-corner bus stop.

Smoke waited till the two men found their post, an outdoor table at a café. Smoke walked past them within a few feet. A final test. They paid him no attention.

Smoke hustled across an intersection narrowly missing a collision with oncoming bicycle Nazis and caught up to Aimer.

"Yo. Where are the other two?"

"Sitting at the café across the street." Smoke made an over the shoulder nod. "Got-um?"

"Yep."

"I think Gurds is in for the night. That place has gotta be a couple of hundred a night. He wouldn't be using it as a no-tell motel."

"499. I looked it up."

"Damn. Anyway, I need some sleep. Can you keep an eye on the tail? My guess is they'll call it soon and maybe you can get a 20 on where they're staying."

Aimer nodded. "No worries."

"Good. I'll head back to the hotel and meet you downstairs in the morning."

Smoke spun to leave. "But if—"

"Yeah, yeah, if something happens, call. What am I, a rookie? Get some fuckin sleep, will ya."

Smoke pointed at his friend, stuck his hands in his pockets, and headed toward a far less expensive bed.

24

NEW YORK CITY

Nowhere does time move slower than in a hospital room, waiting for a doctor to tell one's fate. Sounds of care being distributed to other patients on the floor echoed up and down the green painted-block walls. The ultra-modern facility had every modern up-to-date convenience save one archaic device— a large white-faced wall clock. The sound of seconds ticking became a drumbeat for a song that just wouldn't begin.

They were waiting impatiently for Dr. Brightman and his entourage from Columbia Presbyterian's Neurology Department to deliver the results of the series of tests O was given earlier. Brightman specialized in neurological disorders like concussions, trauma, and brain trauma. He was qualified, experienced, and O had not, as yet, felt the need for a second opinion.

Somewhere down the hall the volume on a TV got loud but, in a few seconds, muffled. The hallway clatter continued but the sounds of life beyond the walls of room 536 fell on deaf ears.

Felix sat in a straight back chair next to O who lay on her side covered with a sheet she had pulled up to just under her nose. Gia planted herself on the windowsill which was just wide enough to support her narrow frame. No one spoke.

A noise suddenly broke the tension.

It was a rumble. A bass that started low, built up, then became unmistakable.

"Sorry," Felix apologized, rubbing his belly.

Gia's face scrunched up. "Jesus, how often do you have to feed that thing?"

O reached her hand out from beneath the sheet and rubbed the big man's forearm.

"Why don't you run down to the cafeteria and get something?"

Felix stood and rubbed his belly. "I'd rather not. Its already angry. If I feed it something it doesn't like it will be bad for everybody."

O cracked the slightest of smiles, leaving her hand extended.

Felix sat down quickly and engulfed her delicate finger in his meaty mitt.

"Felix, really, I'm so tired. It's okay. Gia will call you if the doctor shows up. Didn't you tell me there's a pizza place on the corner that makes an edible pie?"

Felix nodded. "What can I bring for you?"

O smiled weakly. "A few hours of sleep would be nice."

Gia stood and put her hand on Felix's shoulder. "Go, I got this."

Felix nodded reluctantly just as the monster in his belly roared again. "How about you skinny? You want one of those cauliflower things with vegetables and no cheese?"

Gia grinned.

"I'm embarrassed every time I order that for you."

Dr. Brightman tried to walk out of the elevator but his path was blocked. "Mr. Grant, I was just on my way to Dr. Bennet's room." His eyes darted and the entourage became busy with phone notes.

"What?" Felix's tone was demanding.

"I should be speaking with Dr. Bennet."

"Yeah, well, you're not, are you? You're speaking to me and one more time… what?"

Brightman's attitude changed. He motioned to his two assistants to wait down the hall. He reached out and softly guided Felix to a lounge area.

"Felix, may I call you Felix?"

The big man nodded and sat down.

"I don't know what's wrong. The scans didn't show much. There was a small spot, maybe the size of a head of a pin. It doesn't seem like much but it wasn't there this morning. It could be a mass. It could be blood. It could be a fault in the computer program."

"Computer?" Felix was perplexed.

"It's probably not, but it is possible. The scan is a computerized tomography that combines several x-rays to produce an image of the brain. It's like being able to look at one slice of bread inside a loaf. We saw it during the testing but she was so tired I didn't want to chance stressing her any more today. She seems stable right now and we are keeping a close eye on her vitals."

"Okay, so tomorrow?"

"Yes. She needs to get some rest and we will try again in the morning."

Brightman stood to leave, but Felix grabbed his arm.

"Doc. You said she needs rest but your nurses are in there, like every hour on the hour. How can she sleep?"

"Being tired is actually a symptom that could be problematic." He scratched his chin the way thinkers do. "But you make a good point. I'll give her something to relax her and hopefully that will build her strength."

Brightman started to walk away.

"Hey."

Brightman turned around.

"She's going to be okay, right?"

"We're doing everything in our power to make that so."

Felix's blood rushed to his face. "Knock off the 'we' shit. That's not an answer."

Brightman put the team role aside. "I can't answer because I don't know."

Felix's phone vibrated. It was Smoke. He gulped and answered. "Hey, what's happening?" He immediately regretted his choice of words.

There was a pause. "What's wrong?"

"Nothing, really nothing's wrong. I'm just fucking hungry and headed for a pizza joint near the hospital."

Surprise was instantaneous. "Hospital? You're still at the hospital?"

"Yeah. No big deal. There was some kind of problem with a computer that screwed up the results of one of her tests."

"Is she okay?"

"Yeah, sure. Just tired from all the bouncing around. The doc has given her something to help her sleep and they will give her the test again tomorrow morning."

"Felix, are you—"

"How's it going there? You making any progress?"

There was another hesitation but Smoke answered. "Some. I think we may have two ways to make this guy give me the name. Bobby and I are staking out and gathering info."

"So, you think this guy… Gurds… what a stupid name… you think this guy knows who the dead guy in the parking lot was?"

"Yep, I think so. I think Putz is trying to expand without his daddy knowing. Interpol and George, both told me this group doesn't use middlemen to run the local operations, so it is logical that, if the kid is trying to expand his territory, he would know who's working and where. It's not as long a shot as it may seem."

"Great… ah… how long do you think you'll be there?"

"Why?"

"Why? Are you kidding? O's finally getting some sleep and the very first thing she's going to ask when she gets up is, 'did I talk to you' and the second thing is 'did you say when you were coming home'."

"Ahhh."

"Yeah… Ahhhh, some fucking detective you are."

"I'm not a detective, dick."

"Speaking of dicks, how's Aimer? Were you able to drag him out of those brothels yet?"

"You just graduated to big dick."

"Always wanted to graduate— woulda made my mama so proud."

"Right. Listen Felix. Seriously. I really don't know how long we'll be here. A couple more days at least." His voice lowered, leaving the kidding aside. "Felix, promise me that if anything changes, I mean anything … you'll call me."

"Absolutely." He hated lying to his best friend. She wasn't okay. He decided there wasn't anything Smoke could do about her mistaking Lauren for Lo or calling him Henry.

"If I don't pick up—"

"Leave a message, of course."

"Sorry, I'm on edge. I feel like I should be there."

"Smoke, you have a shot right now to get the name. Who knows what happens to that source tomorrow or next week? Besides, there is nothing you can do here. She's getting looked after by, like, the best team in the... anywhere. Stay there. Get what you need."

There was a pause. "You're right."

"I know."

"You're still a dick."

"I know."

The background noise coming from the phone stopped. Smoke had disconnected. He stuck the phone back in his pocket and started down the hall to O's room. His head was down and his thoughts were occupied with hopes he was right. There was nothing Smoke could do.

25

QUANTICO, VA.

George DiSanto had a pile of empty cardboard boxes stacked up in the corner of his office. Files, books, newspapers, keepsakes of almost every description lay on the conference table, the two chairs, the couch, and on the floor. The office had been transformed from its normal disorder to retirement chaos. He hadn't gotten used to the idea that in seven days he would have to turn in his access pass and ID.

Alone in the turmoil was a single file resting neatly in the center of his desk pad. George sat leaning back in his chair, head up, eyes staring at the ceiling. He had copies of the photos Aimer had emailed him on his lap. They were good resolution, front and profile photos of the two men who had followed Quinton Gurds in Amsterdam.

He had done nothing with them. He couldn't.

His cell phone beeped; he looked at the screen and was relieved.

"Smoke, I'm glad you returned my call."

"George, did you ID the photos?"

"I didn't, actually, I can't or shouldn't."

"What?"

"The description Robert put into the email, and what I see in the photos he sent, makes me believe there is a possibility these men have a Middle East connection. It may be a jump but you need to remember that the Taliban obtains much of its income from the sale of heroin and cocaine to the west. We also know this Gurds character is a major drug supplier. Let's assume the men in the photos are from one of the Afghanistan factions moving the Taliban's drugs. If I get a hit in the FBI's or CIA's systems, they'll descend on me instantaneously. They will take over this investigation and it will be years before you'll get any chance of getting a name."

The silence George heard wasn't unexpected.

"Thanks."

George didn't respond.

"What... I mean, I'm not sure how to proceed?"

"My thought is for you reach out to Bram Visser. He said you could call to see if he could help."

"Shouldn't you call? He's your contact."

"No. I don't think so. Getting an ID on these two may only be a beginning of him helping you and possibly you helping him and Interpol."

"How so?"

"Ask if he could help with the photo ID of the men. He'll ask you if you know where they are now."

"We do. Robert followed them to their hotel."

"Good. He'll want to know what hotel."

"You sure about Visser? You trust him?"

"Yes, I do. I've had a lot of professional relationships over the years with people I knew I could trust as long as there was something in it for them, advancement, promotion, good press. But Bram Visser is different. In fact, Bram could have risen much further but he chose, instead, results over advancement, a choice that kept him as Chief of Station instead of the Director of Operations. Smoke, he's a good man and I know he will understand your situation. That said, you'll need to keep him completely in the loop. If he has to move, he will, but he'll respect what you need to accomplish."

"Got ya. I understand."

"I will caution you to not talk over the phone. Brief him in person."

"Thanks, George."

This time it was George who maintained a moment of silence. "Smoke, this could be very dangerous. Please be careful. You know O needs you."

"I know and I will be careful. One more thing, should I call you with updates?"

"Only if you have to… let's maintain plausible deniability for now. It's best for both Bram and me to be helping you 'off the record.' If these two turn out to be connected and I don't report it, could be bad all around. You'll need autonomy on this at least for another seven days. I'll be an official civilian then."

"Okay George. I'll call only if I have to and again thanks."

"You're very welcome, my friend. Stay safe."

The phone went to a blank screen and George rested the phone on his semi-clear desk.

"Godspeed Smoke, I wish I could be there for you."

26

AMSTERDAM, NETHERLANDS

Large blocks of granite stood like soldiers— tall, thick, and orderly. They were placed in an arc comprising the walls of half a building. Halfway up the grey stone edifice was a simple black sign with white letters announcing its purpose, *Van Gogh Museum*. In dramatic contrast, the other half of the building's entrance was all glass, a fragile, vulnerable structure that mirrored the shape of the opposing stone fortress. It was the spectacular home to the work of the master Dutch impressionist. Crowds of people lined up every day to see the tortured soul's infamous work that today would be valued in the billions. The art of a man, who in the entirety of his life, never sold one single painting.

The chill of the fall day warmed with the morning sun. Smoke and Aimer sat on a bench facing the museum, drinking coffee. Smoke felt calm for the first time in a while. His hands held a paper cup and he watched the steam float from the dark brown elixir. He hadn't gotten to speak to O, she was sleeping again when he called but Felix convinced him she was fine and to stay and pursue the lead. He felt he had time.

"What does a Mr. Bram Visser, Bureau Chief of Interpol, look like?"

Smoke took a sip. "He looks English."

"So, an umbrella and tweed?"

Smoke looked back into the cup. "Pretty close. Tweed, but a walking stick instead of the umbrella."

"Like this guy?" Aimer nodded toward a tall man who was walking alone. He stood out from the various groups of tourists and was sporting a tweed jacket and carrying a walking stick.

Smoke looked up and chuckled. "Yep."

As Visser approached, he made eye contact with Smoke and nodded a follow me gesture.

Smoke and Aimer stood and fell in line behind.

Without turning around Visser said, "Did you get tickets to go into the museum?"

"No." Smoke answered curiously.

Visser, without turning around, said, "I have a museum season pass. Get tickets and I'll meet you inside at the sunflower painting on the third floor." He continued walking and entered the museum through the member's door.

Aimer looked at Smoke. "What's with the cloak and dagger routine?"

Smoke shrugged. "No clue."

After getting tickets, Smoke got a map from an information kiosk then they took an escalator to the top level. The floor was somewhat crowded and provided a bit of cover so the man in tweed wasn't immediately visible. Groups were moving from painting to painting, stopping for a few moments, most quiet, standing and staring, listening to pre-recorded guided tours.

Smoke went into recon mode. *Why was the cloak and dagger routine necessary?* He surveyed each group, looking for something out of place.

Aimer pointed to the sunflower painting and they walked in that direction while searching the floor for the man from Interpol.

The painting hung alone on a wall in a large space that accommodated a crowd. There were fifteen or twenty people gathered but no Visser.

It seemed such an unlikely subject to paint, yet somehow this artist managed to put color on canvas that made people stop and look. Some of the people milling about were just kids who had no degree in art history, knew nothing of the artist's backstory, and yet they too, stopped and looked. A couple of droopy flowers possessing no particular beauty, yet somehow this painting possessed some magic power. Something that made even the least likely of observers notice three silly flowers and wonder.

Smoke scanned the groups, watched the escalators, and looked for anyone who didn't fit. He looked for someone who wasn't there to see the brilliance of what a human could accomplish.

An elevator at the far end of the floor dinged and, when the door opened, Visser exited. He spotted Smoke and Aimer and walked past the groups milling around and headed directly to their location.

Smoke challenged Visser when he arrived. "That wasn't exactly a stealthy approach. What's with the intrigue?"

Bram took Smoke's elbow and guided them to the other end of the floor and pushed open the door to the stairs going down and walked into the empty stairwell.

"I was making sure you were not being followed. I hung back when you came in to make certain."

"Wait. What?" Aimer was surprised. "Why would anyone be following us?"

"George told me you took pictures of two men following Quinton Gurds."

"That's right." Aimer nodded. "I did."

"I became concerned when George told me Gurds had a tail. Because of that I thought it prudent to make certain you weren't spotted last night and, in turn, picked up a surveillance team yourself. One can't be too careful with the Penose."

Smoke nodded, acknowledging the concern. "I appreciate that, but really, this isn't our first rodeo."

"Ah…" Bram smiled, "an American western movie reference." Visser nodded toward a space near a window and sat on the sill. "Did the stakeout give you any leads?"

Smoke answered. "As you suspected, he has something going on in the club. He seems to be very friendly with two of the performers. We have names, but we don't think we can do much with that information. The tail, however, that has potential."

Visser tapped his cane on the floor as he leaned forward. "Your goal, as I understand it, is to get some very specific information from a very dangerous man. Quinton Gurds is the son of an important member of Penose— a criminal organization that goes back to the 1800s. It is strong, powerful, and has long-standing connections in almost every part of the Netherlands. The word Penose means livelihood and it has been a generational way of life for many, many people. Their influence has many tentacles, some of which even penetrate law enforcement, even, I'm sorry to say, Interpol. It is important for you to embrace the gravitas of your undertaking. You two foreigners, here only two days, unfamiliar with surroundings and customs and cannot speak a single word of the language are pursuing one Quinton Gurds, in his own city." He shook his head. "And now there is an unknown involved. So, you can see my concern. It is a very dangerous situation and that, my American friends, is why I'm, as you put it, stealthy."

Aimer leaned over and whispered, "Gravitas?"

Smoke elbowed him.

"They were following Gurds, not us." Smoke said confidently. "They didn't see us."

Visser's hand went to his chin. "You're certain?"

"Yes." Aimer responded. "I followed them after the theater. Once Quinton Gurds went to ground for the night at the hotel, they left and walked straight back to their hotel without hesitation. They never looked back, once."

Smoke shrugged his shoulders. "Why is this important?"

"George wrote you had pictures of the two men who followed Gurds." Visser held out his hand. "Let me see them."

Aimer took out his phone and began paging through pictures on the screen. "DiSanto didn't send them to you?"

"No. He too was being cautious. He knows, as I do, that Penose is powerful. His email said you needed help identifying two men who were following Gurds. He didn't attach pictures."

Smoke caught on. "So... you think somebody has access to your email."

Visser shrugged. "Possible. When Penose is involved, nothing is secure or certain."

Aimer handed Visser the phone.

"At first, we thought these two might be hired by the father to keep an eye on the kid. You did mention Quinton had made some trouble for the old man."

"I did." Visser was focused on the pictures on the phone. "Not the father. I know both these men." He looked up; his face drawn serious. "The father has made a small fortune for the family staying under the radar dealing in something that no one pays a lot of attention to. However, he's old and its rumored he's turning the business over to Quinton. The son is ambitious and reckless and, after looking at these pictures, it's possible he is already in charge."

Bram turned the phone around showing Smoke and Aimer an image. "This man is Ahmad Kahn, which in English is equivalate to a name like John Smith. He is a Saudi. Lives here in Amsterdam. And is what he looks like, a blunt object of violence. I've come across him several times, even managed to put him in prison once."

Visser swiped the screen again and then tapped a finger on the image of the tall well-dressed man. "This is Hashim bin Talal, a member of the Saudi royal family." He took a breath like a professor beginning a lecture. "There are about 4,000 princes in the House of Saud in Saudi Arabi whose estimated net worth of the family is in the trillions.

However, in every family there are members, who while possessing the status and name, do not share in the mega-wealth. Now there aren't any middle-class royals, most do well enough, never have to hold a job and live under the protection of the family name. But some, this one in particular, are black sheep."

He held up the picture of the tall, well-groomed bearded man. "Hashim bin Talal is a nephew of Alwaleed bin Talal— a man who is unique in the Saudi royal family. He is the nephew of the man who sued Forbes magazine for underestimating his incredible wealth just years before giving it all to charity."

"Ah… what'd you say?" Aimer scratched his head. "He gave it away?"

"Alwaleed gave up Lamborghinis, Gulf Stream jets, and golden Falcons. He gave away his fortune to charity, thus becoming an outcast and hated by the rest of the royals. He didn't care but some of his immediate family suffered in the backlash. One of the casualties was Hashim bin Talal, a nephew who now only possesses a family name, a European education, and no income."

Visser started pacing around. "bin Talal left Saudi and moved here. He did his best to maintain the mystique of a wealthy image so those who didn't know the background would believe he had influence within the Middle East. To finance this lifestyle, he began brokering deals with Afghanistan, Iraq, Syria… basically any country where he could use his name to gain entry and was being boycotted by the west. He isn't dealing with Mobil or BP, nothing honorable or aboveboard. He deals in illegal trade; guns, drugs, and human trafficking."

"No arrests, I take it?" Smoke mused.

"None. He's been careful and confines himself to making the connection between parties. He never participates in the actual crime, just arranges to make the introductions, facilitates the meetings, then watches over the transactions through completion, always maintaining a safe distance. Somehow, he has managed to never leave enough of a fingerprint to garner an arrest."

"Interesting," Smoke said. "But the question is, why is he following Quinton Gurds?"

"Yes. That is the question, isn't it?" Visser rested his hands on the windowsill, closed his eyes, and lifted his head toward the ceiling.

Aimer offered a thought. "Do you think Gurds is expanding the ecstasy business to the Middle East?"

"Never. Definitely not." Visser responded quickly. "There is no market for drugs in Muslim countries. First, the population is very poor, and second, most are religiously opposed to drugs, alcohol, anything that alters the mind. But—" Visser had started tapping his cane, then stopped suddenly and looked at Aimer. "But there is something we are not considering." Visser pointed a lecture finger. "Afghanistan has been getting support from Iran, Pakistan, and, believe it or not, the country they just humiliated; Russia. These countries were very interested in seeing the Americans defeated so they sent billions in arms and money. Now that the U.S. is gone, Afghanistan's allies are cutting back on aid. I'm wondering if Hashim bin Talal is facilitating a deal to expand the Taliban's heroin trade using—"

"Quinton Gurds," Smoke finished the sentence. "Fuck."

Visser tapped the cane harder. "Exactly. This is a very possible scenario because, as odd as it may seem, Afghanistan produces about 90 percent of the poppies used in making heroin worldwide. Poppies are easy to harvest, ship, and require no refrigeration. They are durable, portable, and profitable. The intention might be to include heroin in Penose's worldwide domination of the ecstasy market."

Smoke nodded. "So, you think this Hassim guy may be following Gurds to make sure he isn't cooperating with Interpol."

Bram grinned. "Exactly. Like I said, he is a very careful man."

Aimer put both hands up, frustrated. "Wait, back up, I don't understand something. Isn't the war over?" Aimer asked. "If Afghanistan doesn't need money to fight a war any more, then… I don't understand."

"You're right. You don't understand. But you're not alone, most westerners only know what's on the TV news. Afghanistan has been devastated by war for centuries. The people are born in, and die in, a constant state-of-war." Bram using a professorial tone said, "Did you know, the United States has been involved in war for about 225 of the 244 years since it was formed in 1776?"

"Really?" Aimer looked astonished.

"Yes, however, out of all those years only nine were fought on American soil, with the Civil War lasting five years. Afghanistan is the exact opposite. Every battle has been fought within its borders for centuries."

Visser leaned on the wall. "Americans understand little of world history but for comparison's sake, starting around the time of the American Revolution, the Afghans were at that time battling with the Ottoman, Maratha and Sikh Empires until the Brits, followed by the Russians, waged war from the 1870s through 1928. Those wars were followed by a civil war that lasted into the 1970s when the Russians invaded again. In that war, the Taliban, largely armed by the CIA, became a world class fighting force. It took ten years for an army a tenth of the size of the invaders to defeat the invincible Russian Bear. In the 90s the Mujahideen managed to gain control of the country but continued to battle with the Taliban and Al-Qaeda. In 2002, the American army attacked, looking for bin-Laden, and began helping Mujahideen and the Islamic State of Afghanistan fight the Taliban and Al-Qaeda. Now, today, twenty years later, and immediately after the Americans pulled out, the Mujahideen regime fell to the Taliban. In short, over about the same time period as the United States has been in existence, Afghanistan has known peace… on its own soil… for about ten years."

"I had no idea." Aimer looked at Smoke who was standing still and deep in thought.

Bram addressed Aimer. "What does that tell you?"

Neither Aimer nor Smoke answered.

"Afghanistan is a country who's only functioning industry is war, rugs, and poppies. The U.S. lost many troops but if the Taliban finds another way to ship its poppies, more Americans will die, but on your own soil."

Smoke filled in the blanks. "Gurds has manufacturing that can convert the poppies to heroin. His distribution goes directly from manufacture to consumer with only one stop, the local dealer." Smoke looked at Visser. "He also might have—"

"Figured out how to add heroin to ecstasy thus making it addictive." Bram nodded.

"Double fuck!" Aimer said loud enough to echo in the stairwell. "Sorry."

Smoke had another thought. "But if bin Talal is still following Gurds around, doesn't that mean the deal isn't done yet?"

Bram nodded. "Maybe."

"Right," Aimer piped in. "These Saudis aren't very good at shadowing anybody. I spotted them immediately."

Smoke agreed. "Because they weren't looking. Like Bram said, Hashim bin Talal is a careful guy."

"Yes, that is the most likely conclusion— nothing has happened yet." Visser checked his watch then put his hand on Smoke's shoulder. "I haven't decided what to do about this information. This escalation by Gurds to include the Taliban will draw serious Interpol attention. Of course, it must be stopped, but I'm going to be very cautious because the whole Penose organization is behind Gurds and they have tentacles everywhere. I'll be selecting people I can trust to conduct a thorough investigation, slowly and carefully." Visser regripped the walking stick. "Smoke, I haven't forgotten why you're here. You need one name. But you need to know sooner or later, the Penose will find out about my efforts and run for cover. I think at best you'll have one, maybe two, days. This means you'll probably have only one opportunity to get what you're looking for from Gurds."

Smoke was grateful. "I don't know what to say, except, thanks."

"Tell George he owes me one." He reached into his jacket pocket. "One more thing, this might help. I got a list of all the properties owned by Gurds from real estate records. There are twelve properties owned by the Gurds family and corporation."

Aimer offered the obvious with a doubting face. "It's not possible that these guys would be running an international drug operation from a property with their name on it."

Smoke and Visser looked at him impassionately.

"As I was saying, this is a list of the properties the Gurds own, most are office, commercial, and light manufacturing.... and unlikely there is any illegal activity." He glanced up at Aimer. "However, there is one property, and mind you this took a bit of looking to find, unlike the others." He pointed to a name on the page. "It's a warehouse and dock facility located at Haven van Amsterdam, our major port facility. The building is old and ill-used but has a ten-foot barbed wire fence, cameras, and twenty-four-hour security." Visser folded then tapped the paper on his hand, grinning.

Smoke couldn't outlast the Interpol Director's sense of dramatic pause. "And?"

"And... the property is owned by Prince Flornell Halleston."

"Just what we need, another member of a royal family." Aimer scoffed.

"This prince is not a royal. It is a dachshund. Prince Flornell Halleston is the family dog."

Smoke laughed, took the paper, then reached for a handshake. "Thanks again, Bram. This is much appreciated."

Visser held on to Smoke's hand with a tight grip. "If you need help, blow the trumpet and I'll be there with the cavalry." Bram smiled and added, "Always wanted to say that, big fan of American westerns."

Visser walked through the door back into the museum.

Aimer looked at Smoke and shrugged. "So, what's the next step, Smoke?"

Smoke scratched his chin. "Get some food… do some recon… then get caught."

Aimer got loud. "That's the plan? That's the best you got? We get caught by a member of the mafia of the Netherlands and a drug pusher for the Taliban?"

Smoke smiled. "Yes, but one part of that is wrong."

Aimer, still loud, said, "What part?"

"We… don't get caught… just me."

27

NEW YORK CITY

Felix and Gia stood in the hallway outside O's room. They had feet spread, hands on hips, and were staring each other down with unblinking eyes. The confrontation was something worthy of a comedy movie. One opponent, a giant, white spike-haired man wore yellow sweatpants and a New York Jets football jersey. He stood a foot and a half over the opposition who was sporting pink yoga pants and a loose Flash dance t-shirt.

"I'm not going." Gia inched closer.

Felix Upton Grant spoke slowly through clenched teeth. "Neither am I."

Gia responded one word at a time. "Yes. You. Are."

Felix gazed down at the svelte dancer and fell back on a last resort. "Oh yeah?"

Gia knew she'd won. She grinned while sticking a finger in his chest. "That's it… that's all you got… oh yeah? That's weak." Gia closed the distance while continuing to poke him. "You're going and that's it. I ordered dinner to be ready for pickup at 6:15 and its now 5:30. You need to leave right now." She pointed down the hall. "So, git."

Felix stammered, but had nothing. "This… this is not fair. I did lunch."

Gia cocked her head and pointed again.

He sighed defeat. "Okay, but tomorrow, breakfast… and lunch, are yours."

"LaBarca, 38th and Broadway. I ordered using your name. And don't forget the plantains."

"Okay, okay. I'm going." Felix looked at his watch then at O. "She's been out for more than an hour; do you think we should wake her up now?"

Gia shook her head and stepped back inside the room. O was motionless, quiet, deep in sleep. "No, I don't think so." Her voice lowered from head-strong adversary to soft loving caretaker.

Felix followed her back into the room and Gia put a finger to her lips wanting him to be quiet. "She didn't sleep well last night," Gia whispered, looking at the wall clock. "It will take you more than an hour to get to the restaurant and back. There's time. I'll roust her before you get back and have her up, washed, and ready for dinner, so don't be late."

"Right, 38th and—"

"Broadway. You want me to write it down for you?" Gia frowned then smiled and touched his arm. "Get on outta here, you oaf. Stop worrying, I got this."

Felix bent the distance and kissed Gia's cheek. "Of course, you do."

The big man turned to leave but stopped in the doorway. He stood for a long moment facing out, but not leaving.

Gia saw him blocking the door and noted the sound from the hallway actually diminish.

Felix turned around. "You know why I like you?"

"Because I'm tough but beautiful?" Gia mugged a pose.

"No." He didn't smile. "I met Smoke in the Army where I was a friendless, six-foot-four-inch, gay soldier who was a joke to everybody

I'd ever met… except him. I was his friend and when the shit hit the fan, he literally saved my life, almost getting killed in the process."

Gia could see the giant's eyes welling up. "This one," he pointed to the Sleeping Beauty. "This one taught me how to love. How to be myself and to not be afraid to let someone see who I really was." Felix sniffed then pointed. "And as far as you go pipsqueak… I see how you care for her and how much she cares for you. You're as close to her as she was to Lo, and I can see how much she has grown to rely on you. And I just want you to know I appreciate you."

Gia, also welling up, turned and walked toward the bed. "You're not the only one with issues, big fella. I have my story as well. She didn't throw herself in front of a bullet for me, but she has changed my life. I think she is…" Gia reached out and gently stroked O's hair.

Felix waited quietly, watching the dancer's perfect poise slump.

Gia's brown eyes widened and she spoke with determination. "She has to be okay. She's going to get better!"

Felix took two giant steps forward and swallowed Gia in a hug. "God damn right, she's going to be okay."

Gia was now chin to chin, both arms pinned against his chest and both feet off the floor. She looked into his eyes. "Thanks." She kissed his cheek then hit his chest with both closed fists. "Now, go get dinner, you oaf."

Gia spent the time waiting, organizing the room. She got the clothes that needed to go to the laundry in a bag, organized the toiletries in the bathroom, placed fresh towels on the vanity, and laid a bathrobe over a chair. Finished, she sat next to her boss and glanced at the clock on the wall. O had been asleep for more than two hours. Felix was due back in a bit, but she decided to let O sleep a little while longer.

She sat back in the chair, and brought her knees up to her chin in a tight tuck position. She extended one leg at a time, each with a ballerina toe point. The wince her face made was something new. What her body used to do effortlessly was now accompanied by a little stiffness. Consciously, she told herself she needed to get to the gym, and start a workout schedule that would get her back in shape. Subconsciously, she knew she would exercise but she also knew she would never go back to the stage.

It had been almost two years since she was in front of footlights. Covid had closed the stage curtains in the beginning but she found O's need for assistance after Lo's death and the aftermath in Hawaii following the kidnapping was more important than the spotlight. The truth was, she was gone too long. There had been so much to do that she hadn't given it much thought. Recently, however, her career change became evident by muscles that weren't responding in a familiar way. But she was okay with it, the dream of starring on Broadway could stay a dream. She had found a different purpose.

She stretched again and thought about Felix who revealed his feelings openly and truthfully. She had started to tell him but stopped. His honesty had challenged her about her feelings about O but she couldn't respond the same way. It was hard for her to admit, because the pain was still there. The pain of her youth.

Gia had been given the gift of a near perfect childhood, with kind, loving parents. A childhood that was shattered into a million pieces by the horror of the accident that killed them both and left her alive. She had no other family, just them. Her parents had no living relatives, just Gia. They had no roots, no restrictions, and did what they loved to do— travel the world. When they died, she became a ward of the court and was alone, growing up in strangers' houses. Her life was dark and lonely. She was alone in a crowd, dreaming about bright lights and applause.

Gia straightened O's sheet and blanket then brushed her hair again.

Where would I be right now if it weren't for you?

O had changed her life. Working at Felix's club allowed her free spirit to fly wherever it wanted to go and O gave her direction. But she was still alone and frightened. It was Dr. O who helped her channel what society would call reckless behavior into a tool that helped people handle deep psychological issues. She became a surrogate who, while helping others, learned to free herself from the pain of her childhood. When Lo was killed, Gia leapt at the opportunity to help and give back to the person who had given so much to her.

"Excuse me." A nurse poked her head in the door.

"Yes?"

"There's a man downstairs in the lobby who has a package for Dr. Bennet."

"Okay..." Gia seemed confused. "Send it up."

"Can't. He says he needs a signature and it's not visiting hours and he's not on the doctor's visit list."

"Can't one of the nurses or someone on staff sign?"

"No, I'm afraid not. Against hospital policy. Just not permitted."

Gia looked over at O who was still asleep.

"Okay, I'll go." She stood and started for the door. She turned in the doorway and said to her charge, "Don't go anywhere while I'm gone." Gia paused for a second, then hustled down the long hallway to the elevators.

The water was warm. Her hand was tilling the water like a rudder on a sailboat. The sun was warming her face and a breeze caressed her face. The air seemed clean, although there was no fragrance of a sea which struck her as odd, but O didn't question the anomaly, because it was so peaceful. The calm, the air, the sun— it was so beautiful.

She wanted to open her eyes and look around but they wouldn't cooperate, and remained steadfast and sealed tight, despite her insistence.

"Olivia."

A grey haze began rolling in from the distance.

"Olivia."

It came upon her fast, rolling across the water, high and deep; boiling, roiling, rising in height.

Her shoulder moved involuntarily, the muscles not under her control.

"Olivia."

Light came in through slits.

"Ahh, you're awake."

O groaned as her body objected.

The calm of the sea was gone. Garbled conversation in the tiled hallway became recognizable. *I'm in the hospital.*

"Olivia, you're looking well."

She blinked hard; her hand went to rub her eyes.

"How do you feel?"

She recognized the voice first. "Abe?"

"Your friendly neighborhood publisher, at your service." His grin was wide, insincere, and almost visible through his beard.

"Abe," her voice cracked. "What are you doing here?"

Abe Filbert acted hurt. "Olivia my dear, I'm your friend as well as your publisher. I'm here to see how you're doing and to cheer you up. I have good news."

"I put you on the visit list?"

Filbert stuttered. "Well, not exactly. I convinced the woman at the desk in the lobby that Dr. Olivia Bennet's publisher had to see her on a matter of great importance."

Olivia shook her head disbelieving. "They wouldn't have let you in. You snuck in, didn't you?" She picked up the control box and raised the bed to a sitting position.

"Well," he stammered, "sort of, but it is a matter of great importance."

O crossed her hands in her lap. Her vision was still a little blurry, and her mouth felt like she'd swallowed a pillow. "Give me the water please." She pointed to the glass on the tray.

"Certainly." Abe spilled some water from a blue plastic pitcher into a glass.

There was silence while she drank.

"Olivia, your book is still number one. Has been for weeks. I know this thing you're going through is difficult, but I'm here to tell you there is a huge silver lining to this... situation." He grinned more broadly and a sliver of teeth became visible.

O dabbed her mouth with her sheet then gave her publisher a sarcastic frown. "Really."

"Yes, really. I just sent out the fourth printing for hardback and paperback and the Kindle sales are off the chart. But..." He folded his arms over his ample belly and expanded chest and grinned again.

"But what?"

"But that's not the best news. Hollywood has come knocking. We have a huge offer on the table for the movie rights from Paramount. I'm also hearing someone from Netflix wants to make it a series."

O remained completely impassive.

Abe stepped up the speed of his delivery. "I think we need a publicity bump to put the deal over the top. You need to understand that a movie deal will make three times what the book makes and foreign rights could double that. The Paramount producer told me top actresses are already fighting over who gets to play you."

Abe stepped back and held up his arms in victory. "It's the mother lode."

O saw a flash of red hair in the hallway outside the open door, instantly recognizing the reporter who had ambushed her twice. "Dear Jesus! You didn't!"

Abe glanced to the door. "Now, don't get upset. She's working for TMZ now. I know she was hard on you before but she has a national audience now and the publicity is—"

He didn't get to finish. Diane Copula burst through the door followed by her line producer carrying a small but expensive looking camera and a sound man holding an extended boom microphone.

"Abe, you son of a bitch." O's face flashed red.

His pudgy fingers went up. "Five minutes, Olivia. That's all she needs, five minutes. We need a publicity boost to get over the top."

"You rolling?" The reporter pointed to the crew but her eyes were riveted on the patient in bed.

"Go." The producer positioned the camera to get the redheaded gossip reporter and Dr. Olivia Bennet in the same frame.

"Dr. Bennet," Copula began her assault. "Your book has been on the best-seller list for weeks. Congratulations. But… you were admitted to Columbia Hospital and no one seems to know why."

O's eyes were wide and she had defensively pulled her blanket up to her chin.

Copula raised her voice and angled to take a bit more of the camera's shot. "O… may I call you O? Is it true you are still recovering from injuries you received while being tortured by Hamilton Lighter, the serial killer?" The redhead's face was flush with anticipation.

Copula didn't get the answer she expected. Her reporter's head was suddenly jerked back, her trademark red hair twisted around.

Gia had hold of her ponytail with one hand and had covered the camera lens with the other.

"Oh my God, my hair." Copula dropped the microphone and reached up to grab Gia's hand but it was too late.

Gia pulled again and the wig, fine as it was, came free.

The reported screamed. "Noooooo."

Gia stood holding the red mess out like a hunter with a dead rabbit, then smiled and threw it into the hallway. She took a wide stance and stuck her face in the reporter's face. "Get the fuck out, you scum sucking bitch."

The woman, now with mousy brown hair streaked with grey, hustled out the door. Following her retreat, the producer was hunched over and cradling his camera. The sound man left as well, but he was laughing hysterically.

Abe Filbert had taken refuge— backing up against a wall. He was muttering, "I… I… I."

Gia heard a commotion in the hall. There was the sound of a cart crashing, a loud voice shouting, followed by the sound of a woman crying.

Felix came through the door carrying a hot food bag and a boatload of attitude.

After he saw Filbert huddled in the corner, he didn't need a recap.

"Get out." Felix's voice was low, like the growl of a lion right before he rips the throat out of a wildebeest.

Gia was pretty sure Abe Filbert shit himself as he ran for the door.

O seemed better, now that protection had arrived, but her face was still flushed and her eyes revealed there was pain.

"Are you okay?" Gia hustled to her bedside and picked up O's hand.

O gulped. "I think so, but—"

Felix immediately panicked. "But what? Should I get the doctor, a nurse, what's wrong?"

O grinned slightly. "But… I think I need another publisher."

28

AMSTERDAM, NETHERLANDS

Aimer and Smoke were back at the café outside of the hotel and halfway through the first real meal they had since arriving two days ago. They were both tired but they had to eat something good. The street carts weren't making it.

"What's this?" There were several brown balls next to a filet of fish on Aimer's plate. "I ordered cod, and its pretty good, but I'm not eating this until I know what it is."

"Shut up and try it, you child. And by the way this isn't Mexico. You can drink the water." Smoke pointed to the full glass of water next to three empty bottles of beer.

Still probing the brown sphere, Aimer swiveled his head around looking for a waiter. "It's not about the water and I'm not going to eat this until I know what it is."

Smoke shook his head. "Will you stop being such a baby? It's probably a rice ball."

"Probably? How come you didn't get them?"

"I didn't give dinner much thought. I ordered from the picture on the menu and this is what came. It's scallops and some rice thing. I just wanted food and didn't care if it was the best Amsterdam had to offer." Smoke pointed his fork at Aimer, frustrated. "You really want to talk about food right now?"

"No, not really, but in my defense, you haven't said six words to me since we left Visser. Obviously, you don't want to talk about what you intend to do next and spring training hasn't started yet. So… what do you want to talk about?"

Smoke pushed some food around on his plate. "I'm thinking we should get back home."

Aimer looked surprised. "Now. Really? This is the first time I thought we've had a real shot at getting what we came for." He leaned across the table demanding Smoke's attention. "Hey."

Smoke dropped the fork and sat back with his arms crossed.

"She'll be okay."

"I don't know that."

"Listen Smoke, Bram said we have a short window on this. One day? Two days? Come on man, pull your shit together and let's do this."

Smoke didn't look at his friend. He grunted and picked up his coffee cup.

"Unless." Aimer ate one of the round things.

"Unless what?"

With a half-full mouth Aimer mumbled, "Hey, this is pretty good."

"Unless what? Finish what you were saying." Smoke tapped the fork.

"Unless… you were just saying that and you don't actually have a plan."

"You're a real prick." Smoke grinned at his friend's challenge. It broke his funky mood. "Of course, I have a plan. I'm just not sure it will work."

"Potatoes." Aimer mumbled.

"What?"

"Potatoes. The round things are potatoes. I like it. Wanna try one?" Aimer stuck a fork in one and held it out across the table.

"Are you kidding?" Smoke put up a flat hand. "I'm not using your fork... cooties."

Aimer broke up laughing. "Now, who's the child?"

Smoke pulled the folded pages with the addresses Bram gave them from his back pocket.

He laid it flat on the table and smoothed the paper. "Bram pointed out this address as suspect and a building that didn't fit the pattern of their business. Their real estate holdings are office buildings, a shopping center, and residential houses. He said this was the anomaly, a warehouse on the dock in the Port of Amsterdam. I think if we're looking for a needle in a haystack this would be the place to start."

Aimer nodded. "Sounds right."

"Let's use that Google Earth thing you have on your phone and see if there are some pictures online that will give us an idea of what we're up against."

Aimer opened the app and plugged in the address. The screen immediately produced an aerial map with a red arrow marking a building on the water. He zoomed in on the satellite picture, then reduced it to a street view. A structure with what seemed to be weathered-grey wood siding appeared. It was surrounded by a tall chain-link fence. In front, the structure's only openings were a large steel garage sliding door, and a solid looking people door. There was no sign with a business name, and not much evidence of traffic.

"Is there a 360-degree view?"

"I'll check." Aimer found and pressed the icon. He was able to maneuver the camera angle to see three of the four sides of the building. There was no picture of the back, which was against the water.

Smoke took the phone and examined each image carefully. "High windows, and judging from the height of the doors, they are at least twelve feet off the ground. The front door is solid, no windows and looks like it's secured with two deadbolts. The garage door is one of those metal roll-ups, most likely on a track and roller, hard to jimmy. We have to assume anything on the back of the building will be similar."

"Can't break-in, then?"

Smoke looked at his friend curiously. "You were… a cop, right?"

"Hey, hey, watch it. I didn't study the best way to commit a felony break-in. I was in homicide, remember? When I needed access to a building, I used two uniforms with battering rams or an SUV with a chain."

"Typical flatfoot, damage as much private property as possible."

"I could shoot you right now."

"Amsterdam, no gun." Smoke looked back to the images.

Aimer chuckled. "Really, seriously Smoke, how are we getting in?"

"No, we. I told you before just me."

"I'm coming?"

"No. You're not going."

"Why?"

"Because."

"Now who's the child? Because why?"

"Because, if you get shot … Mary Pat will kill me."

Aimer mused a second. "You're right, my wife is mean. She would kill you and it would be slow and painful."

They both smiled at the thought of tiny Mary Pat kicking Smoke's ass.

"Are you going to answer me, or not? How are you getting in?"

Smoke put two fingers on the phone screen and enlarged the image then passed it to his friend.

Aimer looked but didn't see it at first. "Ohhh… skylight."

"Yep. Its thirty feet up with no access from the ground. Odds are the skylight isn't well secured. That's how I get in."

"But, wait, thirty feet? How do you get up there and then how do you get down to the floor?"

Smoke shook his head. "I keep forgetting you never worked robbery. Look at the building corner."

Aimer blew the image up again. "Okay, you're going to climb up a downspout but how do you get down to the floor?"

"A rope, dope. I pull the top off the skylight and drop in."

"Window will be unlocked?"

"It's thirty feet in the air. No ladder to the roof so a lock wouldn't be necessary."

"What if it is? Just saying."

"I'll break the window."

"Stealthy."

Smoke ignored him. "I'll use a long rope, long enough to loop from the floor up to the roof and back down again. I repel down from the roof and, just like in the Army, after I hit the floor, I pull one end and the whole thing falls to the floor. I don't want to leave a rope hanging from the ceiling if someone should suddenly show up. The window would still be open but who would look up?"

Aimer nodded. "Okay, so you do have a plan."

Smoke continued. "By the way. I arranged for a car, they're bringing it here to the hotel. Can you find a hardware store? I need a few things."

"Sure, I'll look for Burglars-R-Us on Google."

Smoke ignored him. "When we get there, I need you to post up on the northwest corner. Use the same bat signals we used at the theater, short messages. The light from a phone in a dark place is always a necessary evil. We need to keep messages short."

Aimer paused. He took a sip of beer then asked with a voice that showed concern. "You sure about this?"

"No, I'm not, but given where we are and what we know, which isn't a lot, I think it's our best shot. I just hope we get lucky."

Aimer paused and looked at his friend, concerned.

"Is this where you get caught by the bad guys on purpose?"

"Not yet. At least that's not the plan."

Smoke blew past Aimer's concern. "There's maybe thirty hours left before Visser and Interpol turn this thing upside down." Smoke swiped the phone closed and handed it back to his friend.

Aimer still had the disapproving face. "You know this might be easier if I actually knew what the plan was."

Smoke patted his friend's shoulder. "It's only half a plan, Bobby, but I gotta try."

The smell of an ocean dock is the same everywhere in the world. It's a mixture of salty sea air, diesel fuel, and decaying wood. The Port of Amsterdam was more like a long river than a harbor. Boats of all descriptions were moored at docks that jutted out from every possible land mass. Yellow lights lit the wharfs protruding out into the waterway. They cast triangular spotlights that reflected off the calm water and added wonder to the star-filled night sky.

What was different in the port of Amsterdam from most every other harbor was the sound. There were no waves, no water lapping up against boat hulls, no buoy bells signaling rough water. The port, as well as the city itself, was well below sea level and existed solely because of the Afsluidtijk and Houtribdijk dikes. The port was protected from the open sea by the seawalls so it was rarely affected by storms or high seas. The water level was constant, calm, and controlled. There was another constant, but it wasn't controlled— seagulls and bird shit.

It took only ten minutes with a newly purchased bolt cutter to cut a hole in the fence and a couple more to get to the downspout in the back corner of the building. Smoke pulled on work gloves and coiled the nylon cord he'd purchased around his neck and then put his new cutters in a belt loop. He put a hand on the downspout and discovered the gutter attached to the topside of this downspout must have been a favorite hangout for the feathery sea rats. It was covered with white bird shit.

Smoke put one foot on the wall and both hands behind the five-inch tube. He leaned back, stretching out his arms to full length, then moved one hand up the spout. He pushed off the ground. He reached up for another handhold, then repeated the process he had been taught in the Army. One hand and one foot after another, he slowly walked up the wall, commando style.

The toughest move in the climb came at the top. He had to press his body weight up and over the side of the building using only his arms. It was difficult and it reminded him he could have done it easily when he was young, which he was not. He grunted but eventually got up and over the edge and lay flat onto the roof. His chest was on the metal and he strained to hold his face up off the surface and the white bird paint. He rolled over on his back and caught his breath, then slowly got to his feet. He looked down to the corner where he knew Aimer was posted as lookout. He waved once then crept over to the skylight. It was a piece of reinforced glass set into a metal frame. The whole assembly was built over a curb sticking out of the roof like the lid of a shoebox. There was no lock. Smoke lifted an edge of the box. It moved. Relieved, he lifted it up and off, resting it on the roof. He looped the rope around the base then dropped both loose ends into the hole. He slipped over the side and, recalling more of his military training, wrapped the rope around his waist, leaned into the opening, and repelled quickly to the floor.

The impact of his feet on concrete made a slapping sound. He stood motionless for a long moment. The descent was quiet but not silent. He waited a little longer. Nothing.

He pulled on one side of the rope. The other end went up, unraveled from the skylight, then fell down to the floor. He gathered it up and placed it in a trash can.

He made his way to a shadowed corner, took out his phone, and texted, ***In***.

The high windows let some light in so it wasn't completely black but Smoke had to use a thin but powerful LED flashlight to move around. The first thing that struck him was whatever was going on in here didn't have anything to do with the harbor. Nothing seemed nautical— no boats, no fuel oil smell, no fishing nets.

It didn't feel like a warehouse either. There was no forklift or skids of inventory waiting shipment. There were however, plywood bins filled with unassembled cardboard boxes. Smoke pulled out one and folded the edges. It was a typical box shell, four sides with top and bottom flaps. There were hundreds of them stacked awaiting assembly, all the same small size, and all unmarked.

He examined the floor. There were tire marks in the dust where a truck entered through the front door and stopped. Hand trucks stood in one corner near two long empty tables. Single bulb light fixtures dropped from the ceiling above the tables and, from the remnants left by workers, the tables seemed to be where the boxes were assembled, filled, and labeled.

His eyes had become more accustomed to the darkness. He clicked off the flashlight and walked to the far side of the building. A wood wall had been constructed sectioning off about a third of the building. A cheap wood door was the only entrance. It was windowless and unlocked.

Smoke put an ear to the door and listened then twisted the knob slowly. He pushed it open.

It was the motherlode.

On one side, boxes were filled with empty white plastic pill bottles. On the other wall, a green light blinked on the power button of large professional copy machine. There was a high-backed chair at a table where columns of shipping labels were stacked high.

But the centerpiece of the room was a brightly polished stainless-steel machine. It had a heavy base. At its midpoint there were four round dials and an LED operation screen which apparently controlled cylinders on the top of the machine. Four glass viewing panels allowed an observer to watch as that material flowed inside to what resembled the inside of a watch. A circle of steel and brass pistons interlocked with round gears. It stood silent. Awaiting a human command.

In front of Smoke on the panel next to the dials was a red button.

Smoke held his finger above the button, looked around again, then shrugged and said, "Fuck it," and pushed the button.

Lights came on inside the machine as it came to life. Instantly all the things it looked like it could do, it did. Wheels spun, and gears circled. The metal feeder funnels on top shuddered and the pistons started moving one at a time. One after another the small pistons with little round heads pressed down an inch then rose back up an inch, all in perfect synchrony. It started slow then gained speed. There was noise but it wasn't loud. He took out his phone, set the camera app to video, and ran a minute of the machine in operation.

Smoke stepped to the side of the metal marvel and filmed the product the machine produced. Pill after pill spilled from a metal shoot. The pills came down in a perfectly straight line dropping onto a conveyor with a counter where the white plastic bottles were receiving a measured number of pills. Smoke walked back to the front and hit the red button again and everything stopped.

The printer caught his eye. The labels on the table were blank, devoid of the shipper company name or a delivery address. He pressed the power on button and waited for it to warm up. When it did, he pressed all of the preset buttons, but nothing happened. He opened the paper drawers, which were loaded with the same blank labels. He started to walk away then stopped suddenly. He walked back to the end of the table and pulled off the lid of a trash can. Bingo. Inside were discarded labels; some with bad ink, or blurred copy, crinkled jambs, and double prints.

One man's trash is another man's gold.

He grabbed several handfuls, selected a dozen, and stuffed them in his pocket. He returned to the pill press, grabbed a handful of samples and an empty plastic bottle.

His phone vibrated. ***2 + 4***

"Shit. Almost a clean getaway."

He hustled over and hid in a shadow behind a stack of the boxes containing the empty bottles. The open skylight was the only evidence of his being there.

Hope they don't look up.

The metal garage door screeched as it opened and, as soon as it reached head height, men started in.

The bodyguard came in first, followed by Quintin Gurds. Four more men walked in slower with hands in their pockets.

Workers. Maybe they wouldn't fight.

Gurds waved his finger around the warehouse. "Il will dat al deze spullen worden verplaatst."

The men looked at each other, perplexed.

"Right, don't speak Dutch. English? Italian?"

One of the men volunteered "English."

"Fine. I want all this stuff moved tonight. The boxes, the bottles, the copy machine, the press, everything. Get it?"

"Yes, sir. We understand."

Gurds turned to the bodyguard. "You have the address of the new facility. You have the manpower and you have an empty truck. I am in Interpol's crosshairs, and I don't have time for any mistakes." Gurds got up in the guard's face. "Do not fuck this up."

"Ja meneer."

"Don't fucking, yes sir, me. Just get it done."

The bodyguard nodded.

"I'm taking the car and going to see the girls. You stay with these guys and the truck. Call me on my burner phone when you're done."

The guard nodded. "Ja men—"

A car alarm went off outside. Both Quinton and the bodyguard reached for a gun.

Guns, that's unexpected.

Another alarm went off. They held the pistols gangster style, sideways.

Amateurs.

Gurds and the bodyguard headed for the door. The other four trailed slowly behind. They didn't have guns.

Smoke inched forward and made it to the side of the open garage door.

The six men were standing at the open gate looking down the street at the car with the flashing headlights and ear-splitting horn blowing.

Another car alarm went off on the other side of the building.

Gurds pointed the barrel of his pistol to the left. "Take two men and go that way. I'll take the other two and go this way."

Smoke smiled and shook his head, then walked out of the building and through the front gate just as Aimer rolled up in the car.

Aimer rolled down the passenger window.

"You need a cab mister?"

29

NEW YORK CITY

O was sitting up, her eyes closed. She lay stiff against a heavily pillowed bed. Gia was holding a compress on her forehead and looking at Felix with panic in her eyes. Since the publisher's ambush, O's condition had worsened by the hour. The headache returned with a vengeance and nothing seemed to be relieving the pain.

Gia removed the compress, soaked it in a bowl of water, and wrung it out and reapplied the cloth to O's head. She glanced down at her friend whose complexion was pale and grey. When she looked at Felix, again, she had tears running down both cheeks.

Felix made a firm face and then shook his head back and forth.

Gia understood, and quickly wiped away the tears.

Dr. Brightman was consulting with his team just outside the door. After security removed the publisher and the reporter, Brightman had been summoned and examined O. In addition to the headache, she had stiffness in her neck, was dizzy, and had stumbled when walking to the bathroom. She had also been unable to recall her publisher's name.

Brightman stepped into the room and beckoned Felix to follow him into the hall.

"Mr. Grant—"

"Felix."

"Ah... yes... of course. Felix, Dr. Bennet has indications that the trauma she's suffered has not healed. It is serious and all precaution must be taken. I'm recommending a new treatment which has been used to help with the healing process, called HBOT."

"Sounds ominous." Felix was fighting to control his voice.

"Not to worry. It's not invasive. In fact, it's the exact opposite. It's basically a chamber that provides an increased level of oxygen to stimulate healing. It's also reducing all outside influences that could cause stress. The damage caused by the traumas she's suffered has not healed, or at least has not healed completely."

Felix seemed numb. "Really, that's it? An oxygen tent?"

The doctor handed the file he was holding to one of his white-coated assistants and motioned the group to wait for him down the hall.

Gia had left O's beside and stood next to Felix.

"It's very difficult for us to see if Dr. Bennet's brain injury is healing. We know where the problem is but we cannot see if it's healing when we use a CAT scan. She's had several and there seems to be some improvement."

Felix and Gia both inhaled, slightly relieved.

"The thing to remember is, the scan is not healing anything, and I don't think more scans at this point will serve a purpose. Moreover, the process might cause additional stress."

"I don't understand." Gia piped up. "Is she getting better or not?"

Dr. Brightman took a moment to respond. "There is no way to know. The symptoms she exhibits are very troubling. Neck pain, dizziness, trouble walking, are all neurological and concerning."

"You're going to need to be more specific, doc." Felix was becoming agitated. "What are we looking at?"

Brightman said it quick. "It could be an intracerebral hematoma. I suspect it is possible that a small blood clot has developed deep in her brain. In many cases the body absorbs the clot, the symptoms disappear, and there are no long-term effects."

Gia grabbed the doctor's arm. "In many cases?"

"Yes, in many cases with rest and proper medical attention."

"But?" Felix wanted to know.

"But." Brightman gave the worst case. "She is showing signs that her body is reacting to the injury. It is trying to heal itself and in doing so the body sends fluid to the injured area. The body will continue to produce fluid until the injury is healed. There are two problems with that when the injury is in the brain. The fluid causes swelling which is then confined inside the skull and it also restricts blood flow which increases blood pressure and the likelihood of stroke."

Felix's words creaked out. "If that happens?"

"We'll insert an EVD, an external ventricular drain, to relieve the pressure."

"And..." Felix could only manage one word.

"We wait and see but the worst case and only if it's the last alternative, we would do a craniotomy and remove the subdural hematoma."

Neither Gia or Felix spoke.

"Last resort."

Everyone turned.

O was sitting up, eyes open, and looking at the three with crossed arms and a school teacher's scowl. "Last resort? Really, the only resort I'm interested in is the Four Seasons in Tahiti."

Felix smiled and Gia ran back to her friend.

Brightman stammered, "I'm sorry Dr. Bennet. I should have wakened you before beginning this consult."

O waved him off. "No worries, Bob. Please, its fine talk. You know by now you can speak to them as you would talk to me."

Brightman nodded as he walked over and went for the obligatory taking of the pulse. "How are you feeling?"

"Better, my breathing is regular, no dizziness, and the headache has reduced to 3 of 10. However, now that I mentioned Tahiti, I want a Mai Tai."

Her audience responded with a nervous chuckle.

"I'll be back in an hour or so." Brightman released her wrist, apparently satisfied with her heartbeat, and left the room.

Felix closed the door behind him then stood facing the door with both hands spread out like he was holding back the horde.

"Please, you two have to relax. You're making me think I'm sick."

Gia wiped away a tear. "I'm sorry, I... I mean we are just so concerned."

O patted her hand. "Everything is as it should be and you need to stop worrying."

Felix spun around. "As it should be? What does that mean?"

"Have you heard from Smoke?"

"Don't change the subject, girlfriend. What are you trying to say?"

"What I'm trying to say is... how is Smoke?"

There was a moment of silence.

O's demand won out.

"Yes, I heard from him. You were asleep and I didn't want to wake you." Felix walked slowly over to a chair and plopped down. "He said they broke into a warehouse and got some information he thinks they can trade."

O smiled. "That is the best news I've heard in days."

"I asked him when he's coming back."

O scowled. "Why? I thought we discussed that. Did you tell him about Abe?"

"No." Felix could stand up to a charging bull, but O had always been able to control him with just a smile or a frown. "I didn't tell him. I feel bad about that. I don't think I've ever lied to him... ever."

"Did he ask you if a reporter ambushed me?"

"Well, no—"

"Then you didn't lie." She cut him off and moved to Gia. "And you..."

Gia sputtered. "What… what did I do?"

"Nothing, honey. You haven't done anything but I need you to concentrate on positive energy. You both know I'm trying to heal something that we can't exactly put a Band-aid on."

The two nodded.

"You need to have faith that everything is as it is supposed to be."

"What—" Felix started again.

"What did I just say?" Her voice elevated and Felix shut up immediately. "I need positive energy. Only positive energy."

Again, they both nodded, this time in matching rhythm and speed.

The door opened slowly and two nurses came in, one with a wheelchair. "Dr. Brightman has ordered Hyperbaric oxygen therapy which is on the ninth floor." She looked at Felix and Gia. "He also said that you two may use the doctor's lounge while Dr. Bennet undergoes the treatment."

O started to get out of bed. "How long will—"

The nurse held up her hand "Doctor Bennet, please wait a moment. There's no need to hurry." The other nurse rushed to help. "The treatment will be the rest of the day. Doctor Brightman will see you during evening rounds. We will be monitoring your vitals but the idea is complete and total rest with little or no stimulation." The nurse gave a stern look to Gia and Felix. "Do you have a good book to read?"

O shook her head and smiled. "Felix, honey, could you pop over to Barnes and Noble and pick me up a book on the ten best things to do in Tahiti?"

30

AMSTERDAM, NETHERLANDS

Smoke walked on the pedestrian portion of the color-coded travel lanes of the Jan Evertsenstraat Thorofare, looking to find a quiet spot to finish formulating his plan. He looked at a map folded neatly into quarters and judged there were two more blocks to Overtoomse-Veld Park off Staalmeesterslaan. It wasn't an easy task, finding his way through the city streets. There wasn't a single name on a street sign under four syllables and most were eight, nine, or even ten. It made him homesick for any road named with a number. However, despite the letter-abundant Dutch language and continuous need to dodge relentless bicycle assassins, he managed to negotiate the route to his destination. The park was a broad expanse of calm and reminded him of the parks he grew up with in Philadelphia— respites amidst the bustling and hustling of a modern city.

He walked along the path with his hands in his pockets and his mind running possible variations. It was difficult to concentrate because thoughts of O lying in a hospital bed kept disrupting his planning.

Concentrate.

He glanced at his phone, almost two o'clock, eight a.m. in New York. He found a bench and sat. Sunshine hit his face and he laid his head back and let his shoulders slump. Fatigue rose up on him like a wave and he suddenly felt very tired.

O.

He shook his head vigorously.

Stop it. Concentrate.

The plan was short, uncomplicated, and very direct. It was a one-shot deal and there were just two possible results— get the name or he wouldn't. Gurds would see him coming. There would be no surprise or hope of catching his prey off-guard, which meant an elevated risk of injury or death. Bobby would not be in harm's way but there wasn't any way to minimize his own exposure. The confrontation would be easy. The hard part would be getting away— alive.

A woman passed by with a child in hand waking Smoke from his daze. They were speaking Dutch and he didn't understand a word, but their body language spoke volumes. It was obvious the boy had done something to displease her. Smoke deduced the woman had to be his mother because of the way she was pulling him along, how she was chastising him, and how the boy's face reflected regret, apology, and a little fear. He flashed, for a second, on what it would have been like.

Concentrate.

He stood, checked his phone for the time in Virginia, and pushed a pre-set button.

A buzz, then a click, was followed by a familiar ring. "Hello."

"George."

"Smoke," George DiSanto sounded surprised.

"Good morning, George. Is today the day?"

"It is. And Smoke, I have to say I'm flattered. With everything going on, you remembered I'm being put out to pasture today. Thank you for this."

"You're very welcome, but maybe it will help if you think of it as being put out to stud."

Smoke could almost see the director's face getting red.

"Ahh... ahem... uhm. Indeed. So, how is Olivia?"

"From what I understand she's stable. She's still in the hospital but Felix said she's doing what the doctors want her to do and they're feeling like everything is as it should be."

"As it should be?"

"Yeah," Smoke laughed a little. "I questioned the same phrase you did, but Felix said to stop worrying, that it's what she said. He said she's a doctor and I'm not and he quoted exactly what she said."

"Hey, I'm old, but isn't that a he said she said joke?"

"Did you just make a joke?"

"What, yes. Well, I guess I did. Indeed."

"Good one." Smoke's voice lowered and he got serious. "Listen George, the reason I'm calling is because last night Bobby and I... no wait, I mean just me, not Bobby—"

"Smoke, my God. Did you kill somebody?"

"No, nobody got killed but I did sort of commit a crime and I need a legal opinion and I can't ask Bram Visser."

"Okay, but why did you call me instead of a lawyer?"

"It's complicated. You see... I sort of broke into a warehouse and discovered how Quinton Gurds is shipping the ecstasy. My question is, if I tell Bram about the break-in and he acts on that information, won't the way he obtains the information make it possible for Gurds to beat it in court?"

"No, I don't think so. The fruit of the forbidden tree idiom only applies to how law enforcement gathers information internally, not on what a witness tells them."

"Good."

"So, you'll tell Bram about your adventure?"

"No, not yet, and you can't either."

"I don't understand."

"I came here to get the name and if nothing changes in the next couple of hours, I think I'll have a shot."

"Is that it?"

"No. I emailed you about the two men who were following Gurds."

"Yes, I remember. Did you get an ID?"

"Bram knew who they were. Both live in Amsterdam, one is just a thug; the other a middleman for arms and drugs. Bram thinks it's possible they are brokering a deal with the Taliban. Bram thinks they are going to use Gurds' smuggling operation to ship heroin-laced ecstasy into the U.S. and Europe."

George breathed out one word slow and low. "Fuck."

"That's what I said. So, you can see now why I called. This is way bigger than me just getting a name of a dead guy in an Oklahoma parking lot. It's now about stopping a crime cartel from shipping heroin which is financing terrorism. I think there is time and I need a few more hours to see this through. What do you think?"

There was a pause on the line.

"George, did I lose you?"

"No, I'm here. When will you notify Bram?"

"If things go the way I expect, tonight."

Another pause.

Smoke added, "And you can't call him either, not yet."

"I understand, but if I don't hear from you, I will have to call Interpol."

"Of course. I'll call you tonight."

"How are you going to approach Gurds?"

"With cunning and guile."

His pace was quick and determined on the way back to the hotel. He walked in a straight line and discovered the bicyclers would magically move around him like schools of fish around snorkelers. He pulled the phone out again.

Aimer answered on the first ring. “Yo.”

“Bobby, use my computer, go online and get the first available back to New York, late tonight or first thing in the morning. My credit card will automatically show on the payment page.”

“What happened? We giving up?”

“No. Just get packed so we can bolt.”

“Cool, first class coming up.”

Smoke ignored him. “I’ll get the car and pick you up in front of the hotel in thirty minutes. Bring that list of Gurds’ properties addresses. Bram underlined the office where Quinton and his father work.”

“What’s the plan?”

“We’re gonna fuck some shit up.”

Aimer laughed. “Atta boy.”

31

AMSTERDAM, NETHERLANDS

The voice from the Waze app guided Smoke and Aimer through the city and they found the building. It was in the middle of a block of uniform, brick, seven- and eight-story buildings. The architecture of the entire block was simple, most had tall windows and few adornments. It was a street like most other residential cities, stores, offices, and restaurants on the first floor and offices or apartments above. Gurds International spanned two units, had tall, sparkling-clean glass on the first floor giving it the appearance of an art gallery. Above the foyer were six floors of brick and black-tinted windows. From street level one could see an expansive foyer with art hanging on every wall and bronze and marble statues positioned around small conversation couches. A long, red mahogany reception desk seemed to be the door to OZ.

Aimer pulled up to the front door.

Smoke started to pull the handle.

"Wait." Aimer grabbed Smoke's arm. "I really don't like you going in alone."

"That makes two of us."

Aimer took a beat. "No other way?"

Smoke shook his head. "We passed the entrance to the underground parking lot back on the corner. Go around and pull in. You can wait there without getting hassled."

"Thirty minutes, right?"

Smoke nodded.

Aimer nodded.

Smoke got out and walked for the door without looking back.

There was no security to be seen anywhere. No black suits with white curly wires in their ears, no uniforms with black utility belts loaded with handcuffs, mace, and large caliber handguns. The only person on the floor was a central-casting, Danish blond perched behind a long-curved reception desk. She wore a black jacket over a collared blouse that was almost as white as her teeth.

"Hej, hvordan kan jeg hjaelpe dig?"

"Sorry, I don't speak your language."

Without a moment's hesitation, she responded in perfect English. "Hello, how can I help you?"

"I would like to see Quinton Gurds."

"Do you have an appointment?"

"Ah, no. No appointment."

Her smile diminished slightly. "I'm sorry sir, but Mr. Gurds is in meetings."

"How would you know that?"

The smile was gone. "Mr. Gurds sees no one without an appointment."

Smoke looked around the room. Still no security. "Why don't you call his office and see if he has a few minutes?"

He saw her reposition herself in the seat. The call button for security must be on the floor.

"And what exactly would you want me to tell him?"

He heard an elevator motor start. "Tell him the guy who broke into his warehouse is here and wants to talk to him."

Her reaction indicated this wasn't in her playbook. She sat frozen in indecision.

"I think it's a mistake not to call him, don't you?"

She reached for the phone, pushed one button, then turned her head and whispered in Dutch.

"I don't speak the language. You don't have to whisper." He chuckled as he walked toward one of the sculptures.

An elevator bell rang and two black suits emerged, and zoned on him immediately.

The Danish blond stood up and started snapping her fingers at them. "Vente, Vente."

The men walked to her, keeping eyes on Smoke.

She leaned forward and started whispering to them.

Smoke yelled out again. "I don't speak the language. You don't have to whisper."

One of the men picked up the handset of the phone, pushed a button. A few seconds passed then he nodded to his partner and together they approached Smoke. "You, come follow."

Smoke started for the elevator before they got to him. They quick stepped, catching up and bookending him. Smoke was bigger than both of them.

The elevator was old and slow, taking almost a minute to reach the seventh floor. The door slid open and Smoke exited looking up and down the hallway. Both of the black suits were on the floor of the elevator, unconscious.

A man carrying several files and a coffee cup came out of an office and nodded to Smoke politely. When he saw the guards, he dropped his cup.

"Where is Quinton Gurds?"

"Undskyldning mig?" The man shook as he backed up.

"Gurds… Quinton Gurds?"

The man pulled the files to his chest then pointed shakily toward the end of the hall.

Smoke used the only Danish word he had learned. "Tak. Like… thanks."

The man scurried off in the opposite direction to where Smoke assumed he would call the police.

The hallway was wide, had four closed doors on each side, and double doors at its end.

"Quinton Gurds." Smoke bellowed as he moved toward the end of the hall. "Quinton Gurds."

The double doors opened and the stout bodyguard Smoke had seen with Gurds in the Red-Light District came out. He had his head tilted forward and his eyes fixed on Smoke.

Smoke stopped, leaving about six feet between them. "Speak English?"

The bodyguard didn't respond, but his hands were clenched into white-knuckle fists.

"I want to talk to your boss and believe me he needs to talk to me."

Smoke had seen You Tube videos of lions on the African plains stalking their victims. The big cats would sometimes get within a few feet of striking distance then freeze before lunging forward for the kill. The victims were defenseless and paralyzed with fear. From the position the bodyguard had chosen, Smoke assumed the man thought himself a king of the jungle because he hadn't fought anyone who could fight back.

“You’re making a mistake.” Smoke said softly.

The man was quick, faster than he looked. Leaping forward he turned his body sideways getting his right hand onto Smoke’s shoulder. His left hand was down, cocked, and about to throw a punch.

Smoke shifted most of his weight to his right foot and launched an uppercut that hit the bodyguard’s chin full force.

It was a one-punch fight. The sound of a jaw breaking, teeth shattering and the body hitting the floor echoed down the hall.

Smoke nudged the fallen king with a toe then headed for the open door.

“Anybody home?” Smoke walked carefully inside the cool dark room, stepping to one side out of the backlight of the hallway. No need to be the deer in headlights.

“Come in.”

Smoke saw a puff of smoke rise from behind the back of a desk chair.

“Oh good. I don’t have to do the I don’t speak your language thing. Quinton Gurds, I presume?”

A moan emanated from the hall.

Gurds swung his chair around. “I see you have dispatched my welcoming committee.”

“I did, but I understand you have really excellent health care in the Netherlands.”

“Okay, you have my attention funny man, now what the… fuck do you want?”

“Great, right to the point. Like I told Miss Netherlands downstairs, I’m the guy who broke into your warehouse on the dock last night.”

“So?”

“So, I need one piece of information. A name I believe you know. If you give me what I need, I will go away and everything will return to normal.”

Gurds blew another puff of smoke and twirled the cigar in his fingers. “What makes you think I’ll give you what you want?”

"Because I know about what you're doing now, what you're about to do, and who you're going to do it with."

Gurds stared silently at Smoke then tapped the cigar ash off into in an ashtray. "You get nothing until I know what you know."

"I thought you would say that and it's a lot. Actually..." Smoke reached into his pocket and Gurds reached for a drawer.

Gun.

"Hold up there, cowboy. No need for weaponry. Just getting some notes." Smoke took out a folded piece of paper. "Lots of numbers."

Gurds pushed back in the chair.

Smoke took a step closer to the desk and began. "Your father built an organization with the Penose that controls about ninety percent of the ecstasy market. You don't have to ship in bulk because you've eliminated the middleman and ship to local suppliers. The drug is illegal everywhere but nobody really gives a shit about it because it's not killing people like coke, crack, or heroin."

Gurds picked up his cigar.

"So, last night I broke into your warehouse and found, no doubt, just one of your many pill mills. There was one machine that can pump out thousands of pills every hour. I found the little plastic bottles and hundreds of boxes."

Gurds pushed forward and slapped his desk with an open palm. "I don't know what you're talking about. I went to inspect my warehouse today because its being readied for sale. It was totally empty." He leaned across the table. "There's nothing there."

Smoke shrugged. "I was there last night and heard you give that order. But it doesn't matter. You're still fucked."

Gurds smiled nervously. "Oh yeah?"

Smoke chuckled. "Why do people always say that? Oh yeah? I've done this more than a couple of times and they always say... oh yeah, right before the boom comes down on their heads."

Gurds tried to take a puff but the cigar had gone out.

"Anyway, like I was saying, and this is where I need my cheat sheet." Smoke held up the note. "Each pill weighs about .101 grams which means thirty pills weigh about 3.2 grams." Smoke waved the paper. "Do you mind if I do this in pounds instead of metrics? I'm American and we're kinda backward in weights and measures."

Gurds was motionless.

"Good. So, thirty pills in a bottle would mean fifty bottles would contain about a pound of whatever your pill-mill is making."

Gurds shifted around in his chair. "And?"

"And… four out of five American adults take vitamins, most of which are unregulated. Nobody is really paying much attention. They're just vitamins, right? Two hundred million Americans taking almost five trillion pills a year. Amazing huh? It also means hundreds of millions of pills are shipped to the U.S. from other countries."

Smoke took a breath. "Actually, your system is really pretty ingenious. You use white plastic pill bottles and small shipping boxes that I saw in the warehouse and ship direct. There's no middleman to break down bricks of powder into little bags."

Smoke looked at the stone-faced man, leaned forward, and spoke slowly. "I know about Hashim bin Talal. You're going to buy heroin from the Taliban. You'll have the ability to ship hundreds of pounds of heroin anywhere in the world completely undetected. While everyone is looking for shipping containers filled with bricks of powder, nobody will be looking for heroin in little bottles marked Vitamin C."

"You can't prove anything." Gurds tried to sound convincing.

"Oh, but I can. I found labels in the trash."

There was the sound of a door creaking and Smoke turned around. A hidden panel door on a side wall was open. An old man with a cane stood with another man, a very large man, behind him.

"How?" The old man's voice was weak but authoritative. He nodded to the man behind him who grabbed his elbow and helped him to a chair. "How do you think we're doing it?"

"The labels." Smoke tried to adjust to the unexpected. "You've eliminated the middleman by shipping direct from dozens of fake companies. You ship small amounts, less than a pound at a time. Fifty to a hundred bottles labeled as vitamins, actually containing ecstasy, and soon heroin, are addressed to a carefully constructed network of fake names and drop boxes."

The old man sat silent.

"What you don't know is your son is making a move to expand the business and is making a deal with the Taliban to ship heroin along with or mixed with the ecstasy you're manufacturing."

"Not my son."

Smoke was surprised again. "Huh?"

"Not my son… stepson. His mother died years ago, and I got stuck with this witless piece of shit."

Smoke regrouped and tried to get back on course. "Mr. Gurds, I'm here for one reason and one reason only. I need one name. Tell me the name and I'm gone."

"Whose name would that be?"

"Some weeks ago, a man who worked for you was shot and killed by police in a parking lot in Oklahoma. I need his name."

The man tapped his cane. "Why?"

"He murdered my wife and took my child twenty years ago in Philadelphia."

Quinton started to say something and the old man instantly reacted. "Shut up fool."

Smoke started planning an exit and took a step backwards, closer to the desk.

The old man started to get up but didn't. He just pointed his cane at Quinton. "I can't believe how anyone would think I would let this idiot run anything. He's a worthless showboat who hangs around with whores from the district. I am Penose, a word that means 'way of life.' What I built belongs to Penose not him."

Quinton sunk in his chair.

Smoke shifted a bit again which gained the big man's attention.

The old man's voice was soft but strong. "You sir, are a problem. You claim you need one name and you'll be gone but you are a man who obviously possesses some skills and has a lot of knowledge you could have only gotten from Interpol. You might even think having friends in law enforcement is an advantage, but I assure you my friends are more powerful than yours. You are alone. And by the way, don't think police will show up because you created a ruckus in the lobby. They've been and gone. False alarm. But back to you." Anton Gurds tried to get up again and this time succeeded.

The big man held both of the old man's elbows as he rose.

"I think you haven't told anyone about what you've learned because if you had, there would be a lot of people in this room with handcuffs. But I know you have connections at Interpol and they know you're trying to talk to this idiot. That could be troublesome. Mind you I said only troublesome. I will have to take steps now to recover and please don't bother assuring me of your silence."

"Wouldn't, but can I ask you something?"

The old man nodded.

"Do you know the name of the man in Oklahoma?"

"Of course, I do. The man worked for me for years, setting up distributors all around the U.S. He was also my enforcer. If there was a problem, he handled it. He never had an issue until Oklahoma. What is surprising to me is how anyone could think Quinton had the brains to manage the expansion of this thing of ours. You also thought he was making a deal with the Taliban. A conclusion you reached when you saw men following Quinton. Whom, with the help of Interpol, you identified, but you made the wrong assumption. You thought the son was pushing the old man out." He shook his head and smiled. "You were wrong. Hashim bin Talal was following whore-boy for me. I'm making the deal with the Taliban."

Quinton had gone white. “You had someone follow me around? I was just having fun and—”

“Shut up.” The old man barked as he shuffled off to the side of the room. When he stopped, he nodded at the bodyguard. “I know the name you want but you don’t need it anymore. You won’t need anything anymore.”

The big man reached behind his back and withdrew a pistol. It was a Glock with a long black silencer attached.

Smoke flinched.

The old man said, “Do it.”

The bodyguard snapped the gun up and pulled the trigger. The bullet hit Quinton Gurds in the middle of his forehead.

32

NEW YORK CITY

White surrounded her entire body. O lay flat on her back, unable to move, and in pain. She knew if she didn't stay still the technicians would have to start the MRI over again. It was the fourth time she was in the tube in four days and it hadn't gotten easier. She was a doctor and knew magnetic resonance imaging showed more detail of soft tissue than a CAT scan but the noise was difficult to tolerate. The multitude of intense pulsating beats were a result of computer-generated radio waves that passed through the body creating detailed images.

She had been in the tube more than a half an hour. The pain in her head was excruciating.

I have to get out.

The pounding in her head was matching the beat of the machine. Her eyes were wide, her fists clenched.

I'm going to scream.

It stopped.

The platform began to move.

"Way to go doc. Way to hang in there." A tech in a blue hospital uniform took her hand then her pulse. "You did great."

She couldn't talk. She just nodded.

An RN came in with a wheelchair. "Let's get you back to your room."

O remained on the platform. "I need something for the pain right now."

"I can't do anything till doctor sees you. He'll be making rounds in about an hour."

O grabbed her wrist and squeezed hard. "Get him now!"

The nurse tried to peel O's hand away and at first couldn't, but O weakened and let go.

Tears were running down O's face. "Please go get him now."

The RN hesitated for a second then looked at the tech. "Help her into the chair. I'll be back in a minute."

Ten minutes later, Dr. Brightman came into the room followed by the RN. "Bad time doctor?" He lifted O's hand and took her pulse.

O looked up, her face white and tension squeezing her eyes closed. "Occipital, radiating and intense. Nine on the ten scale. I need eight mg of lorazepam and a dark room, stat."

Brightman turned to the nurse. "You heard the doctor, stat. I'll wait here till you get back."

O tapped his hand. "Thank you."

Brightman rolled another wheelchair up next to hers. "Olivia, this isn't good. You know that."

She nodded.

"Any numbness, confusion, dizziness?"

She nodded.

Brightman took out a pen light and looked at her pupils. "Unequal pupils."

She nodded again.

"I'll look at the MRI and consult with Doctor Lee." He looked at his watch. "I should be in your room in about an hour."

The RN walked back in with a tray.

Brightman nodded and the nurse injected O.

"That will help take the edge off. I'll see you in a bit, okay?"

O nodded. "Thanks, Bob."

Curtains were drawn, all lights were off, and the room was dark. Felix and Gia were alternating shifts, one in a chair near O's bed, and one standing guard in the hall. She was asleep. The sedative had temporarily turned off the pain switch allowing O a few minutes of pain-free sleep.

Felix was at the door when Brightman and his entourage emerged from the elevator. Felix tossed his *Sports Illustrated* on the chair as he stood up in front of the door. "What's up doc?"

Brightman was all business. "Felix, this isn't good. The MRI showed two abnormalities. The previous scans showed inflammation which has not retreated and today's indicated there may be a small bleed. We are moving her to intensive care right now so I can keep her under constant observation."

Felix staggered a bit.

"You need to be aware; it may become necessary to do a craniotomy to relieve the pressure."

"But… but," Felix stammered, "what's wrong?"

"We are not sure yet. I'm consulting with several specialists but what I'm seeing on the MRI is bleeding, most likely a result of the traumas, however it could be a small tumor. We need more time and more tests to be sure."

"You can't put her in that tube again."

"If it's necessary, I'll have her sedated. Okay?"

Felix remained in front of the door.

"Can I go in?"

"If it's necessary? She's asleep."

"No, I guess it can wait a bit but there will be people here to move her to the ICU, shortly."

"When they get here, I'll wake her, but not until then."

Brightman nodded and left with his team in tow.

Felix took a breath, then cracked the door to catch Gia's attention. He had to tell her the bad news.

33

AMSTERDAM, NETHERLANDS

Half of Quinton Gurds' head was on the wall behind his chair. The smell of blood and gunpower overpowered the trappings of the plush office. Smoke hadn't moved from his spot in front of Gurds' desk. A part of him thought he would be next. Another part was working on escape.

"I can't tell you how fortunate I am that you decided to take on this one-man quest. Quinton has been a tremendous burden for me and the Penose. Naturally, while his mother lived, I could do nothing to curb his behavior. He defied every directive and flaunted his lifestyle, relishing in the publicity." Anton Gurds moved to sit in a chair as the bodyguard continued to train the Glock on Smoke.

Smoke, facing the gun, moved an inch backward closer to the desk.

"Other members encouraged me to deal with my stepson sooner but I chose to be cautious and wait for the moment when the spotlight that followed his demise would fall on someone else."

"And the man in that spotlight is now me. Correct?"

"For an incredibly stupid man, you're pretty smart. And... yes, you're it. You told the receptionist that you broke into our warehouse, you assaulted two guards in the elevator, and severely injured another. Then, for some inexplicable reason you shot and killed Quinton."

Smoke took another inch of space toward the desk.

"Your quest ends now. Your fingerprints will be on the gun and your body will disappear, never to be seen again." Gurds nodded toward the assassin.

"You'll need to get my fingerprints on that gun."

Gurds waved a hand at the huge man.

The man put the gun back in his belt and took a step forward.

Smoke had his hands behind his back searching for the pen set on Quinton's desk.

Anton Gurds spoke impatiently. "Come on, get this done. Break his neck then get a print on the gun. I'm tired and want to go home."

Smoke stood still, facing the man, hands behind his back.

The big man raised both arms, gripped Smoke's neck, and squeezed.

Smoke began turning red from the grip but smiled in the big man's face.

Suddenly, the man sucked in a great amount of air though a mouth that had become contorted.

Smoke thrust both his arms up, breaking the man's grip.

The bodyguard staggered backwards, his hands and fingers outstretched, his mouth open with no sound coming out. A gold-plated pen was sticking out of his groin.

"Oh, that really had to hurt." Smoke reached out and flicked the pen and the big man fell to his knees then flat on his back.

Anton Gurds seemed unaffected. "That was unexpected."

Smoke stepped toward the old man. "I think I'll be going now. But before I do, I really think you should reconsider giving up that name." He spun a matching gold pen around in his fingers.

Gurds looked at him dispassionately. "Do you think I have lived this long without having backup?"

Four men came though the panel door and surrounded Smoke.

Gurds stared hard at Smoke. “Amateur.” He then pointed a boney finger. “Strap this man, get his prints on the gun, then take him down to the parking lot.”

Smoke didn’t resist.

Two men held Smoke’s arms while another secured his wrists with a plastic tie. The fourth man, who was wearing medical gloves, removed the gun from the big man’s belt. He wiped it clean, stuck it in Smoke’s hand, then dropped it on the floor next to the body.

Gurds pointed his cane at Smoke. “You cannot escape. I think you didn’t know how far Penose can reach. Before you got into the elevator to come up to this floor a call was made. There is a van in the lot with a crew, waiting to take you to the farm. Some of these men will ride along with them and make sure no one ever hears from you again.” Anton waved to one of the men to help him get up. “I want to go home.”

Two suits pushed Smoke through the door and into the hall. The two guards he had disabled in the elevator had recovered and joined the group making the count six to one.

Two of the men had Smoke by his arms and pushed his face into the wall when Anton Gurds was being helped to the elevator.

“Last chance to give me that name.” Smoke’s words were labored as his head was being crushed into a block wall.

Gurds shook his head. “Amateur.”

A couple of minutes went by before Smoke was manhandled into the elevator accompanied by the entourage of suits. The group stood silent watching the floor numbers change. Musak was playing.

Aimer hadn’t been on a stakeout in a very long time, being a lieutenant in the homicide division had its perks. It was the perk he most enjoyed, because he despised sitting in a parked car waiting for something to happen. The parking lot was as expected, concrete pillars, painted concrete walls, and signs in Dutch. Fortunately, he was bright enough to be able to follow the painted arrows. Several people had emerged, got into their cars and left, but no Smoke.

He checked his watch, forty minutes. Smoke said thirty. His phone was leaning against the windshield. In that position, he could keep an eye on the glass doors leading to the elevators for the floors above and for a text from Smoke. He was getting antsy. He hated the waiting.

A single man came out, walked to his car and Aimer watched as he left. The car passed an incoming van. It was an older van, with panel doors. He slumped down in his seat as it passed by. The passenger window was down and the man inside was wearing motorcycle gang colors. It pulled up near the glass doors to the elevators and stopped.

That's wrong.

There was activity inside the glass enclosure. A group got out of the elevators.

Four, five... no six.

The van doors opened and two men got out, both wearing the same colors.

In the middle of the group, he saw Smoke.

Fuck.

Aimer pushed the trunk button, got out of the car, ran to the back, and began searching.

Two suits had Smoke by the arms leading him out the door. Two were in front and two behind. Through the glass he saw two more men wearing gang colors waiting.

"Now it's a party."

The man on his right yanked his elbow. "Hou je mond."

"I don't speak... never mind."

The lead men pushed the door open and they squeezed through the opening in a group.

"Hey mother fuckers!" Aimer came in fast, swinging a tire iron.

Smoke reacted like a linebacker, lowering his head, bowling over the two men in front. With his hands behind his back, he was unable to maintain balance and fell forward.

Aimer knocked one of the motorcycle guys out and was swinging the tire iron back and forth while the other men encircled him. One rushed forward and caught the bar on his shoulder but a second man knocked Aimer to the ground.

Smoke got up and charged again but was immediately knocked to the concrete.

Three men were punching and kicking him and the other three were doing the same to Aimer.

Suddenly, red and blue lights were flashing and tires screeched through the gate into the lot. Six cars flew around the corner and slid to a stop. All the doors opened at once and police jumped into the fray.

Two of the men ran back through the enclosure headed for the emergency stairs but were met by police coming down.

It was over in seconds.

Smoke, cut and bleeding, rolled to his side and a police officer cut the plastic restraint on his wrists. He got to his feet and hustled to Aimer who was still down on the ground. He grabbed his friend and rolled him over. His face was almost as bad as his own. Aimer's eyes were closed, blood was coming from gashes on his forehead, his lip was split, and a lump on his head had already begun swelling.

"You alright?" Smoke shook Aimer's shoulder.

Aimer slowly opened his eyes. "Mary Pat is going to kill you."

Smoke grinned. "Tire iron?"

Aimer spit blood. "I left my pistol in my other pants."

A man in tweed approached. "Good show, gentlemen."

Both Smoke and Aimer looked up at Bram Visser.

"How?" Smoke winced in pain as he tried to stand.

"You didn't really think I was going to let you tackle the century-old Penose organization on your own, did you?"

Smoke helped Aimer to his feet. "I had a feeling, but how did you know about this little escapade?"

"Interpol is a worldwide intelligence organization with connections in every corner of the world."

Smoke spit blood. "Ah un, but again, how did you know?"

Bram chuckled. "We put a bug in your phone on the first day we met. We've been listening to every word you've said since we met two days ago."

Smoke nodded. "I guess you won't be needing this then." He took his phone out of his pocket and showed Visser the screen. The recorder had been running for forty minutes.

Visser took Smoke's phone and beckoned to an officer. "Download the recording on this phone and return it to Mr. Smoke immediately. He has a plane to catch."

The uniform nodded and hurried off.

"What about the old man?"

Visser walked between Smoke and Aimer and started them toward the open door of his car. "We took him into custody coming out of his private elevator. He'll be charged with conspiracy, drug trafficking, financing terrorism and of course, murder. He'll be looking at bars for the rest of his life."

Smoke nodded. "When you see him again tell him the amateur said hi."

Bram beckoned to two officers to help Smoke and Aimer. "Do you want the medical staff to take a look?"

Smoke looked to Aimer who shook his head. "No thanks, we have tickets on the United to New York at nine o'clock. Will you need us to stay?"

Visser shook his head. “We have what we need right now. I have a feeling Gurds will be making a deal before this gets to court.”

“Okay then, we’d like to go.”

Visser put Aimer in the car and walked Smoke to the other door. “You didn’t get what you came for, did you?”

Smoke’s attitude changed instantly. “No. I didn’t. I was close, almost got it from Quinton but the old man changed the game. Anton knows the name too but refused to tell me what it was.”

“Well, don’t give up hope.”

Smoke just shrugged.

Visser beckoned to the driver. “Get these men back to their hotel and wait there. Take them to the airport when they’re ready.”

Smoke plopped into the back seat and looked up. “Thanks, Bram. You saved our asses.”

“Happy to help someone who helped break up a very dangerous drug cartel.”

Bram started to close the door and Smoke stopped him. “You know I never blew the trumpet for the Calvary.”

Bram laughed loud. “Yes, that’s true but I still got to lead the charge.”

34

NEW YORK CITY

It was cold and dark. Her fingers found the edge of the blanket and tried to pull it up but couldn't. It was stuck under her hip and wouldn't move. A shiver ran down her spine, and she let out a low groan when the second attempt to cover up failed.

The sound of the groan didn't have a chance to reach the ceiling before Felix and Gia arrived at the side of her bed.

Gia leaned close. "What do you need, honey?"

O's voice was barely audible. "Cold."

Felix's giant feet slapped the tile floor as he hustled to get another blanket from the closet. Within seconds Gia and he were tucking it around their friend.

She hadn't said more than two or three words to them since she'd returned to her room after the MRI. She had gone out free of monitors and tubes but came back with a port in her arm and three IVs; fluids for hydration, antibiotics and a sedative for pain. She knew why the doctors ordered the medications but Felix and Gia didn't.

O smiled weakly at her well-meaning personal nurse and bodyguard and beckoned them closer. She looked up at Felix. "Get Brightman."

Felix took off like he was shot out of a cannon.

O looked over at Gia. She coughed a little, trying to clear her throat. “There is an envelope in the nightstand by my bed at home. If anything happens, give it to Smoke.”

Gia gripped O’s hand and laid her head on O’s shoulder. “Everything’s going to be alright.”

O squeezed Gia’s hand lightly.

Dr. Brightman came through the door first being shoved along by Felix. An RN with a really pissed-off face was pulling the big man in the opposite direction. Felix easily won the tug of war.

“Dr. Bennet, I was in the corridor on my way here when… your friend hustled me along.”

Felix let go and so did the RN.

O waved Brightman to come close and lean over. “I know what’s next. Tell them.”

Dr. Brightman turned around and faced Gia and Felix. “Would you like to sit?”

They stood silent and where they were.

“Right… okay. The MRI revealed an area of swelling in the occipital section of Dr. Bennet’s brain. There is cerebral bleeding most likely caused by an intercranial aneurysm causing a hematoma to form outside the wall of the blood vessel.”

“Aneuryam… Hematuma?” Felix questioned.

“Aneurysm is a bulging of a weakened blood vessel causing a hematoma, which is blood pooling in the damaged area. Understand?”

Felix nodded.

“Because the damaged area is enclosed inside the cranium, the swelling creates pressure within the cavity causing a great deal of pain.”

Gia sucked in a gulp of air.

“We need to do two things immediately. First, we will perform a craniotomy. Dr. Lee and I will remove a small portion of the skull bone which will release the pressure and allow time for the swelling to recede.”

Gia gasped, her hand covering an open mouth.

O beckoned to her and Gia sat in a chair next to the bed then waved at Brightman to continue.

"Dr. Bennet will be closely monitored and as soon as her vitals normalize, Dr. Lee and I will operate again and repair the damage to the blood vessel by installing a permanent titanium clip on the artery, isolating it from general circulation."

Felix asked a very intelligent question. "So, you know what to fix. I mean you know exactly what's wrong and you can fix it, right?"

Brightman didn't answer immediately. He looked at O who nodded and waved him on.

"Actually, we don't know exactly what's wrong. The MRI shows the area and the hematoma but we don't as yet have a clear picture of what caused it."

Felix and Gia looked at O with wide eyes and drawn faces.

O cleared her throat and spoke. "Best surgeons in the world. They got this. Stop worrying."

It helped but her friends seemed still unconvinced.

O waved Felix closer. "Smoke?"

"He called."

O's eyes winced with pain. "And?"

"I told him what's going on. He's getting on a plane. He'll be here tonight."

O smiled. "I want…" She coughed a bit.

Felix became instantly frantic. "What… what do you need?"

"Tonight. Oso Bucco from Masstro's."

Felix sat up. "What?"

She smiled. "For four."

35

NEW YORK CITY

The yellow cab pulled up to 710 West 168 Street, the front of the Neurological Institute off Columbia University's Irving Medical Center. Smoke pulled his weary body out of the taxi and scanned the street, getting his bearings. There were sidewalks and railings and trees in planters. It was modern and sleek and known to be on the leading edge of medical care in the country but when Smoke looked at the façade he wondered why there were room air conditioners sticking out of the walls.

It was three in the morning and there was no one on the street but him. He slung his gym bag, containing the minimum needed for a couple of days in Amsterdam, over his shoulder and hustled up the ramp. The light from the other side of the glass door gave him hope that he could get inside.

He pushed on the door but it was locked.

"Shit."

He cupped his hands on the glass and peered inside.

"You need something buddy?"

Smoke spun around. A police officer stood a few feet away with a stern look on his face and his right hand on the handle of his nightstick.

"Officer, my wife is inside. I need to get in."

"Visitor hours are—"

"I understand that but I just got off a plane from overseas and I think they are operating on her or she's been operated on or… I don't know. I just need to get inside and find her."

The policeman's hand didn't come off the stick but his face got a little less intense.

"You can't get in through —"

Smoke raised his voice. "I have to get inside."

"Calm down and listen to me."

Smoke anticipated a confrontation but didn't get it.

"All I'm telling you is, you can't get in through that door. The entrance to the hospital is around the corner."

Smoke was confused. "But this is the—"

"Offices, not the hospital… round the corner."

"Oh." Smoke was embarrassed.

"I'll show you. Come on." The officer nodded for Smoke to follow. "You look like shit, pal. What happened to your face… car accident?"

Smoke fell in step. "No. Actually, I assisted in breaking up an international drug cartel."

The policeman shook his head. "Another funny man. Three o'clock in the morning and I'm stuck with Jay Leno. I am never switching beats with Harvey again."

"No, really. I was involved with Interpol—"

"The Comedy Cellar is up on McDoogle Street." The cop pointed to a two-story arch. "The entrance is over there."

"Thanks." Smoke started walking quickly.

"Hey."

Smoke turned around.

"Wife huh?"

"Yeah."

"Good luck, then."

"Thanks.

The door was open and there were people in the lobby. A woman behind a desk searched on her computer and found Dr. Olivia Bennet was on the seventh floor.

The elevators were old, a part of the original building no doubt. The buttons were faced with a real brass plate and a bell rang on every floor. There was no Musak.

Two nurses entered from the fourth floor then left on the fifth. A doctor got on when they came to six and got off with Smoke on seven.

Smoke stopped when he exited and looked both ways. Wall sconces lit the hallway but the fluorescent overheads were off.

The doctor from the elevator came up behind him. "Who are you looking for?"

"My wife, Dr. Bennet."

He shook his head. "Don't know any—"

"A patient, not a doctor. No, I mean she's a doctor but a patient too." Smoke looked up at the ceiling. Somehow, he had turned into a teenager unable to finish a complete thought.

"Okay." He gave Smoke a once over.

"I just got off a plane from Europe. I know I look bad but…" Smoke hesitated, "I received these injuries in an accident just before I left."

The doctor looked him over again then said, "Follow me."

They walked down the hallway in the low light past a lot of closed doors. Smoke could feel the weight of his fatigue. He hadn't slept on the plane, never could, even when he didn't have anything to worry about. Not being here when O needed him the most was something he would never get past.

There were plastic chairs near an empty floor station. "Wait here. I'll send someone to help."

The wait was more painful than the cuts on his face or what he thought must be a broken rib. Finally, a young pinstriped nurse bobbed down the hall. "Mr. Bennet?"

"Ah..." he got up from the chair, wincing.

The pinstriper winced with concern at his pain.

"Are you okay?"

"Yes, I'm fine, thank you." He decided not to confuse the situation any further. "And yes, I'm Mr. Bennet. My wife is a patient here and I need to see her as soon as possible."

She didn't move instantly but did eventually, apparently making a decision of which only she knew the parameters. "She's down the hall on the right."

As they walked, the pinstriper was sneaking peeks at his face.

"Got it breaking up an international drug cartel."

She went speechless until they reached a closed door at the end of the hall.

"She's sleeping so be very quiet."

Smoke pushed the door open a crack and peeked in.

Gia was awake and sitting on a chair with her feet up. She slapped her hand over her mouth, surpassing any sound and leaped off the chair like a ballerina and flew across the floor.

Smoke caught her as she threw her arms around his neck pushing him back toward the door. She whispered in his ear. "Outside."

With the door closed behind them Gia gushed, "Oh my god I'm so glad you're back. She'll be so happy."

"How is she?"

Gia's voice caught in her throat. "She was in surgery for two hours. Doctor Brightman said she did fine but didn't give me a lot of details. He said the best thing that could happen is that she rest tonight. He said he would be here first thing this morning and let her know what's next."

"Next?"

Gia stood motionless. Her eyes were as wide as saucers. "They had to do something called a craniotomy."

Smoke looked at her blankly.

"They had to remove a part of her skull to relieve the pressure on her brain."

Neither spoke.

Gia cried.

Smoke looked toward the sound of footsteps coming down the hall fast.

Felix, without saying anything, bear hugged Smoke.

Gia still had tears on her face.

Felix held him by both shoulders and Smoke winced.

"Busted rib?"

Smoke nodded.

"Gia and I will head out and give you some privacy. Text me when you want us back. We'll be in the lobby."

Smoke nodded and watched them walk away. He turned and pushed the door open very slowly. He walked as light footed as he could to the chair next to the bed and sat. O lay on her side with her back to him. A blanket was pulled up to her shoulders and he could see they had shaved half of the hair off her head. A white patch, several inches square, covered a portion of the shaved area. There was no blood, just gauze and white tape.

He stretched out and pulled the blanket down to cover an exposed toe.

"You need a shower."

He choked down a quick breath.

Her arm came out from under the blanket and she rolled over, her hand extended. She wiggled her fingers. "Come to me."

He leaned onto the bed and laid his head close to hers on the pillow.

"Hi baby."

"Hi."

Her hand stroked his face. "You look like shit."

"International drug cartel."

"I know a really good doctor. You should hang around."

They lay eye to eye. "I'm not going anywhere."

36

NEW YORK CITY

The noise coming from the hallway flooded into the room when the nurse pushed open the door and hit the light switch. O was on her side, covered up, except for her arm, which hung over the side of her bed.

Smoke was stretched out on the floor— his hand in hers.

Both awoke; O, quickly, brightly, and smiling until she stroked her half-bald head and found the bandage. Smoke until the damage of his recent beating and the last few hours on a cold concrete floor caught up to his body.

"Ah… good morning, Dr. Bennet. And you are?"

O lifted his arm and kissed his hand. "The husband, back from the war."

The nurse stepped toward the bed and got a better look at his face. "Would you like me to look at those injuries? The gash on your forehead looks like it might need a stitch."

Smoke waved her off as he stretched his back. "No thanks, I'm okay."

The nurse shrugged then did the mandatory inspection of tubes, temperature, pulse, and pressure while Smoke sat silently on a hard metal chair.

"Doctors will be here shortly."

"Brightman?" O queried.

"Doctor Brightman and Lee will be here shortly." The nurse replaced the medical gear and scurried out the door.

"Why do they always—"

"Drop the article… doctor will be here instead of the doctor will be here. Why does that bother you so much?"

"It doesn't."

"Every time you hear it, you comment."

Smoke scratched his head. "Really, I do? I didn't realize. I guess I think its pretentious."

O looked at him with loving eyes. "You know when you use three syllable words, I get all hot and bothered."

Smoke leaned over close. "Counterintuitive."

"Oh my." O fanned her face with her hand.

A team of white coats interrupted the moment. Brightman, Lee, two assistants, two nurses, and a man in a suit entered the room.

O whispered to Smoke, "Later."

"Abb so positively."

She laughed.

Brightman stuck out his hand to Smoke. "Good to see you again." He shook hands but then pointed a finger to Smoke's face. "That might need a stitch."

"I'm fine. What's going on with O?"

"The Craniectomy went well, no complications. I trust you're feeling better."

"I haven't felt this good in months. There is no headache. My vision is clear, no neck pain and I have energy. When can I check out?"

Brightman peered over his glasses like he was looking at a child. "Dr. Bennet, you know better than that." He turned to Smoke. "She feels better because the removal of a small portion of bone near the injury allowed us to drain the fluid caused by the injury which was causing swelling and pressure to build up. The intracranial pressure was the reason for all of the outward symptoms and pain but not the cause."

Smoke didn't say anything and continued staring at the now unnerved doctor.

The doctor continued but was more respectful. "The MRI has identified two areas of concern. One is in the occipital." He cupped his hand on the back of his head. "This one is more identifiable and we will perform an endovascular procedure to seal the bleed and remove a ventricular aneurysm, if there is one."

"Careful with the six syllable words, doc."

O slapped Smoke's hand.

Brightman was confused but continued. "The second area on the MRI is a bit more concerning. The most recent screens indicated there is some intracerebral swelling."

Smoke saw O's face instantly reflect fear.

"We will monitor it closely and act if we need to. In surgery today, I will be doing the vascular repair. Dr. Lee is one of the finest brain surgeons in the country and will assist me with the repair and will be there if additional procedures are required."

O spoke low. "You said today?"

"Dr. Bennet, time is not on our side. We need to act quickly."

"When?"

"We'll begin to prep you in about an hour."

Brightman nodded to the door and his entourage left the room. After the last of them left he moved closer and said firmly, "Olivia, this is the best route to take. The longer we wait the greater the chances for a hemorrhage."

O nodded. "It's okay, Bob. I just got caught off guard for a second."

"It will be fine. Don't worry." He patted her hand, smiled, then left the room.

O turned her face away.

Smoke did the only thing he could think of, straightened her blanket.

The door creaked open and Felix stuck his head through the opening. "All good?"

Smoke motioned him in. Gia was right behind.

O feigned a smile. "They're going to prep me for surgery in about an hour."

Nobody spoke.

"Listen, I'm a doctor and I'm telling you it's going to be fine."

Her assurance didn't break the ice.

The silence became awkward.

"You know they're going to have to put a plate in my head."

Gia punched Felix in the stomach.

Felix started laughing. "What's that for?"

"I don't want to hear any screw loose, or getting stopped by airport security, jokes from you."

"Well, I can't now, can I? You just did."

O laughed. Gia laughed. Felix laughed. Smoke walked to the window.

"Right, okay, now here's the game plan." O took control. "You all will wait with me and keep me entertained until I have to go up. Then my husband is going to go to the condo, shower, change clothes, and return redressed and refreshed."

"Thank you." Felix waved his hand in front of his nose. "Man, you are... r- i -p -e."

Smoke continued to look out the window.

The hour went by quickly, Felix providing entertainment while Gia straightened the room for the tenth time.

A nurse came in several times, checking nurse stuff, poking, prodding, and taking temperatures. Her last visit was to say they would be taking her up in a few minutes, a cue for the visitors to leave.

Gia took direction well but had to pull Felix to the door.

Felix, resisting Gia's efforts, spoke to O as he backed up. "I called Andre at the Four Seasons. He's making a special dinner for you. Don't let them keep you up there too long, everything will get cold."

Gia pushed him again while turning to blow O a kiss.

The door slowly closed.

Smoke leaned close and took her hand. “I don’t know what to do.”

“You can’t fix this by punching it in the mouth.”

He ducked his head.

“Look at me.”

He raised his head and met her eyes.

“Listen to me you big oaf. I waited my whole life for what I thought was love to come along. There were many, many nights I went to sleep thinking I was a fool, that I was delusional, that what I thought was love was just a fantasy.” A tear welled up. “Then you show up, and my little girl fantasy became this woman’s reality. You are my prince charming, my hero, my protector… my love. Nothing can take that away, not today, not tomorrow, not ever.”

A gurney banged though the door followed by two nurses in surgical blues.

Smoke gripped her hand and leaned to her.

Their lips touched.

Their eyes open.

Their breath, one.

37

PHILADELPHIA, PA.
ONE YEAR LATER

Mary Pat Aimer was in bed, asleep— a well-deserved sleep. It had been a long day, babysitting three visiting grandkids who seemed to have an endless amount of energy. She had her head on her pillow, and drifted into the comfort of deep sleep— when the phone rang. She woke startled, next to a husband who hadn't responded to the disturbance.

"Answer the phone." She shoved her husband, then rolled to her side, mumbling. "I thought this ended when you retired." She yanked on the blanket in a really not-happy way.

Aimer slowly lifted his head from the pillow, propped it on one hand, then reached for the receiver. "Hello."

"Lieutenant, it's George DiSanto."

"George? I thought I told you not to call me... never mind, forget it. What's up? And what time is it anyway?"

"Oh... I'm sorry. I didn't realize. Is it late?" There was a pause as Bobby heard a rustling sound. "Oh my, 12:30. I apologize. Please forgive me. I'll call you tomorrow."

"No, wait. Don't hang up." Aimer swung his feet over the bed. "Give me a minute."

Mary Pat grunted as Bobby headed for the stairs and the downstairs phone.

"Okay, I'm back." Aimer settled into a chair. "What can I do for you?"

"I got the name you and Smoke were looking for in Amsterdam."

"Really, how?"

"Bram Visser got it. Anton Gurds made a deal with Interpol— a plea bargain."

"What kinda deal was he looking for? He's a million years old, a drug kingpin, and there are audio tapes of him murdering his own son."

"Stepson." George corrected. "It turns out he has two daughters from a previous marriage. Bram told Gurds they were going to take everything he has under their version of our RICO Act. So, he made a deal that the kids could keep a trust fund he set up."

"Is that legal?"

"I guess so. Gurds made a full confession which gave Interpol the grounds to apprehend the two Saudis, both of whom by the way, are being deported."

"Whoa, wouldn't want to be them."

"You're right about that. Being arrested for drug smuggling in the Middle East is a fate worse than death. Anyway, Bram negotiated with Gurds and got the information you were looking for. Bram said to tell you both it was a reward for your efforts in breaking up the cartel."

"No shit. I am really coming to like that guy."

"Me too."

"Did he have to give Gurds something for the name?"

"He didn't really say but I think it was something like a window in his cell."

Aimer laughed. "George, did you just make a joke?"

The former FBI man chuckled a bit. "Indeed, I think I did."

"Outstanding."

George recovered his demeanor and continued. "Anyway, the name is Phillipe Laurent. The old man sent him to Philadelphia in 2001 to open a new supply chain for drugs. While Laurent was living in Philadelphia, he hooked up with a woman, a nurse, who had a nasty drug habit. They moved in together and, apparently, she wanted a baby but couldn't have one. The woman worked in the maternity ward where Helen had the boy. Gurds told George when the woman learned Smoke was overseas and Helen lived alone, she talked Laurent into breaking into the house and stealing the baby but Helen woke up and..."

"I know the rest." Aimer cut him off. The memory was still vivid. He didn't need a recap.

George continued. "The crime was hard to solve because it wasn't a murder of opportunity or a kidnapping for ransom. It wasn't a conspiracy, a crime of passion, or a random act of violence. It was just bad people doing bad things."

"But what about the boy?"

"I'm coming to that." George took a beat. "Gurds said when he heard what Laurent had done, he was furious, afraid of the backlash from police, and almost had them all killed. A few weeks after kidnapping the kid, the woman is DOA of an overdose. Gurds said he demanded Laurent leave the boy on a doorstep or at a firehouse, anywhere, but to handle it as soon as possible. Gurds didn't want anything to connect him to the murder. He told Laurent the baby would just disappear in the system which is exactly what happened."

"Again, what about the boy?"

"Be patient. I took Bram's info and got busy. I knew the date of the crime and the approximate date of the woman's overdose. I searched all the records for abandoned children in Philadelphia, Camden, New Jersey and Wilmington, Delaware during that period and found only two possible. One boy and one girl."

"Oh my God." Aimer jumped to his feet and dropped the phone. It rattled around before he got himself under control and picked it up.

"Makes me cry too." George said softly.

"I wasn't crying, George. I dropped the phone."

"Oh, I just thought I heard—"

Aimer had his composure back. "It's been twenty years. Are you sure?"

"I called in every favor I had at the FBI and received a lot of help. Bottomline, I got a name, a history, and a location. I'll send you an email with all the particulars. Bobby, believe me, even without a DNA test… I'd bet the farm."

Aimer was silent.

George waited a minute then pressed him. "When will you tell him?"

"That is the question."

"I tried to call Smoke, before I called you, but he never picks up. His mailbox is full so I can't leave a message. Is he alright?"

"Actually, no, not really. He doesn't answer my calls either, or Felix for that matter. He's been holed up in his apartment since the funeral."

"How does he avoid the publicity? Aren't there still reporters tailing him around?"

"He's kinda hiding in plain sight. He's from the neighborhood where almost everybody knows him and where there are like a thousand people always on the look-out for strangers. He can go anywhere around there and nobody sees nothin'. I suspect if a reporter parked anywhere near his apartment, they might return to their car up on blocks."

"I know it's tough, but he can't just hide forever."

"He can… and he's done it before. When Helen died, he hid out in that apartment and was intolerable for years. Felix and I eventually wore him down and then he met Olivia. But now… I gotta tell ya George… I'm not sure what to do."

"If you tell him his son is alive, he's going to want to find him."

"Not sure of that either. I had one conversation with him after the funeral. He's convinced himself everybody he touches comes to harm, Helen, Lo, Olivia. I think he might decide to not go near him."

"What will you do?"

"Be like Smoke, I guess. I'll get a plan."

"Bobby, you're a good friend."

"That's the first time you called me Bobby. I'm getting all teary eyed."

George laughed. "Call me and let me know how it goes, okay?"

"Absolutely, I will. But now I have to go upstairs and tell the ball and chain who was on the phone."

"Ball and chain!" Mary Pat yelled into the bedroom phone.

"I thought you hung up the extension." Aimer said out loud.

Mary Pat paid no attention. "Ball and chain, imagine that, George, thank you for helping Smoke, he's a sweet man and has had a bunch of bad breaks, but he's lucky he has friends like you. Anytime you're in Philadelphia you better stop here, or I'm going to be very angry with you—"

Aimer interrupted. "George, believe me… you don't want that."

"Oh really. Me… the ball and chain, angry? I don't get angry, I get even and I think you should hang up the phone, Mister-I'm-So-Important because I used to be a homicide detective and come to bed before—"

"You know there is something called punctuation, Mary Pat."

"Okay now you're really in trouble, you just wait, and you…"

"Good night, George. And thanks."

"Are you going to tell Smoke all about—"

The phone line went dead.

38

18TH STREET BALLFIELD
NORTH EAST PHILADELPHIA

Smoke came out of the dugout and walked to third base with his head down and his hands in his pockets. He had seen Felix and Aimer arriving in the middle of the fourth inning but paid them no mind nor gave them any recognition. He didn't know what they wanted and didn't care.

"Coach, I need a batter here." A burly man with an umpire's mask at his side, and a lot of attitude, yelled at Smoke. It wasn't the first time Smoke's indifference received this umpire's wrath.

Smoke beckoned to the dugout. "Let's go. Marcus, you're up."

A five-foot-two boy, with shaggy black hair, and an ill-fitting uniform, grabbed a bat and a helmet.

Smoke called again to his team. "Ricky on deck." A boy a foot taller with a similarly fitting uniform, reluctantly gathered himself, and a bat.

The American Legion Post 125 from Kensington fielded its first baseball team in its history. Every Legion Post in Philadelphia had teams, except the 125. Most of the boys from the neighborhood where the Post was located played in the Catholic Leagues, so a Legion team didn't matter but the neighborhood had changed since Smoke was of age, and so did the part the church played in the lives of this part of the city called the Great Northeast. Smoke's boyhood Catholic League team was no more. It was replaced by the 125's from Post 125.

Marcus went down on three pitches, Ricky followed him to the bench after four more, but Tony hit a frozen rope off the fence in left for a double. Petey followed and killed the rally with another three-pitch strikeout.

The boys playing the field ran past Coach Smoke without saying a word to him. He walked back slowly, head down, still ignoring his visitors.

Felix and Aimer were among only a few fans rooting for 125. Several parents in fold-out chairs had the parent package of water bottles, snacks, and iPhone with the unlimited viewing service as their son's team was dismal and hard to watch.

"How did you get him to do this?" Felix asked.

"Well, I played on his community spirit. This is where we grew up. We played ball on this field. It's where he got noticed which led to a full scholarship at LaSalle. Our neighborhood hasn't had a team since the Catholic League shut down. I got him to volunteer. To help the kids. The neighborhood."

Felix weighed the information carefully. "Nah. That's crap. How did you really do it?"

"Swear, that's the truth."

Felix shook his head. "No, it isn't."

Aimer stared at Felix for a beat. "Okay... Mary Pat... my wife... she went with me to see him in his apartment. She told Smoke her nephew couldn't play baseball and demanded he coach because he almost got me killed in Amsterdam and he owed her."

Felix laughed. "Now that's believable."

"Yeah, she can be very persuasive."

Felix looked out over the field. "Who's the nephew?"

Aimer pointed to a tall gawky kid playing right field. "There. He can't hit for shit but he has a decent arm and loves the game."

They sat and watched. It was sunny and warm and for a minute the past was not present.

"You sure they're right about this?"

Aimer nodded. "I talked to George for an hour again last night. He convinced me."

"I know but if he's wrong—"

"He's not. Trust me."

Felix saw Smoke sitting in the dugout. There was a rough beard on a face with no expression. "I hope you're right."

Marcus was up again in the bottom of the ninth and rolled a seeing-eye grounder past the shortstop for a single. It was only the fifth hit of the game for the 125's, however somehow, they had all happened at the right moment putting the team within a couple of runs of the lead. The Roxborough Bandits had the opposite baseball luck, compiling twelve hits but only four runs.

The Bandit coach, a serious looking man wearing a shiny white uniform, walked slowly to the mound. Halfway there he signaled for a left-handed pitcher from the bullpen.

The hottest pitcher in the Legion emerged from the right field gate. He was six-foot tall, short blond hair, an athletic frame and a confident stroll. He was a senior out of the number one program in Philadelphia, Malvern Prep, had a full ride at Penn locked up, and was being scouted by major league baseball for the draft coming up in a couple of weeks.

Ricky, who had been in the batter's box waiting his turn to strike out, walked back into the dugout shaking his head. "Fuck'n Duggan. I hate this guy. He always throws inside trying to scare me."

The gawky kid playing right field threw his glove on the ground and quick-stepped to Smoke's corner of the bench. "You want to say something here, coach?"

Smoke looked up and said nothing.

"Nothin…? Right. What a joke." He stuck his finger in Smoke's face. "I really hate my Uncle Bob for hooking your sorry ass up with us. We want to win or at least we want to try to win which is more than we can say about you. You just sit there, make no effort, and don't even pay attention. You're a fucking joke."

Smoke looked straight into the kid's face then stood up. His head barely fit under the roof of the dugout. He looked up and down the dugout and then walked to the chain-link fence and gripped the metal with his fingers.

The phenom was finishing his warm-up pitches.

Smoke stared wordless for a full minute.

The players looked at each other wondering what's next.

"Yo, asshole." Uncle Bob's nephew wasn't giving up. "What's the play? Ricky is 0 for the month and we're two runs down."

Smoke turned around. "Ricky, come here."

The mophead walked down the bench, adjusting a loose helmet.

Smoke looked down. "How you doin'?"

Ricky squeaked out, "I'm okay coach, how are you?"

Smoke almost smiled. "Step into one."

Ricky's mouth dropped. "What?"

"He throws you inside, so step into it. I need you on first base."

The umpire yelled out. "Coach, I need a batter here."

"Go." Smoke pointed to the exit and Ricky walked head down ready for some pain.

"Tony."

"Yea." A boy who looked like a supersized Ricky stood up. He was big, broad, and thick. He looked more like a linebacker than a first baseman but the kid could swing a bat.

"You hit this kid in the opener in April and twice in May, right?"

"Yeah, I can hit his fastball but that fucking slider kills me."

"Right." Smoke walked to him and put his arm around his shoulder. "I watched him warm up. He kept looking at the stands. I think there is a scout here watching him so he'll be throwing heat right away."

"And?"

"Swing but don't come close to the first pitch. It'll be a fastball outside. Nothing you can hit, but swing anyway."

"Huh?"

"Swing way late, like he blew it past you."

"I don't understand."

"The next pitch will be another fastball and you'll do the same thing. Swing way late."

"Okay." The boy agreed but seemed still unsure what was next.

"He won't throw a waste pitch. He'll come right after you trying to impress the scout. He'll give you a fastball right down the middle."

Tony grinned. "Sure thing, coach."

A sound of a ball hitting meat was followed with Ricky yelling. The mophead limped down to first.

The pitcher smiled as he rubbed up a new ball.

Smoke walked to the end of the dugout and put a foot on the top step.

Tony stepped into the box and swung wildly at the first pitch. He swung again badly missing the second pitch, this time acting frustrated and banging the plate with his bat.

Smoke saw the pitcher grin with confidence.

The nephew came up beside Smoke. "Do you think he'll throw Tony the fastball?"

"Absolutely."

There's a particular sound that occurs when a ball hits the fat part of a bat. There is a tone, the sound of a triumphant result of a perfect swing. Those who have the game in their blood don't actually have to see it happen. They know when they hear it. But it is fun to watch.

Tony's ball landed in the parking lot, twenty over the fence.

The team emptied the dugout to welcomed the hero to home plate.

Smoke grabbed his jacket and headed out to his car.

"Coach, coach." The nephew ran out from the field.

Smoke didn't stop walking.

"Thanks. That was really great."

Smoke didn't say anything.

"Uncle Bob is here." The nephew pointed to the stands.

Smoke kept walking.

"Practice Friday, right coach?"

"Friday."

Before reaching the parking lot, Smoke turned around and saw the nephew jump onto Tony's back. They were laughing and yelling along with the rest of the team.

Felix and Uncle Bob ambushed Smoke at his car.

"Nice." Felix came from behind a van and stood with his arms crossed. "I drive all the way down from New York for a fucking Legion game, nice win by the way, and you try to sneak off. Nice."

"I wasn't sneaking off. I just don't want to talk to you."

Aimer stepped out next. "Or me?"

"Especially you."

"What?"

"You made me coach this team—"

"Hold on, Mary Pat made you an offer you couldn't refuse, not me."

"And you won't stop bugging me. I just want to be left alone. Get it?" Smoke stuck a rude finger in Aimer's direction.

Felix growled at Smoke. "You better not point that thing at me. You'll bring back a bloody stump if you do."

Smoke grunted and stuck his hand in his pocket, looking for his keys.

"Forget your keys, you're coming with us." Felix stepped up close.

"The fuck I am."

"The. Fuck. You. Are." Felix said it slowly and with force.

Smoke and Felix stood face to face.

A moment was approached where it could go either way.

"Coach."

Smoke looked down. Ricky was there, his mother in tow.

"Go ahead, tell him." Ricky's mother nudged him. "Go on."

"Coach, I just wanted to say thanks. I mean, I didn't get a hit, I only got hit with a ball. But it was the first time in my whole life I ever felt like a hero. All the other kids were treating me like I did something really great. I mean getting hit hurt... a lot but... I guess what I'm saying is... it was worth it. So, thanks coach." He broke into a big smile.

Smoke rubbed his head. "Okay, Ricky. See you Friday."

The mom smiled and followed the boy as he ran back to the team.

"I got a tear in my eye." Felix faked a sob.

"Shut the fuck up." Smoke pushed his friend away. "What do you want anyway? You didn't drive down here to watch his nephew."

Aimer looked at Smoke. "I need a favor."

"No."

Felix stepped in. "Okay, I need a favor."

Smoke didn't answer immediately.

People were walking by and couldn't help but notice the standoff.

Smoke broke first. "What?"

"You need to come with us... now."

"Why?"

"Because."

"You're a fucking child. And, no. I'm not going with you."

Felix stood strong. "You're coming or we're rolling in the stones, right here, and right now."

Another beat went by.

Smoke breathed out. “Where?”

“We’ll tell you when we get there.” Aimer started for his car.

Felix pushed his friend and together they followed behind Aimer toward his car.

Smoke was walking behind Aimer and Felix stepped to his side. “You doing alright?”

“Not really, no.”

“We got your back. You know that, right?”

Smoke nodded and kept walking.

39

LASALLE UNIVERSITY
PHILADELPHIA, PA.

They parked in the lot off of 20th street near the Gatehouse. Smoke hadn't been on campus in more than twenty-five years but not much had changed. The buildings were in the same place, the sidewalks right where he left them, but the trees were a little older.

"Where you headed?" A security guard confronted the three as they walked past Wister Hall.

Aimer was in front and answered. "Headed to DeVincent Stadium."

The guard was paid to be suspicious of three old men walking around a college campus. "Why youse going to the baseball field? No games there anymore."

Smoke stopped walking. "Wait, what, because of Covid?"

"No, they played all though last year. Been around since 47, but no more. I saw them go to the NCAA finals in 85. Now that was a good team. Softball, tennis, swimming… seven teams… all pulled, no money. Yeah, last year was the last season for baseball at LaSalle."

Smoke breathed out a slow, "That sucks," then turned to Aimer. "Why are we here if there is no game?"

"Well, actually, there's a kid here who played last year who needs some help moving on. Coach Anderson called me when he couldn't reach you and now, you're here."

Smoke looked at the two and said, "I ain't buying any of this."

Aimer and Felix starting walking, leaving Smoke standing by himself. He stood for a minute, ducked his head, and followed.

At the end of the tunnel leading into the field Smoke saw Coach Anderson waiting. "Hey Smoke, Bobby, and you are?"

"Felix Upton Grant, coach. Pleasure to meet you." Felix hardly ever had to look up at anyone but he did to this man. The older, taller, heavier man looked like a defensive tackle, if a defensive tackle could hit a ball over four hundred feet.

"Nice to meet you too." Anderson shook hands then put an arm around Smoke and walked him out onto the field. "I'm so sorry to hear of all your troubles, son. Carol sends her best to you and told me to tell you there's a home cooked meal waiting for you at our house, any day, any time."

"Thanks coach. Please tell her that means a lot to me. Now, what can I do for you?"

Anderson stepped back. "You know they shut us down, right?"

Smoke nodded.

"Well, I'm sure Bobby told you by now, there's a kid that played for me as a freshman last year. He's good, Smoke. Shortstop, great arm, and he can hit. I think there's a chance he could get drafted like you did, but he'll need some help getting there. You played your ball here. You know the drill. I think you can help him."

They walked from the shadows onto a field that in spite of the shutdown was still being maintained. The smell of fresh cut grass drifted across the field, along with the memories of a long home run, a line drive caught at the last moment of its flight, and the joy of victory and the heartbreak of defeat.

Smoke saw a batting cage set up behind home plate and a bucket of balls on the mound behind a pitcher's screen. He also saw a young man who was stretching out at home plate.

"Smoke, will you do me a huge favor? Throw a couple to him and see what you think?"

"Sure coach, no problem."

"Great, thanks."

Smoke walked alone toward the mound.

The young man had broad shoulders and well-developed arms that were sticking out of a sleeveless t-shirt. Smoke watched his warm-up swings. The young man had a warmup routine which was good and a flaw which was bad.

Smoke walked to the mound and picked three baseballs with one hand from a basket next to the protective screen. "Hey." He yelled to the young man. "Coach asked me to throw you a few. Up for it?"

The young man responded immediately and with enthusiasm. "Sure. Thanks. You got a name mister?"

"Smoke, you can call me Smoke."

The boy stood for a second gripping and re-gripping the bat then suddenly turned to Smoke. "Hey, sorry, you want to throw first? Warm up? I can get my glove."

"Nah. That's okay. I won't be throwing hard. I just want to see your swing."

"Okay."

Smoke rolled the ball in his fingers, set up, and threw a straight fastball down the middle of the plate.

The boy's timing was off a bit and he topped it down the third baseline.

Smoke threw another.

The kid just got under it and hit a fly ball to center field.

Smoke corrected his swing. "Your hands are drifting. Stay back."

The third pitch Smoke threw went over the wall in left.

Smoke yelled, "Hit the next one to right."

The young man laced a grounder between first and second.

Smoke announced the next pitch. "Breaking ball." He threw a slow curve and the young man swung early. Swing and a miss.

The young man set himself again and yelled. "Again."

This time Smoke's slow breaking ball went over the center field wall.

Smoke dropped the ball he was holding back into the basket and walked to the batter's box.

The young man looked confused and a little disappointed.

Smoke took the bat from him and felt the weight. "You can hit, that's a given, but what kind of hitter do you want to be?"

"Sorry? I don't understand."

"Home runs or line drives? What do you want to achieve, home runs or getting on base?"

"Both?" The young man smiled.

"I understand, but no. Two different swings. The home run swing is hard and violent, comes from the shoes. Every pitch is the same swing. But line drives, hitting on the screws to all fields, that's a totally different mindset."

"But I like doing both."

Smoke looked down and shook his head a little. "Can't do both and you have to choose. If you want just home runs, you wait for your pitch. If you want to get on base then every pitch is a study in different methodology. Some will go over the fence but every swing is taking what is given and hitting it where its supposed to be, not where you want it to be. Understand?"

The young man seemed honest when he said, "I think so but it will be a while to get it to sink in."

"That I guarantee is the smartest thing you've said all day."

The young man smiled. "Can you throw a couple more?"

"Sure." Smoke started toward the mound but turned back. "Hey, what's your name?"

"Hank."

"Nice. Great name. Like Hank Aaron."

The young man ducked his head. "Yeah, almost."

Smoke didn't let it go. "What's that mean, almost?"

"Not for Hank Aaron. My name isn't Hank, it's Henry."

Smoke instantly froze then looked back toward the tunnel for his friends.

The young man said, "Hey, are you okay, mister?"

Smoke saw Aimer and Felix standing side by side with huge grins on their faces.

The boy was still standing in the batter's box spinning the bat. "I never really liked the name Henry, so I made people call me Hank. It actually was a lot of work because I was in foster homes when I was a kid and had to re-educate everybody to call me Hank instead of Henry."

"You were adopted?"

"No, never adopted. I got dropped off at a firehouse in Wilmington and spent my childhood in foster care."

Smoke's face was ashen. He stood, hands at his sides, motionless.

"You alright mister? You don't look so good."

"If you were dropped off when you were a baby, how did you know your name was Henry?"

"Oh, that was easy." He held up his arm. "I had this beaded bracelet on my wrist when I got dropped off. I still wear it. Made it bigger a bunch of times. See? It has beads that spell out Henry."

The boy spun his wrist around a couple of times showing Smoke a baby bracelet on a thin silver chain. "See, Henry."

Smoke walked back to the young man, took his arm in his hand, and read the name spelled in beads. "Henry."

"That's right."

"Your name is Henry and so is mine."

The boy took a step back, shaking his hand loose. "This is getting weird."

Smoke looked at the young man. "I know for a fact that your mother, whose name was Helen, put that bracelet on you after you were born."

The boy said nothing.

"I know that because the bracelet you have on your wrist is the same bracelet my mother put on my wrist when I was born."

The young man dropped the bat.

"Son, you are Henry Robert Smokehouse and I am your father."

THE END

ABOUT THE AUTHOR

Paul Eberz authored *Henry* as the final edition of a trilogy. The first novel, *Smoke-White Collar Crimes* was published in 2020 and the second, *Reckoning* published in 2021. In addition to this series, he is preparing two additional novels for publication, an Historical-Fiction mystery about the death of JFK and a Call of the Wild adventure story set in 1849. Eberz has retired from the construction industry where he held executive positions in Fortune 500 companies and traveled the country working with Native Americans. Born in Philadelphia, he now resides in Virginia.

www.ingramcontent.com/pod-product-compliance
Lightning Source LLC
Chambersburg PA
CBHW020609310726
48979CB00008B/1400/J

* 9 7 8 1 7 3 5 2 5 6 6 9 6 *